THE
FEAST
OF
ST.
DIONYSUS
Five Science Fiction Stories

Books by Robert Silverberg

Unfamiliar Territory
The Book of Skulls
Dying Inside
Tower of Glass

▽▲▽▲▽

THE
FEAST
OF
ST.
DIONYSUS

FIVE SCIENCE FICTION STORIES

by Robert Silverberg

▼▲▽▲▼

CHARLES SCRIBNER'S SONS ▼ *New York*

Library of Congress Cataloging in Publication Data

Silverberg, Robert.
  The feast of St. Dionysus.

  CONTENTS: The feast of St. Dionysus.—Schwartz
between the galaxies.—Trips. [etc.]
  1. Science fiction, American. I. Title.
PZ4.S573Fe [PS3569.I472]   813'.5'4   74-11078
ISBN 0-684-13998-7

1 3 5 7 9 11 13 15 17 19 V/C 20 18 16 14 12 10 8 6 4 2

Printed in the United States of America

For Barry Malzberg

▼▲▼▲▼

CONTENTS

THE FEAST OF ST. DIONYSUS 3

SCHWARTZ BETWEEN THE GALAXIES 79

TRIPS 107

IN THE HOUSE OF DOUBLE MINDS 153

THIS IS THE ROAD 181

▼▲▼▲▼

THE
FEAST
OF
ST.
DIONYSUS

Sleepers, awake. Sleep is separateness; the cave of solitude is the cave of dreams, the cave of the passive spectator. To be awake is to participate, carnally and not in fantasy, in the feast; the great communion.
—Norman O. Brown: *Love's Body*

*T*his is the dawn of the day of the Feast. Oxenshuer knows roughly what to expect, for he has spied on the children at their catechisms; he has had hints from some of the adults; he has spoken at length with the high priest of this strange apocalyptic city; and yet, for all his patiently gathered knowledge, he really knows nothing at all of today's event. What will happen? They will come for him, Matt who has been appointed his brother, and Will and Nick, who are his sponsors. They will lead him through the labyrinth to the place of the saint, to the god-house at the city's core. They will give him wine until he is glutted, until his cheeks and chin drip with it and his robe is stained with red. And he and Matt will struggle, will have a contest of some sort, a wrestling match, an agon: whether real or symbolic, he does not yet know. Before the whole community they will contend. What else, what else? There will be hymns to the saint, to the god—god and saint, both are one, Dionysus and Jesus, each an aspect of the other. Each a manifestation of the divinity we carry within us, so the Speaker has said. Jesus and Dionysus, Dionysus and Jesus, god and saint, saint and god, what do the terms matter? He has heard the people singing:

This is the god who burns like fire
This is the god whose name is music
This is the god whose soul is wine

Fire. Music. Wine. The healing fire, the joining fire, in which all things will be made one. By its leaping blaze he will drink and drink and drink, dance and dance and dance. Maybe there will be some sort of sexual event, an orgy, perhaps, for sex and religion are closely bound among these people: a communion of the flesh opening the way toward communality of spirit.

I go to the god's house and his fire consumes me
I cry the god's name and his thunder deafens me
I take the god's cup and his wine dissolves me

And then? And then? How can he possibly know what will happen, until it has happened? "You will enter into the ocean of Christ," they have told him. An ocean? Here in the Mojave Desert? Well, a figurative ocean, a metaphorical ocean. All is metaphor here. "Dionysus will carry you to Jesus," they say. Go, child, swim out to God. Jesus waits. The saint, the mad saint, the boozy old god who is their saint, the mad saintly god who abolishes walls and makes all things one, will lead you to bliss, dear John, dear tired John. Give your soul gladly to Dionysus the Saint. Make yourself whole in his blessed fire. You've been divided too long. How can you lie dead on Mars and still walk alive on Earth?

Heal yourself, John. This is the day.

From Los Angeles the old San Bernardino Freeway rolls eastward through the plastic suburbs, through Alhambra and Azusa, past the Covina Hills branch of Forest Lawn Memorial-Parks, past the mushroom sprawl of San Bernardino, which is becoming a little Los Angeles, but not so little. The highway pushes onward into the desert like a flat, gray cincture holding the dry, brown hills asunder. This was the road by which John Oxenshuer finally chose to make his escape. He had had no particular destination in mind but was seeking only a parched place, a sandy place, a place where he could be alone: he needed to recreate, in what might well be his last weeks of life, certain aspects of barren Mars. After considering a number of possibilities he fastened upon this route, attracted to it by the way the freeway seemed to lose itself in the desert north of the Salton Sea. Even in this overcivilized epoch a man could easily disappear there.

Late one November afternoon, two weeks past his fortieth birthday, he closed his rented apartment on Hollywood Boulevard; taking leave of no one, he drove unhurriedly toward the freeway entrance. There he surrendered control to the electronic highway net, which seized his car and pulled it into the traffic flow. The net governed him as far as Covina; when he saw Forest Lawn's statuary-speckled hilltop coming up on his right, he readied himself to resume driving. A mile beyond the vast cemetery a blinking sign told him he was on his own, and he took the wheel. The car continued to slice inland at the same velocity, as mechanical as iron, of 140 kilometers per hour. With each moment the recent past dropped from him, bit by bit.

Can you drown in the desert? Let's give it a try, God. I'll make a bargain with you. You let me drown out there. All right? And I'll give myself to you. Let me sink into the sand; let me bathe in it; let it wash Mars out of my soul; let it drown me, God; let it drown me. Free me from Mars and

I'm yours, God. Is it a deal? Drown me in the desert and I'll surrender at last. I'll surrender.

At twilight he was in Banning. Some gesture of farewell to civilization seemed suddenly appropriate, and he risked stopping to have dinner at a small Mexican restaurant. It was crowded with families enjoying a night out, which made Oxenshuer fear he would be recognized. Look, someone would cry, there's the Mars astronaut, there's the one who came back! But of course no one spotted him. He had grown a bushy, sandy mustache that nearly obliterated his thin, tense lips. His body, lean and wide-shouldered, no longer had an astronaut's springy erectness; in the nineteen months since his return from the red planet he had begun to stoop a little, to cultivate a roundedness of the upper back, as if some leaden weight beneath his breastbone were tugging him forward and downward. Besides, spacemen are quickly forgotten. How long had anyone remembered the names of the heroic lunar teams of his youth? Borman, Lovell, and Anders. Armstrong, Aldrin, and Collins. Scott, Irwin, and Worden. Each of them had had a few gaudy weeks of fame, and then they had disappeared into the blurred pages of the almanac, all, perhaps, except Armstrong: children learned about him at school. His one small step: he would become a figure of myth, up there with Columbus and Magellan. But the others? Forgotten. Yes. Yesterday's heroes. Oxenshuer, Richardson, and Vogel. Who? Oxenshuer, Richardson, and Vogel. That's Oxenshuer right over there, eating tamales and enchiladas, drinking a bottle of Double-X. He's the one who came back. Had some sort of breakdown and left his wife. Yes. That's a funny name, Oxenshuer. Yes. He's the one who came back. What about the other two? They died.

Where did they die, daddy? They die
enshuer came back. What were their nai
son and Vogel. They died. Oh. On Ma
enshuer didn't. What were their names aga

Unrecognized, safely forgotten, Oxensh
meal and returned to the freeway. Night ha
time. The moon was nearly full; the mountain.
lined against the darkness, glistened with a co   y sheen.
There is no moonlight on Mars except the feeble, hasty glow
of Phobos, dancing in and out of eclipse on its nervous journey from west to east. He had found Phobos disturbing; nor
had he cared for fluttery Deimos, starlike, a tiny rocketing
point of light. Oxenshuer drove onward, leaving the zone of
urban sprawl behind, entering the true desert, pockmarked
here and there by resort towns: Palm Springs, Twentynine
Palms, Desert Hot Springs. Beckoning billboards summoned
him to the torpid pleasures of whirlpool baths and saunas.
These temptations he ignored without difficulty. Dryness
was what he sought.

Once he was east of Indio he began looking for a place to
abandon the car; but he was still too close to the southern
boundaries of Joshua Tree National Monument, and he did
not want to make camp this near to any area that might be
patrolled by park rangers. So he kept driving until the moon
was high and he was deep into the Chuckwalla country, with
nothing much except sand dunes and mountains and dry
lakebeds between him and the Arizona border. In a stretch
where the land seemed relatively flat he slowed the car almost to an idle, killed his lights, and swerved gently off the
road, following a vague northeasterly course; he gripped the
wheel tightly as he jounced over the rough, crunchy terrain.
Half a kilometer from the highway Oxenshuer came to a
shallow sloping basin, the dry bed of some ancient lake. He

...ed down into it until he could no longer see the long yellow tracks of headlights on the road, and knew he must be below the line of sight of any passing vehicle. Turning the engine off, he locked the car—a strange prissiness here, in the midst of nowhere!—took his backpack from the trunk, slipped his arms through the shoulder straps, and, without looking back, began to walk into the emptiness that lay to the north.

As he walks he composes a letter that he will never send.

Dear Claire, I wish I had been able to say goodbye to you before I left Los Angeles. I regretted only that: leaving town without telling you. But I was afraid to call. I draw back from you. You say you hold no grudge against me over Dave's death; you say it couldn't possibly have been my fault, and of course you're right. And yet I don't dare face you, Claire. Why is that? Because I left your husband's body on Mars and the guilt of that is choking me? But a body is only a shell, Claire. Dave's body isn't Dave, and there wasn't anything I could do for Dave. What is it, then, that comes between us? Is it my love, Claire, my guilty love for my friend's widow? Eh? That love is salt in my wounds, that love is sand in my throat, Claire. Claire. Claire. I can never tell you any of this, Claire. I never will. Goodbye. Pray for me. Will you pray?

His years of grueling NASA training for Mars served him well now. Powered by ancient disciplines, he moved swiftly, feeling no strain even with forty-five pounds on his back. He had no trouble with the uneven footing. The sharp chill in the air did not bother him, though he wore only light clothing, slacks and shirt and a flimsy cotton vest. The solitude, far from oppressing him, was actually a source of energy: a couple of hundred kilometers away in Los Angeles it might be the ninth decade of the twentieth century, but this was a prehistoric realm, timeless, unscarred by man, and his spirit expanded in his self-imposed isolation. Conceivably every footprint he made was the first human touch this land had felt. That gray, pervasive sense of guilt, heavy on him since his return from Mars, held less weight here beyond civilization's edge.

This wasteland was the closest he could come to attaining Mars on Earth. Not really close enough, for too many things broke the illusion: the great gleaming scarred moon, and the succulent terrestrial vegetation, and the tug of Earth's gravity, and the faint white glow on the leftward horizon that he imagined emanated from the cities of the coastal strip. But it was as close to Mars in flavor as he could manage. The Peruvian desert would have been better, only he had no way of getting to Peru.

An approximation. It would suffice.

A trek of at least a dozen kilometers left him still unfatigued, but he decided, shortly after midnight, to settle down for the night. The site he chose was a small level quadrangle bounded on the north and south by spiky, ominous cacti—chollas and prickly pears—and on the east by a maze of scrubby mesquite; to the west, a broad alluvial fan of tumbled pebbles descended from the nearby hills. Moonlight, raking the area sharply, highlighted every contrast of contour: the shadows of cacti were unfathomable inky pits and the tracks of small animals—lizards and kangaroo rats—were steep-walled canyons in the sand. As he slung his pack to the ground two startled rats, browsing in the mesquite, noticed him belatedly and leaped for cover in wild, desperate bounds, frantic but delicate. Oxenshuer smiled at them.

On the twentieth day of the mission Richardson and Vogel went out, as planned, for the longest extravehicular on the schedule, the ninety-kilometer crawler-jaunt to the Gulliver site. Goddamned well about time, Dave Vogel had muttered, when the EVA okay had at last come floating up, time-lagged and crackly, out of far-off Mission Control. All during the eight-month journey from Earth, while the brick-red face of Mars was swelling patiently in their portholes, they had argued about the timing of the big Marswalk, an argument that had begun six months before launch date. Vogel, insisting that the expedition was the mission's most important scientific project, had wanted to do it first, to get it done and out of the way before mishaps might befall them and force them to scrub it. No matter that the timetable decreed it for Day 20. The timetable was too conservative. We can overrule Mission Control, Vogel said. If they don't like it, let them reprimand us when we get home. Bud Richardson, though, wouldn't go along. Houston knows best, he kept saying. He always took the side of authority. First we have to get used to working on Mars, Dave. First we ought to do the routine stuff close by the landing site, while we're getting acclimated. What's our hurry? We've got to stay here a month until the return window opens, anyway. Why breach the schedule? The scientists know what they're doing, and they want us to do everything in its proper order, Richardson said. Vogel, stubborn, eager, seething, thought he would find an ally in Oxenshuer. You vote with me, John. Don't tell me *you* give a crap about Mission Control! Two against one and Bud will have to give in. But Oxenshuer, oddly, took Richardson's side. He hesitated to deviate from the schedule. He wouldn't be making the long extravehicular himself in any case; he had drawn the short straw; he was the man who'd be keeping close to the ship all the time. How then could he vote to alter the carefully designed schedule and send Richardson off, against his will, on a risky and perhaps ill-timed adventure? No, Oxenshuer said. Sorry, Dave, it isn't my place to decide such things. Vogel appealed anyway to Mission Control, and Mission Control said wait till Day 20, fellows. On Day 20 Richardson and Vogel suited up and went out. It was the ninth EVA of the mission, but the first that would take anyone more than a couple of kilometers from the ship.

Oxenshuer monitored his departing companions from his safe niche in the control cabin. The small video screen showed him the path of their crawler as it diminished into the somber red plain. You're well named, rusty old Mars. The blood of fallen soldiers stains your soil. Your hills are the color of the flames that lick conquered cities. Jouncing westward across Solis Lacus, Vogel kept up a running commentary. Lots of dead nothing out here, Johnny. It's as bad as the Moon. A prettier color, though. Are you reading me? I'm reading you, Oxenshuer said. The crawler was like a submarine mounted on giant preposterous wheels. Joggle, joggle, joggle, skirting craters and ravines, ridges and scarps. Pausing now and then so Richardson could pop a geological specimen or two into the gunnysack. Then onward, westward, westward. Heading bumpily toward the site where the unmanned Ares IV Mars Lander, almost a decade earlier, had scraped some Martian microorganisms out of the ground with the Gulliver sampling device.

      *   *   *

"Gulliver" is a culture chamber that inoculates itself with a sample of soil. The sample is obtained by two 7½-meter lengths of kite line wound on small projectiles. When the projectiles are fired, the lines unwind and fall to the ground. A small motor inside the chamber then reels them in, together with adhering soil particles. The chamber contains a growth medium whose organic nutrients are labeled with radioactive carbon. When the medium is inoculated with soil, the accompanying microorganisms metabolize the organic compounds and release radioactive carbon dioxide. This diffuses to the window of a Geiger counter, where the radioactivity is measured. Growth of the microbes causes the rate of carbon dioxide production to increase exponentially with time—an indication that the gas is being formed biologically. Provision is also made for the injection, during the run, of a solution containing a metabolic poison which can be used to confirm the biological origin of the carbon dioxide and to analyze the nature of the metabolic reactions.

*   *   *

All afternoon the crawler traversed the plain, and the sky deepened from dark purple to utter black, and the untwinkling stars, which on Mars are visible even by day, became more brilliant with the passing hours, and Phobos came streaking by, and then came little hovering Deimos; and Oxenshuer, wandering around the ship, took readings on this and that and watched his screen and listened to Dave Vogel's chatter; and Mission Control offered a comment every little while. And during these hours the Martian temperature began its nightly slide down the Centigrade ladder. A thousand kilometers away, an inversion of thermal gradients unexpectedly developed, creating fierce currents in the tenuous Martian atmosphere, ripping gouts of red sand loose from the hills, driving wild scarlet clouds eastward toward the Gulliver site. As the sandstorm increased in intensity, the scanner satellites in orbit around Mars detected it and relayed pictures of it to Earth, and after the normal transmission lag it was duly noted at Mission Control as a potential hazard to the men in the crawler, but somehow—the NASA hearings did not succeed in fixing blame for this inexplicable communications failure—no one passed the necessary warning along to the three astronauts on Mars. Two hours after he had finished his solitary dinner aboard the ship, Oxenshuer heard Vogel say, "Okay, Johnny, we've finally reached the Gulliver site, and as soon as we have our lighting system set up we'll get out and see what the hell we have here." Then the sandstorm struck in full fury. Oxenshuer heard nothing more from either of his companions.

Making camp for the night, he took first from his pack his operations beacon, one of his NASA souvenirs. By the sleek instrument's cool, inexhaustible green light he laid out his bedroll in the flattest, least pebbly place he could find; then, discovering himself far from sleepy, Oxenshuer set about assembling his solar still. Although he had no idea how long he would stay in the desert—a week, a month, a year, forever—he had brought perhaps a month's supply of food concentrates with him, but no water other than a single canteen's worth, to tide him through thirst on this first night. He could not count on finding wells or streams here, any more than he had on Mars, and, unlike the kangaroo rats, capable of living indefinitely on nothing but dried seeds, producing water metabolically by the oxidation of carbohydrates, he would not be able to dispense entirely with fresh water. But the solar still would see him through.

He began to dig.

Methodically he shaped a conical hole a meter in diameter, half a meter deep, and put a wide-mouthed two-liter jug at its deepest point. He collected pieces of cactus, breaking off slabs of prickly pear but ignoring the stiletto-spined chollas, and placed these along the slopes of the hole. Then he lined the hole with a sheet of clear plastic film, weighted by rocks in such a way that the plastic came in contact with the soil only at the hole's rim, and hung suspended a few centimeters above the cactus pieces and the jug. The job took him twenty minutes. Solar energy would do the rest: as sunlight passed through the plastic into the soil and the plant material, water would evaporate, condense in droplets on the underside of the plastic, and trickle into the jug. With cactus as juicy as this, he might be able to count on a liter a day of sweet water out of each hole he dug. The still was emergency gear developed for use on Mars; it hadn't done anyone any good there, but Oxenshuer had no fears of running dry in this far more hospitable desert.

Enough. He shucked his pants and crawled into his sleeping bag. At last he was where he wanted to be: enclosed, protected, yet at the same time alone, unsurrounded, cut off from his past in a world of dryness.

He could not yet sleep; his mind ticked too actively. Images out of the last few years floated insistently through it and had to be purged, one by one. To begin with, his wife's face. (Wife? I have no wife. Not now.) He was having difficulty remembering Lenore's features, the shape of her nose, the turn of her lips, but a general sense of her existence still burdened him. How long had they been married? Eleven years, was it? Twelve? The anniversary? March 30, 31? He was sure he had loved her once. What had happened? Why had he recoiled from her touch?

——No, please, don't do that. I don't want to yet.

——You've been home three months, John.

Her sad green eyes. Her tender smile. A stranger, now.

His ex-wife's face turned to mist and the mist congealed into the face of Claire Vogel. A sharper image: dark glittering eyes, the narrow mouth, thin cheeks framed by loose streamers of unbound black hair. The widow Vogel, dignified in her grief, trying to console him.

——I'm sorry, Claire. They just disappeared, is all. There wasn't anything I could do.

——John, John, it wasn't your fault. Don't let it get you like this.

——I couldn't even find the bodies. I wanted to look for them, but it was all sand everywhere, sand, dust, the craters, confusion, no signal, no landmarks, no way, Claire, no way.

——It's all right, John. What do the bodies matter? You did your best. I know you did.

Her words offered comfort but no absolution from guilt. Her embrace—light, chaste—merely troubled him. The pressure of her heavy breasts against him made him tremble. He remembered Dave Vogel, halfway to Mars, speaking lovingly of Claire's breasts. Her jugs, he called them. Boy, I'd like to have my hands on my lady's jugs right this minute! And Bud Richardson, more annoyed than amused, telling him to cut it out, to stop stirring up fantasies that couldn't be satisfied for another year or more.

Claire vanished from his mind, driven out by a blaze of flashbulbs. The hovercameras, hanging in midair, scanning him from every angle. The taut, earnest faces of the newsmen, digging deep for human interest. See the lone survivor of the Mars expedition! See his tortured eyes! See his gaunt cheeks! There's the President himself, folks, giving John Oxenshuer a great big welcome back to Earth! What thoughts must be going through this man's mind, the only human being to walk the sands of an alien world and return to our old down-to-Earth planet! How keenly he must feel the tragedy of the two lost astronauts he left behind up there! There he goes now, there goes John Oxenshuer, disappearing into the debriefing chamber——

Yes, the debriefings. Colonel Schmidt, Dr. Harkness, Commander Thompson, Dr. Burdette, Dr. Horowitz, milking him for data. Their voices carefully gentle, their manner informal, their eyes all the same betraying their single-mindedness.

——Once again, please, Captain Oxenshuer. You lost the signal, right, and then the backup line refused to check out, you couldn't get any telemetry at all. And then?

——And then I took a directional fix, I did a thermal scan and tripled the infrared, I rigged an extension lifeline to the sample–collector and went outside looking for them. But the collector's range was only 10 kilometers. And the dust storm was too much. The dust storm. Too damned much. I went 500 meters and you ordered me back into the ship. Didn't want to go back, but you ordered me.

——We didn't want to lose you too, John.

——But maybe it wasn't too late, even then. Maybe.

——There was no way you could have reached them in a short-range vehicle.

——I would have figured some way of recharging it. If only you had let me. If only the sand hadn't been flying around like that. If. Only.

——I think we've covered the point fully.

——Yes. May we go over some of the topographical data now, Captain Oxenshuer?

——Please. Please. Some other time.

It was three days before they realized what sort of shape he was in. They still thought he was the old John Oxenshuer, the one who had amused himself during the training period by reversing the inputs on his landing simulator, just for the hell of it, the one who had surreptitiously turned on the unsuspecting Secretary of Defense just before a Houston press conference, the one who had sung bawdy carols at a pious Christmas party for the families of the astronauts in '86. Now, seeing him darkened and turned in on himself, they concluded eventually that he had been transformed by Mars, and they sent him, finally to the chief psychiatric team, Mendelson and McChesney.

——How long have you felt this way, Captain?

——I don't know. Since they died. Since I took off for Earth. Since I entered Earth's atmosphere. I don't know. Maybe it started earlier. Maybe it was always like this.

——What are the usual symptoms of the disturbance?

——Not wanting to see anybody. Not wanting to talk to anybody. Not wanting to be with anybody. Especially myself. I'm so goddamned sick of my own company.

——And what are your plans now?

——Just to live quietly and grope my way back to normal.

——Would you say it was the length of the voyage that upset you most, or the amount of time you had to spend in solitude on the homeward leg, or your distress over the deaths of——

——Look, how would I know?

——Who'd know better?

——Hey, I don't believe in either of you, you know? You're figments. Go away. Vanish.

——We understand you're putting in for retirement and a maximum disability pension, Captain.

——Where'd you hear that? It's a stinking lie. I'm going to be okay before long. I'll be back on active duty before Christmas, you got that?

——Of course, Captain.

——Go. Disappear. Who needs you?

——John, John, it wasn't your fault. Don't let it get you like this.

——I couldn't even find the bodies. I wanted to look for them, but it was all sand everywhere, sand, dust, the craters, confusion, no signal, no landmarks, no way, Claire, no way.

The images were breaking up, dwindling, going. He saw scattered glints of light slowly whirling overhead, the kaleidoscope of the heavens, the whole astronomical psychedelia swaying and cavorting, and then the sky calmed, and then only Claire's face remained, Claire and the minute red disk of Mars. The events of the nineteen months contracted to a single star-bright point of time, and became as nothing, and were gone. Silence and darkness enveloped him. Lying tense and rigid on the desert floor, he stared up defiantly at Mars, and closed his eyes, and wiped the red disk from the screen of his mind, and slowly, gradually, reluctantly, he surrendered himself to sleep.

Voices woke him. Male voices, quiet and deep, discussing him in an indistinct buzz. He hovered a moment on the border between dream and reality, uncertain of his perceptions and unsure of his proper response; then his military reflexes took over and he snapped into instant wakefulness, blinking his eyes open, sitting up in one quick move, rising to a standing position in the next, poising his body to defend itself.

He took stock. Sunrise was maybe half an hour away; the tips of the mountains to the west were stained with early pinkness. Thin mist shrouded the lowlying land. Three men stood just beyond the place where he had mounted his beacon. The shortest one was as tall as he, and they were desert-tanned, heavy-set, strong and capable-looking. They wore their hair long and their beards full; they were oddly dressed, shepherd-style, in loose belted robes of light green muslin or linen. Although their expressions were open and friendly and they did not seem to be armed, Oxenshuer was troubled by awareness of his vulnerability in this emptiness, and he found menace in their presence. Their intrusion on his isolation angered him. He stared at them warily, rocking on the balls of his feet.

One, bigger than the others, a massive thick-cheeked blue-eyed man, said, "Easy. Easy, now. You look all ready to fight."

"Who are you? What do you want?"

"Just came to find out if you were okay. You lost?"

Oxenshuer indicated his neat camp, his backpack, his bedroll. "Do I seem lost?"

"You're a long way from anywhere," said the man closest to Oxenshuer, one with shaggy yellow hair and a cast in one eye.

"Am I? I thought it was just a short hike from the road."

The three men began to laugh. "You don't know *where* the hell you are, do you?" said the squint-eyed one. And the third one, dark-bearded, hawk-featured, said, "Look over thataway." He pointed behind Oxenshuer, to the north. Slowly, half anticipating trickery, Oxenshuer turned. Last night, in the moonlit darkness, the land had seemed level and empty in that direction, but now he beheld two steeply rising mesas a few hundred meters apart, and in the opening between them he saw a low wooden palisade, and behind the palisade the flat-roofed tops of buildings were visible, tinted orange-pink by the spreading touch of dawn. A settlement out here? But the map showed nothing, and, from the looks of it, that was a town of some two or three thousand people. He wondered if he had somehow been transported by magic during the night to some deeper part of the desert. But no: there was his solar still, there was the mesquite patch; there were last night's prickly pears. Frowning, Oxenshuer said, "What is that place in there?"

"The City of the Word of God," said the hawk-faced one calmly.

"You're lucky," said the squint-eyed one. "You've been brought to us almost in time for the Feast of St. Dionysus. When all men are made one. When every ill is healed."

Oxenshuer understood. Religious fanatics. A secret retreat in the desert. The state was full of apocalyptic cults, more and more of them now that the end of the century was only about ten years away and millenary fears were mounting. He scowled. He had a native Easterner's innate distaste for Californian irrationality. Reaching into the reservoir of his own decaying Catholicism, he said thinly, "Don't you mean St. Dionysius? With an *i?* Dionysus was the Greek god of wine."

"Dionysus," said the big blue-eyed man. "Dionysius is somebody else, some Frenchman. We've heard of him. Dionysus is who we mean." He put forth his hand. "My name's Matt, Mr. Oxenshuer. If you stay for the Feast, I'll stand brother to you. How's that?"

The sound of his name jolted him. "You've heard of me?"

"Heard of you? Well, not exactly. We looked in your wallet."

"We ought to go now," said the squint-eyed one. "Don't want to miss breakfast."

"Thanks," Oxenshuer said, "but I think I'll pass up the invitation. I came out here to get away from people for a little while."

"So did we," Matt said.

"You've been called," said Squint-eye hoarsely. "Don't you realize that, man? You've been called to our city. It wasn't any accident you came here."

"No?"

"There aren't any accidents," said Hawk-face. "Not ever. Not in the breast of Jesus, not ever a one. What's written is written. You were called, Mr. Oxenshuer. Can you say no?" He put his hand lightly on Oxenshuer's arm. "Come to our city. Come to the Feast. Look, why do you want to be afraid?"

"I'm not afraid. I'm just looking to be alone."

"We'll let you be alone, if that's what you want," Hawk-face told him. "Won't we, Matt? Won't we, Will? But you can't say no to our city. To our saint. To Jesus. Come along, now. Will, you carry his pack. Let him walk into the city without a burden." Hawk-face's sharp, forbidding features were softened by the glow of his fervor. His dark eyes gleamed. A strange, persuasive warmth leaped from him to Oxenshuer. "You won't say no. You won't. Come sing with us. Come to the Feast. Well?"

"Well?" Matt asked also.

"To lay down your burden," said squint-eyed Will. "To join the singing. Well? Well?"

"I'll go with you," Oxenshuer said at length. "But I'll carry my own pack."

They moved to one side and waited in silence while he assembled his belongings. In ten minutes everything was in order. Kneeling, adjusting the straps of his pack, he nodded and looked up. The early sun was full on the city now, and its rooftops were bright with a golden radiance. Light seemed to stream upward from them; the entire desert appeared to blaze in that luminous flow.

"All right," Oxenshuer said, rising and shouldering his pack. "Let's go." But he remained where he stood, staring ahead. He felt the city's golden luminosity as a fiery tangible force on his cheeks, like the outpouring of heat from a crucible of molten metal. With Matt leading the way, the three men walked ahead, single file, moving fast. Will, the squint-eyed one, bringing up the rear, paused to look back questioningly at Oxenshuer, who was still standing entranced by the sight of that supernal brilliance. "Coming," Oxenshuer murmured. Matching the pace of the others, he followed them briskly over the parched, sandy wastes toward the City of the Word of God.

There are places in the coastal desert of Peru where no rainfall has ever been recorded. On the Paracas Peninsula, about eleven miles south of the port of Pisco, the red sand is absolutely bare of all vegetation, not a leaf, not a living thing; no stream enters the ocean nearby. The nearest human habitation is several miles away where wells tap underground water and a few sedges line the beach. There is no more arid area in the western hemisphere; it is the epitome of loneliness and desolation. The psychological landscape of Paracas is much the same as that of Mars. John Oxenshuer, Dave Vogel, and Bud Richardson spent three weeks camping there in the winter of 1987, testing their emergency gear and familiarizing themselves with the emotional texture of the Martian environment. Beneath the sands of the peninsula are found the desiccated bodies of an ancient people unknown to history, together with some of the most magnificent textiles that the world has ever seen. Natives seeking salable artifacts have rifled the necropolis of Paracas, and now the bones of its occupants lie scattered on the surface, and the winds alternately cover and uncover fragments of the coarser fabrics, discarded by the diggers, still soft and strong after nearly two millennia.

Vultures circle high over the Mojave. They would pick the bones of anyone who died here. There are no vultures on Mars. Dead men become mummies, not skeletons, for nothing decays on Mars. What has died on Mars remains buried in the sand, invulnerable to time, imperishable, eternal. Perhaps archaeologists, bound on a futile but inevitable search for the remains of the lost races of old Mars, will find the withered bodies of Dave Vogel and Bud Richardson in a mound of red soil, ten thousand years from now.

At close range the city seemed less magical. It was laid out in the form of a bull's-eye, its curving streets set in concentric rings behind the blunt-topped little palisade, evidently purely symbolic in purpose, that rimmed its circumference between the mesas. The buildings were squat stucco affairs of five or six rooms, unpretentious and undistinguished, all of them similar if not identical in style: pastel-hued structures of the sort found everywhere in southern California. They seemed to be twenty or thirty years old and in generally shabby condition; they were set close together and close to the street, with no gardens and no garages. Wide avenues leading inward pierced the rings of buildings every few hundred meters. This seemed to be entirely a residential district, but no people were in sight, either at windows or on the streets, nor were there any parked cars; it was like a movie set, clean and empty and artificial. Oxenshuer's footfalls echoed loudly. The silence and surreal emptiness troubled him. Only an occasional child's tricycle, casually abandoned outside a house, gave evidence of recent human presence.

As they approached the core of the city, Oxenshuer saw that the avenues were narrowing and then giving way to a labyrinthine tangle of smaller streets, as intricate a maze as could be found in any of the old towns of Europe; the bewildering pattern seemed deliberate and carefully designed, perhaps for the sake of shielding the central section and making it a place apart from the antiseptic, prosaic zone of houses in the outer rings. The buildings lining the streets of the maze had an institutional character: they were three and four stories high, built of red brick, with few windows and pinched, unwelcoming entrances. They had the look of nineteenth-century hotels; possibly they were warehouses and meeting-halls and places of some municipal nature. All were deserted. No commercial establishments were visible, no shops, no restaurants, no banks, no loan companies, no theaters, no newsstands. Such things were forbidden, maybe, in a theocracy such as Oxenshuer suspected this place to be. The city plainly had not evolved in any helter-skelter free-enterprise fashion, but had been planned down to its last alleyway for the exclusive use of a communal order whose members were beyond the bourgeois needs of an ordinary town.

Matt led them sure-footedly into the maze, infallibly choosing connecting points that carried them steadily deeper toward the center. He twisted and turned abruptly through juncture after juncture, never once doubling back on his track. At last they stepped through one passageway barely wide enough for Oxenshuer's pack, and he found himself in a plaza of unexpected size and grandeur. It was a vast open space, roomy enough for several thousand people, paved with cobbles that glittered in the harsh desert sunlight. On the right was a colossal building two stories high that ran the entire length of the plaza, at least 300 meters; it looked as bleak as a barrack, a dreary utilitarian thing of clapboard and aluminum siding painted a dingy drab green, but all down its plaza side were tall, radiant stained-glass windows, as incongruous as pink gardenias blooming on a scrub oak. A towering metal cross rising high over the middle of the pointed roof settled all doubts: this was the city's church. Facing it across the plaza was an equally immense building, no less unsightly, built to the same plan but evidently secular, for its windows were plain and it bore no cross. At the far side of the plaza, opposite the place where they had entered it, stood a much smaller structure of dark stone in an implausible Gothic style, all vaults and turrets and arches. Pointing to each building in turn, Matt said, "Over there's the house of the god. On this side's the dining hall. Straight ahead, the little one, that's the house of the Speaker. You'll meet him at breakfast. Let's go eat."

. . . *Captain Oxenshuer and Major Vogel, who will spend the next year and a half together in the sardine-can environment of their spaceship as they make their round trip journey to Mars and back, are no strangers to one another. Born on the same day—November 4, 1949—in Reading, Pennsylvania, they grew up together, attending the same elementary and high schools as classmates and sharing a dormitory room as undergraduates at Princeton. They dated many of the same girls; it was Captain Oxenshuer who introduced Major Vogel to his future wife, the former Claire Barnes, in 1973. "You might say he stole her from me," the tall, slender astronaut likes to tell interviewers, grinning to show he holds no malice over the incident. In a sense Major Vogel returned the compliment, for Captain Oxenshuer has been married since March 30, 1978, to the major's first cousin, the former Lenore Reiser, whom he met at his friend's wedding reception. After receiving advanced scientific degrees—Captain Oxenshuer in meteorology and celestial mechanics, Major Vogel in geology and space navigation—they enrolled together in the space program in the spring of 1979 and shortly afterward were chosen as members of the original thirty-six-man group of trainees for the first manned flight to the red planet. According to their fellow astronauts, they quickly distinguished themselves for their quick and imaginative responses to stress situations, for their extraordinarily deft teamwork, and also for their shared love of high-spirited pranks and gags, which got them in trouble more than once with sober-sided NASA officials. Despite occasional reprimands, they were regarded as obvious choices for the initial Mars voyage, to which their selection was announced on March 18, 1985. Colonel Walter ("Bud") Richardson, named that day as command pilot for the Mars mission, cannot claim to share the life-long bonds of companionship that link Captain Oxenshuer and Major Vogel, but he has been closely associated with them in the astronaut program for the past ten years and long ago established himself as their most intimate friend. Colonel Richardson, the third of this country's three musketeers of interplanetary exploration, was born in Omaha, Nebraska, on the 5th of June, 1948. He hoped to become an astronaut from earliest childhood onward, and. . . .*

They crossed the plaza to the dining hall. Just within the entrance was a dark-walled low-ceilinged vestibule; a pair of swinging doors gave access to the dining rooms beyond. Through windows set in the doors Oxenshuer could glimpse dimly-lit vastnesses to the left and the right, in which great numbers of solemn people, all clad in the same sort of flowing robes as his three companions, sat at long bare wooden tables and passed serving-bowls around. Nick told Oxenshuer to drop his pack and leave it in the vestibule; no one would bother it, he said. As they started to go in, a boy of ten erupted explosively out of the left-hand doorway, nearly colliding with Oxenshuer. The boy halted just barely in time, backed up a couple of paces, stared with shameless curiosity into Oxenshuer's face, and, grinning broadly, pointed to Oxenshuer's bare chin and stroked his own as if to indicate that it was odd to see a man without a beard. Matt caught the boy by the shoulders and pulled him against his chest; Oxenshuer thought he was going to shake him, to chastise him for such irreverence, but no, Matt gave the boy an affectionate hug, swung him far overhead, and tenderly set him down. The boy clasped Matt's powerful forearms briefly and went sprinting through the right-hand door.

"Your son?" Oxenshuer asked.

"Nephew. I've got two hundred nephews. Every man in this town's my brother, right? So every boy's my nephew."

——If I could have just a few moments for one or two questions, Captain Oxenshuer.

——Provided it's really just a few moments. I'm due at Mission Control at 0830, and——

——I'll confine myself, then, to the one topic of greatest relevance to our readers. What are your feelings about the Deity, Captain? Do you, as an astronaut soon to depart for Mars, believe in the existence of God?

——My biographical poop-sheet will tell you that I've been known to go to Mass now and then.

——Yes, of course, we realize you're a practicing

member of the Catholic faith, but, well, Captain, it's widely understood that for some astronauts religious observance is more of a public-relations matter than a matter of genuine spiritual urgings. Meaning no offense, Captain, we're trying to ascertain the actual nature of your relationship, if any, to the Divine Presence, rather than——

——All right. You're asking a complicated question and I don't see how I can give an easy answer. If you're asking whether I literally believe in the Father, Son, and Holy Ghost, whether I think Jesus came down from heaven for our salvation and was crucified for us and was buried and on the third day rose again and ascended into heaven, I'd have to say no. Not except in the loosest metaphorical sense. But I do believe—ah—suppose we say I believe in the existence of an organizing force in the universe, a power of sublime reason that makes everything hang together, an underlying principle of rightness. Which we can call God for lack of a better name. And which I reach toward, when I feel I need to, by way of the Roman Church, because that's how I was raised.

——That's an extremely abstract philosophy, Captain.

——Abstract. Yes.

——That's an extremely rationalistic approach. Would you say that your brand of cool rationalism is characteristic of the entire astronaut group?

——I can't speak for the whole group. We didn't come out of a single mold. We've got some all-American boys who go to church every Sunday and think that God Himself is listening in person to every word they say, and we've got a couple of atheists, though I won't tell you who, and we've got guys who just don't care one way or the other. And I can tell you we've got a few real mystics, too, some out-and-out guru types. Don't let the uniforms and haircuts fool you.

Why, there are times when I feel the pull of mysticism myself.

——In what way?

——I'm not sure. I get a sense of being on the edge of some sort of cosmic breakthrough. An awareness that there may be real forces just beyond my reach, not abstractions but actual functioning dynamic entities, which I could attune myself to if I only knew how to find the key. You feel stuff like that when you go into space, no matter how much of a rationalist you think you are. I've felt it four or five times, on training flights, on orbital missions. I want to feel it again. I want to break through. I want to reach God, am I making myself clear? I want to reach God.

——But you say you don't literally believe in Him, Captain. That sounds contradictory to me.

——Does it really?

——It does, sir.

——Well, if it does, I don't apologize. I don't have to think straight all the time. I'm entitled to a few contradictions. I'm capable of holding a couple of diametrically opposed beliefs. Look, if I want to flirt with madness a little, what's it to you?

——Madness, Captain?

——Madness. Yes. That's exactly what it is, friend. There are times when Johnny Oxenshuer is tired of being so goddamned sane. You can quote me on that. Did you get it straight? There are times when Johnny Oxenshuer is tired of being so goddamned sane. But don't print it until I've blasted off for Mars, you hear me? I don't want to get bumped from this mission for incipient schizophrenia. I want to go. Maybe I'll find God out there this time, you know? And maybe I won't. But I want to go.

——I think I understand what you're saying, sir. God bless you, Captain Oxenshuer. A safe voyage to you.
——Sure. Thanks. Was I of any help?

Hardly anyone glanced up at him, only a few of the children, as Matt led him down the long aisle toward the table on the platform at the back of the hall. The people here appeared to be extraordinarily self-contained, as if they were in possession of some wondrous secret from which he would be forever excluded, and the passing of the serving-bowls seemed far more interesting to them than the stranger in their midst. The smell of scrambled eggs dominated the great room. That heavy, greasy odor seemed to expand and rise until it squeezed out all the air. Oxenshuer found himself choking and gagging. Panic seized him. He had never imagined he could be thrown into terror by the smell of scrambled eggs. "This way," Matt called. "Steady on, man. You all right?" Finally they reached the raised table. Here sat only men, dignified and serene of mien, probably the elders of the community. At the head of the table was one who had the unmistakable look of a high priest. He was well past seventy—or eighty or ninety—and his strong-featured leathery face was seamed and gullied; his eyes were keen and intense, managing to convey both a fierce tenacity and an all-encompassing warm humanity. Small-bodied, lithe, weighing at most 100 pounds, he sat ferociously erect, a formidably commanding little man. A metallic embellishment of the collar of his robe was, perhaps, the badge of his status. Leaning over him, Matt said in exaggeratedly clear, loud tones, "This here's John. I'd like to stand brother to him when the Feast comes, if I can. John, this here's our Speaker."

Oxenshuer had met popes and presidents and secretaries-general, and, armored by his own standing as a celebrity, had never fallen into foolish awe-kindled embarrassment. But here he was no celebrity; he was no one at all, a stranger, an outsider, and he found himself lost before the Speaker. Mute, he waited for help. The old man said, his voice as melodious and as resonant as a 'cello, "Will you join our meal, John? Be welcome in our city."

Two of the elders made room on the bench. Oxenshuer sat at the Speaker's left hand; Matt sat beside him. Two girls of about fourteen brought settings: a plastic dish, a knife, a fork, a spoon, a cup. Matt served him: scrambled eggs, toast, sausages. All about him the clamor of eating went on. The Speaker's plate was empty. Oxenshuer fought back nausea and forced himself to attack the eggs. "We take all our meals together," said the Speaker. "This is a closely knit community, unlike any community I know on Earth." One of the serving-girls said pleasantly, "Excuse me, brother," and, reaching over Oxenshuer's shoulder, filled his cup with red wine. Wine for breakfast? They worship Dionysus here, Oxenshuer remembered.

The Speaker said, "We'll house you. We'll feed you. We'll love you. We'll lead you to God. That's why you're here, isn't it? To get closer to Him, eh? To enter into the ocean of Christ."

———What do you want to be when you grow up, Johnny?
———An astronaut, ma'am. I want to be the first man to fly to Mars.
No. He never said any such thing.

Later in the morning he moved into Matt's house, on the perimeter of the city, overlooking one of the mesas. The house was merely a small green box, clapboard outside, flimsy beaverboard partitions inside: a sitting-room, three bedrooms, a bathroom. No kitchen or dining room. ("We take all our meals together.") The walls were bare: no ikons, no crucifixes, no religious paraphernalia of any kind. No television, no radio, hardly any personal possessions at all in evidence: a shotgun, a dozen worn books and magazines, some spare robes and extra boots in a closet, little more than that. Matt's wife was a small quiet woman in her late thirties, soft-eyed, submissive, dwarfed by her burly husband. Her name was Jean. There were three children, a boy of about twelve and two girls, maybe nine and seven. The boy had had a room of his own; he moved uncomplainingly in with his sisters, who doubled up in one bed to provide one for him, and Oxenshuer took the boy's room. Matt told the children their guest's name, but it drew no response from them. Obviously they had never heard of him. Were they even aware that a spaceship from Earth had lately journeyed to Mars? Probably not. He found that refreshing: for years Oxenshuer had had to cope with children paralyzed with astonishment at finding themselves in the presence of a genuine astronaut. Here he could shed the burdens of fame.

He realized he had not been told his host's last name. Somehow it seemed too late to ask Matt directly, now. When one of the little girls came wandering into his room he said, "What's your name?"

"Toby," she said, showing a gap-toothed mouth.

"Toby what?"

"Toby. Just Toby."

No surnames in this community? All right. Why bother with surnames in a place where everyone knows everyone else? Travel light, brethren, travel light, strip away the excess baggage.

Matt walked in and said, "At council tonight I'll officially apply to stand brother to you. It's just a formality. They've never turned an application down."

"What's involved, actually?"

"It's hard to explain until you know our ways better. It means I'm, well, your spokesman, your guide through our rituals."

"A kind of sponsor?"

"Well, sponsor's the wrong word. Will and Nick will be your sponsors. That's a different level of brotherhood, lower, not as close. I'll be something like your godfather, I guess; that's as near as I can come to the idea. Unless you don't want me to be. I never consulted you. Do you want me to stand brother to you, John?"

It was an impossible question. Oxenshuer had no way to evaluate any of this. Feeling dishonest, he said, "It would be a great honor, Matt."

Matt said, "You got any real brothers? Flesh kin?"

"No. A sister in Ohio." Oxenshuer thought a moment. "There once was a man who was like a brother to me. Knew him since childhood. As close as makes no difference. A brother, yes."

"What happened to him?"

"He died. In an accident. A long way from here."

"Terrible sorry," Matt said. "I've got five brothers. Three of them outside; I haven't heard from them in years. And two right here in the city. You'll meet them. They'll accept you as kin. Everyone will."

"What did you think of the Speaker?" Matt asked.

"A marvelous old man. I'd like to talk with him again."

"You'll talk plenty with him. He's my father, you know."

Oxenshuer tried to imagine this huge man springing from the seed of the spare-bodied, compactly built Speaker and could not make the connection. He decided Matt must be speaking metaphorically again. "You mean, the way that boy was your nephew?"

"He's my true father," Matt said. "I'm flesh of his flesh." He went to the window. It was open about eight centimeters at the bottom. "Too cold for you in here, John?"

"It's fine."

"Gets cold, sometimes, these winter nights."

Matt stood silent, seemingly sizing Oxenshuer up. Then he said, "Say, you ever do any wrestling?"

"A little. In college."

"That's good."

"Why do you ask?"

"One of the things brothers do here, part of the ritual. We wrestle some. Especially the day of the Feast. It's important in the worship. I wouldn't want to hurt you any when we do. You and me, John, we'll do some wrestling before long, just to practice up for the Feast, okay? Okay?"

They let him go anywhere he pleased. Alone, he wandered through the city's labyrinth, that incredible tangle of downtown streets, in early afternoon. The maze was cunningly constructed, one street winding into another so marvelously that the buildings were drawn tightly together and the

bright desert sun could barely penetrate; Oxenshuer walked
in shadow much of the way. The twisting mazy passages
baffled him. The purpose of this part of the city seemed
clearly symbolic: everyone who dwelled here was compelled
to pass through these coiling interlacing streets in order to
get from the commonplace residential quarter, where people
lived in isolated family groupings, to the dining hall, where
the entire community together took the sacrament of food,
and to the church, where redemption and salvation were to
be had. Only when purged of error and doubt, only when familiar with the one true way (or was there more than one
way through the maze, Oxenshuer wondered?) could one attain the harmony of communality. He was still uninitiated,
an outlander; wander as he would, dance tirelessly from
street to cloistered street, he would never get there unaided.

He thought it would be less difficult than it had first
seemed to find his way from Matt's house to the inner plaza,
but he was wrong: the narrow, meandering streets misled
him, so that he sometimes moved away from the plaza when
he thought he was going toward it, and, after pursuing one
series of corridors and intersections for fifteen minutes, he
realized that he had merely returned himself to one of the
residential streets on the edge of the maze. Intently he tried
again. An astronaut trained to maneuver safely through the
trackless wastes of Mars ought to be able to get about in one
small city. Watch for landmarks, Johnny. Follow the pattern
of the shadows. He clamped his lips, concentrated, plotted a
course. As he prowled he occasionally saw faces peering
briefly at him out of the upper windows of the austere ware-
house-like buildings that flanked the streets. Were they smiling? He came to one group of streets that seemed familiar to
him, and went in and in, until he entered an alleyway closed
at both ends, from which the only exit was a slit barely wide

enough for a man if he held his breath and slipped through sideways. Just beyond, the metal cross of the church stood outlined against the sky, encouraging him: he was nearly to the end of the maze. He went through the slit and found himself in a cul-de-sac; five minutes of close inspection revealed no way to go on. He retraced his steps and sought another route.

One of the bigger buildings in the labyrinth was evidently a school. He could hear the high, clear voices of children chanting mysterious hymns. The melodies were conventional see-saws of piety but the words were strange:

> Bring us together. Lead us to the ocean.
> Help us to swim. Give us to drink.
> > Wine in my heart today,
> > Blood in my throat today,
> > Fire in my soul today,
> All praise, O God, to thee.

Sweet treble voices, making the bizarre words sound all the more grotesque. Blood in my throat today. Unreal city. How can it exist? Where does the food come from? Where does the wine come from? What do they use for money? What do the people do with themselves all day? They have electricity: what fuel keeps the generator running? They have running water. Are they hooked into a public utility district's pipelines, and if so why isn't this place on my map? Fire in my soul today. Wine in my heart today. What are these feasts, who are these saints? This is the god who burns like fire. This is the god whose name is music. This is the god whose soul is wine. You were called, Mr. Oxenshuer.

Can you say no? You can't say no to our city. To our saint.
To Jesus. Come along, now?

Where's the way out of here?

Three times a day, the whole population of the city
went on foot from their houses through the labyrinth
to the dining hall. There appeared to be at least half a dozen
ways of reaching the central plaza, but, though he studied
the route carefully each time, Oxenshuer was unable to keep
it straight in his mind. The food was simple and nourishing,
and there was plenty of it. Wine flowed freely at every meal.
Young boys and girls did the serving, jubilantly hauling huge
platters of food from the kitchen; Oxenshuer had no idea
who did the cooking, but he supposed the task would rotate
among the women of the community. (The men had other
chores. The city, Oxenshuer learned, had been built entirely
by the freely contributed labor of its own inhabitants. Several new houses were under construction now. And there
were irrigated fields beyond the mesas.) Seating in the dining
hall was random at the long tables, but people generally
seemed to come together in nuclear-family groupings. Oxenshuer met Matt's two brothers, Jim and Ernie, both
smaller men than Matt but powerfully built. Ernie gave Oxenshuer a hug, a quick, warm, impulsive gesture. "Brother,"
he said. "Brother! Brother!"

The Speaker received Oxenshuer in the study of
his residence on the plaza, a dark ground-floor room, the
walls of which were covered to ceiling height with shelves of
books. Most people here affected a casual hayseed manner,
an easy drawling rural simplicity of speech, that implied

little interest in intellectual things, but the Speaker's books ran heavily to abstruse philosophical and theological themes, and they looked as though they had all been read many times. Those books confirmed Oxenshuer's first fragmentary impression of the Speaker: that this was a man of supple, well-stocked mind, sophisticated, complex. The Speaker offered Oxenshuer a cup of cool tart wine. They drank in silence. When he had nearly drained his cup, the old man calmly hurled the dregs to the glossy slate floor. "An offering to Dionysus," he explained.

"But you're Christians here," said Oxenshuer.

"Yes, of course we're Christian! But we have our own calendar of saints. We worship Jesus in the guise of Dionysus and Dionysus in the guise of Jesus. Others might call us pagans, I suppose. But where there's Christ, is there not Christianity?" The Speaker laughed. "Are you a Christian, John?"

"I suppose. I was baptized. I was confirmed. I've taken communion. I've been to confession now and then."

"You're of the Roman faith?"

"More that faith than any other," Oxenshuer said.

"You believe in God?"

"In an abstract way."

"And in Jesus Christ?"

"I don't know," said Oxenshuer uncomfortably. "In a literal sense, no. I mean, I suppose there was a prophet in Palestine named Jesus, and the Romans nailed him up, but I've never taken the rest of the story too seriously. I can accept Jesus as a symbol, though. As a metaphor of love. God's love."

"A metaphor for *all* love," the Speaker said. "The love of God for mankind. The love of mankind for God. The love of man and woman, the love of parent and child, the love of brother and brother, every kind of love there is. Jesus is love's spirit. God is love. That's what we believe here. Through communal ecstasies we are reminded of the new commandment He gave unto us, That ye love one another. And as it says in Romans, Love is the fulfilling of the law. We follow His teachings; therefore we are Christians."

"Even though you worship Dionysus as a saint?"

"Especially so. We believe that in the divine madnesses of Dionysus we come closer to Him than other Christians are capable of coming. Through revelry, through singing, through the pleasures of the flesh, through ecstasy, through union with one another in body and in soul—through these we break out of our isolation and become one with Him. In the life to come we will all be one. But first we must live this life and share in the creation of love, which is Jesus, which is God. Our goal is to make all beings one with Jesus, so that we become droplets in the ocean of love which is God, giving up our individual selves."

"This sounds Hindu to me, almost. Or Buddhist."

"Jesus is Buddha. Buddha is Jesus."

"Neither of them taught a religion of revelry."

"Dionysus did. We make our own synthesis of spiritual commandments. And so we see no virtue in self-denial, since that is the contradiction of love. What is held to be virtue by other Christians is sin to us. And vice versa, I would suppose."

"What about the doctrine of the virgin birth? What about the virginity of Jesus himself? The whole notion of purity through restraint and asceticism?"

"Those concepts are not part of our belief, friend John."

"But you do recognize the concept of sin?"

"The sins we deplore," said the Speaker, "are such things as coldness, selfishness, aloofness, envy, maliciousness, all those things that hold one man apart from another. We punish the sinful by engulfing them in love. But we recognize no sins that arise out of love itself or out of excess of love. Since the world, especially the Christian world, finds our principles hateful and dangerous, we have chosen to withdraw from that world."

"How long have you been out here?" Oxenshuer asked.

"Many years. No one bothers us. Few strangers come to us. You are the first in a very long time."

"Why did you have me brought to your city?"

"We knew you were sent to us," the Speaker said.

At night there were wild frenzied gatherings in certain tall windowless buildings in the depths of the labyrinth. He was never allowed to take part. The dancing, the singing, the drinking, whatever else went on, these things were not yet for him. Wait till the Feast, they told him, wait till the Feast, then you'll be invited to join us. So he spent his evenings alone. Some nights he would stay home with the children. No babysitters were needed in this city, but he became one anyway, playing simple dice-games with the girls, tossing a ball back and forth with the boy, telling them stories as they fell asleep. He told them of his flight to Mars, spoke of watching the red world grow larger every day, described the landing, the alien feel of the place, the iron-red sands, the tiny glinting moons. They listened silently, perhaps fascinated, perhaps not at all interested: he suspected they thought he was making it all up. He never said anything about the fate of his companions.

Some nights he would stroll through town, street after quiet street, drifting in what he pretended was a random way toward the downtown maze. Standing near the perimeter of the labyrinth—even now he could not find his way around in it after dark, and feared getting lost if he went in too deep—he would listen to the distant sounds of the celebration, the drumming, the chanting, the simple, repetitive hymns:

This is the god who burns like fire
This is the god whose name is music
This is the god whose soul is wine

And he would also hear them sing:

Tell the saint to heat my heart
Tell the saint to give me breath
Tell the saint to quench my thirst

And this

Leaping shouting singing stamping
Rising climbing flying soaring
Melting joining loving blazing
Singing soaring joining loving

Some nights he would walk to the edge of the desert, hiking out a few hundred meters into it, drawing a bleak pleasure from the solitude, the crunch of sand beneath his boots, the knifeblade coldness of the air, the forlorn gnarled cacti, the timorous kangaroo rats, even the occasional scorpion. Crouching on some gritty hummock, looking up through the cold brilliant stars to the red dot of Mars, he would think of Dave Vogel, would think of Bud Richardson, would think of Claire, and of himself, who he had been, what he had lost. Once, he remembered, he had been a high-spirited man who laughed easily, expressed affection readily and openly, enjoyed joking, drinking, running, swimming, all the active outgoing things. Leaping shouting singing stamping. Rising climbing flying soaring. And then this deadness had come over him, this zombie absence of response, this icy shell. Mars had stolen him from himself. Why? The guilt? The guilt, the guilt, the guilt—he had lost himself in guilt. And now he was lost in the desert. This implausible town. These rites, this cult. Wine and shouting. He had no idea how long he had been here. Was Christmas approaching? Possibly it was only a few days away. Blue plastic Yule trees were sprouting in front of the department stores on Wilshire Boulevard. Jolly red Santas pacing the sidewalk. Tinsel and glitter. Christmas might be an appropriate time for the Feast of St. Dionysus. The Saturnalia revived. Would the Feast come soon? He anticipated it with fear and eagerness.

Late in the evening, when the last of the wine was gone and the singing was over, Matt and Jean would return, flushed, wine-drenched, happy, and through the thin partition separating Oxenshuer's room from theirs would come the sounds of love, the titanic poundings of their embraces, far into the night.

——Astronauts are supposed to be sane, Dave.
——Are they? Are they really, Johnny?
——Of course they are.

——Are *you* sane?

——I'm sane as hell, Dave.

——Yes. Yes. I'll bet you think you are.

——Don't you think I'm sane?

——Oh, sure, you're sane, Johnny. Saner than you need to be. If anybody asked me to name him one sane man, I'd say John Oxenshuer. But you're not all that sane. And you've got the potential to become very crazy.

——Thanks.

——I mean it as a compliment.

——What about you? You aren't sane?

——I'm a madman, Johnny. And getting madder all the time.

——Suppose NASA finds out that Dave Vogel's a madman?

——They won't, my friend. They know I'm one hell of an astronaut, and so by definition I'm sane. They don't know what's inside me. They can't. By definition, they wouldn't be NASA bureaucrats if they could tell what's inside a man.

——They know you're sane because you're an astronaut?

——Of course, Johnny. What does an astronaut know about the irrational? What sort of capacity for ecstasy does he have, anyway? He trains for ten years; he jogs in a centrifuge; he drills with computers, he runs a thousand simulations before he dares to sneeze; he thinks in spaceman jargon; he goes to church on Sundays and doesn't pray; he turns himself into a machine so he can run the damndest machines anybody ever thought up. And to outsiders he looks deader than a banker, deader than a stockbroker, deader than a sales manager. Look at him, with his 1975 haircut and his 1965 uniform. Can a man like that even know what a mystic experience *is?* Well, some of us are really like that. They fit the official astronaut image. Sometimes I think you do, Johnny, or at least that you want to. But not me. Look, I'm a yogi. Yogis train for decades so they can have a glimpse of the All. They subject their bodies to crazy disciplines. They learn highly specialized techniques. A yogi and an astronaut aren't all that far apart, man. What I do, it's not so different from what a yogi does, and it's for the same reason. It's so we can catch sight of the White Light. Look at you, laughing! But I mean it, Johnny. When that big fist knocks me into orbit, when I see the whole world hanging out there, it's a wild moment for me, it's ecstasy, it's nirvana. I live for those moments. They make all the NASA crap worthwhile. Those are breakthrough moments, when I get into an entirely new realm. That's the only reason I'm in this. And you know something? I think it's the same with you, whether you know it or not. A mystic thing, Johnny, a crazy thing, that powers us, that drives us on. The yoga of space. One day you'll find out. One day you'll see yourself for the madman you really are. You'll open up to all the wild forces inside you, the lunatic drives that sent you to NASA. You'll find out you weren't just a machine after all; you weren't just a stockbroker in a fancy costume, you'll find out you're a yogi, a holy man, an ecstatic. And you'll see what a trip you're on, you'll see that controlled madness is the only true secret and that you've always known the Way. And you'll set aside everything that's left of your old straight self. You'll give yourself up completely to forces you can't understand and don't want to understand. And you'll love it, Johnny. You'll love it.

When he had stayed in the city about three weeks—it seemed to him that it had been about three weeks, though perhaps it had been two or four—he decided to leave. The decision was nothing that came upon him suddenly; it had always been in the back of his mind that he did not want to be here, and gradually that feeling came to dominate him. Nick had promised him solitude while he was in the city, if he wanted it, and indeed he had had solitude enough, no one bothering him, no one making demands on him, the city functioning perfectly well without any contribution from him. But it was the wrong kind of solitude. To be alone in the middle of several thousand people was worse than camping by himself in the desert. True, Matt had promised him that after the Feast he would no longer be alone. Yet Oxenshuer wondered if he really wanted to stay here long enough to experience the mysteries of the Feast and the oneness that presumably would follow it. The Speaker spoke of giving up all pain as one enters the all-encompassing body of Jesus. What would he actually give up, though—his pain or his identity? Could he lose one without losing the other? Perhaps it was best to avoid all that and return to his original plan of going off by himself in the wilderness.

One evening after Matt and Jean had set out for the downtown revels, Oxenshuer quietly took his pack from the closet. He checked all his gear, filled his canteen, and said goodnight to the children. They looked at him strangely, as if wondering why he was putting on his pack just to go for a walk, but they asked no questions. He went up the broad avenue toward the palisade, passed through the unlocked gate, and in ten minutes was in the desert, moving steadily away from the City of the Word of God.

It was a cold, clear night, very dark, the stars almost painfully bright, Mars very much in evidence. He walked roughly eastward, through choppy countryside badly cut by ravines, and soon the mesas that flanked the city were out of sight. He had hoped to cover eight or ten kilometers before making camp, but the ravines made the hike hard going; when he had been out no more than an hour one of his boots began to chafe him and a muscle in his left leg sprang a cramp. He decided he would do well to halt. He picked a campsite near a stray patch of Joshua trees that stood like grotesque sentinels, stiff-armed and bristly, along the rim of a deep gully. The wind rose suddenly and swept across the desert flats, agitating their angular branches violently. It seemed to Oxenshuer that those booming gusts were blowing him the sounds of singing from the nearby city:

> I go to the god's house and his fire consumes me
> I cry the god's name and his thunder deafens me
> I take the god's cup and his wine dissolves me

He thought of Matt and Jean, and Ernie who had called him brother, and the Speaker who had offered him love and shelter, and Nick and Will his sponsors. He retraced in his mind the windings of the labyrinth until he grew dizzy. It was impossible, he told himself, to hear the singing from this place. He was at least three or four kilometers away. He prepared his campsite and unrolled his sleeping bag. But it was too early for sleep; he lay wide awake, listening to the wind, counting the stars, playing back the chants of the city in his head. Occasionally he dozed, but only for fitful intervals, easily broken. Tomorrow, he thought, he would cover twenty-five or thirty kilometers, going almost to the foothills of the mountains to the east, and he would set up half a dozen solar stills and settle down for a leisurely reexamination of all that had befallen him.

The hours slipped by slowly. About three in the morning he decided he was not going to be able to sleep, and he got up, dressed, paced along the gully's edge. A sound came to him: soft, almost a throbbing purr. He saw a light in the distance. A second light. The sound redoubled, one purr overlaid by another. Then a third light, farther away. All three lights in motion. He recognized the purring sounds now: the engines of dune-cycles. Travelers crossing the desert in the middle of the night? The headlights of the cycles swung in wide circular orbits around him. A search party from the city? Why else would they be driving like that, cutting off arcs of desert in so systematic a way?

Yes. Voices. "John? Jo—ohn! Yo, John!"

Looking for him. But the desert was immense; the searchers were still far off. He need only take his gear and hunker down in the gully, and they would pass him by.

"Yo, John! Jo—ohn!"

Matt's voice.

Oxenshuer walked down the slope of the gully, paused a moment in its depths, and, surprising himself, started to scramble up the gully's far side. There he stood in silence a few minutes, watching the circling dune-cycles, listening to the calls of the searchers. It still seemed to him that the wind was bringing him the songs of the city people. This is the god who burns like fire. This is the god whose name is music. Jesus waits. The saint will lead you to bliss, dear tired John. Yes. Yes. At last he cupped his hands to his mouth and shouted, "Yo! Here I am! Yo!"

Two of the cycles halted immediately; the third, swinging out far to the left, stopped a little afterward. Oxenshuer waited for a reply, but none came.

"Yo!" he called again. "Over here, Matt! Here!"

He heard the purring start up. Headlights were in motion once more, the beams traversing the desert and coming to rest on him. The cycles approached. Oxenshuer recrossed the gully, collected his gear, and was waiting again on the cityward side when the searchers reached him. Matt, Nick, Will.

"Spending a night out?" Matt asked. The odor of wine was strong on his breath.

"Guess so."

"We got a little worried when you didn't come back by midnight. Thought you might have stumbled into a dry wash and hurt yourself some. Wasn't any cause for alarm, though, looks like." He glanced at Oxenshuer's pack, but made no comment. "Long as you're all right, I guess we can leave you finish what you were doing. See you in the morning, okay?"

He turned away. Oxenshuer watched the men mount their cycles.

"Wait," he said.

Matt looked around.

"I'm all finished out here," Oxenshuer said. "I'd appreciate a lift back to the city."

"It's a matter of wholeness," the Speaker said. "In the beginning, mankind was all one. We were in contact. The communion of soul to soul. But then it all fell apart. '*In Adam's Fall we sinned all,*' remember? And that Fall, that original sin, John, it was a falling apart, a falling away from one another, a falling into the evil of strife. When we were in Eden we were more than simply one family, we were one being, one universal entity; and we came forth from Eden as individuals, Adam and Eve, Cain and Abel. The original universal being broken into pieces. Here, John, we seek to put the pieces back together. Do you follow me?"

"But how is it done?" Oxenshuer asked.

"By allowing Dionysus to lead us to Jesus," the old man said. "And in the saint's holy frenzy to create unity out of opposites. We bring the hostile tribes together. We bring the contending brothers together. We bring man and woman together."

Oxenshuer shrugged. "You talk only in metaphors and parables."

"There's no other way."

"What's your method? What's your underlying principle?"

"Our underlying principle is mystic ecstasy. Our method is to partake of the flesh of the god, and of his blood."

"It sounds very familiar. Take; eat. This is my body. This is my blood. Is your Feast a High Mass?"

The Speaker chuckled. "In a sense. We've made our synthesis between paganism and orthodox Christianity, and we've tried to move backward from the symbolic ritual to the literal act. Do you know where Christianity went astray? The same place all other religions have become derailed. The point at which spiritual experience was replaced by rote worship. Look at your lamas, twirling their prayer-wheels. Look at your Jews, muttering about Pharaoh in a language they've forgotten. Look at your Christians, lining up at the communion rail for a wafer and a gulp of wine, and never once feeling the terror and splendor of knowing that they're eating their god! Religion becomes doctrine too soon. It becomes professions of faith, formulas, talismans, emptiness. 'I believe in God the Father Almighty, creator of heaven and earth, and in Jesus Christ his only son, our Lord, who was conceived by the Holy Spirit, born from the Virgin Mary—' Words. Only words. We don't believe, John, that religious worship consists in reciting narrative accounts of ancient history. We want it to be immediate. We want it to be real. We want to *see* our god. We want to *taste* our god. We want to *become* our god."

"How?"

"Do you know anything about the ancient cults of Dionysus?"

"Only that they were wild and bloody, with plenty of drinking and revelry and maybe human sacrifices."

"Yes. Human sacrifices," the Speaker said. "But before the human sacrifices came the divine sacrifices, the god who dies, the god who gives up his life for his people. In the prehistoric Dionysiac cults the god himself was torn apart and eaten, he was the central figure in a mystic rite of destruction in which his ecstatic worshipers feasted on his raw flesh, a sacramental meal enabling them to be made full of the god and take on blessedness, while the dead god became the scapegoat for man's sins. And then the god was reborn and all things were made one by his rebirth. So in Greece, so in Asia Minor, priests of Dionysus were ripped to pieces as surrogates for the god, and the worshipers partook of blood and meat in cannibalistic feasts of love, and in more civilized times animals were sacrificed in place of men, and still later, when the religion of Jesus replaced the various Dionysiac religions, bread and wine came to serve as the instruments of communion, metaphors for the flesh and blood of the god. On the symbolic level it was all the same. To devour the god. To achieve contact with the god in the most direct way. To experience the rapture of the ecstatic state, when one is possessed by the god. To unite that which society has forced asunder. To break down all boundaries. To rip off all shackles. To yield to our saint, our mad saint, the drunken god who is our saint, the mad saintly god who abolishes walls and makes all things one. Yes, John? We integrate through disintegration. We dissolve in the great ocean. We burn in the great fire. Yes, John? Give your soul gladly to Dionysus the Saint, John. Make yourself whole in his blessed fire. You've been divided too long." The Speaker's eyes had taken on a terrifying gleam. "Yes, John? Yes? Yes?"

In the dining hall one night Oxenshuer drinks much too much wine. The thirst comes upon him gradually and unexpectedly; at the beginning of the meal he simply sips as he eats, in his usual way, but the more he drinks, the more dry his throat becomes, until by the time the meat course is on the table he is reaching compulsively for the carafe every few minutes, filling his cup, draining it, filling, draining, filling, draining. He becomes giddy and boisterous; someone at the table begins a hymn, and Oxenshuer joins in, though he is unsure of the words and keeps losing the melody. Those about him laugh, clap him on the back, sing even louder, beckoning to him, encouraging him to sing with them. Ernie and Matt match him drink for drink, and now whenever his cup is empty they fill it before he has a chance. A serving-girl brings a full carafe. He feels a prickling in his earlobes and the tip of his nose, feels a band of warmth across his chest and shoulders, and realizes he is getting drunk, but he allows it to happen. Dionysus reigns here. He has been sober long enough. And it has occurred to him that his drunkenness perhaps will inspire them to admit him to the night's revels. But that does not happen. Dinner ends. The Speaker and the other old men who sit at his table file from the hall; it is the signal for the rest to leave. Oxenshuer stands. Falters. Reels. Recovers. Laughs. Links arms with Matt and Ernie. "Brothers," he says. "Brothers!" They go from the hall together, but outside, in the great cobbled plaza, Matt says to him, "You better not go wandering in the desert tonight, man, or you'll break your neck for sure." So he is still excluded. He goes back through the labyrinth with Matt and Jean to their house, and they help him into his room and give him a jug of wine in case he still feels the thirst, and then they leave him. Oxenshuer sprawls on his bed. His head is spinning. Matt's boy looks in and asks if everything's all right. "Yes," Oxenshuer tells him. "I just need to lie down some." He feels embarrassed over being so helplessly intoxicated, but he reminds himself that in this city of Dionysus no one need apologize for taking too much wine. He closes his eyes and waits for a little stability to return. In the darkness a vision comes to him: the death of Dave Vogel. With strange brilliant clarity Oxenshuer sees the landscape of Mars spread out on the screen of his mind, low snubby hills sloping down to broad crater-pocked plains, gnarled desolate boulders, purple sky, red gritty particles blowing about. The extravehicular crawler well along on its journey westward toward the Gulliver site, Richardson driving, Vogel busy taking pictures, operating the myriad sensors, leaning into the microphone to describe everything he sees. They are at the Gulliver site now, preparing to leave the crawler, when they are surprised by the sudden onset of the sandstorm. Without warning the sky is red with billowing capes of sand, driving down on them like snowflakes in a blizzard. In the first furious moment of the storm the vehicle is engulfed; within minutes sand is piled a meter high on the crawler's domed transparent roof; they can see nothing, and the sandfall steadily deepens as the storm gains in intensity. Richardson grabs the controls, but the wheels of the crawler will not grip. "I've never seen anything like this," Vogel mutters. The vehicle has extendible perceptors on stalks, but when Vogel pushes them out to their full reach he finds that they are even then hidden by the sand. The crawler's eyes are blinded; its antennae are buried. They are drowning in sand. Whole dunes are descending on them. "I've never seen anything like this," Vogel says again. "You can't imagine it, Johnny. It hasn't been going on five minutes and we must be under three or four meters of sand already." The crawler's engine strains to free them. "Johnny? I can't hear you, Johnny. Come in, Johnny." All is silent on the ship-to-crawler transmission belt. "Hey, Houston," Vogel says, "we've got this goddamned sandstorm going, and I seem to have lost contact with the ship. Can you raise him for us?" Houston does not reply. "Mission Control, are you reading me?" Vogel asks. He still has some idea of setting up a crawler-to-Earth-to-ship relay, but slowly it occurs to him that he has lost contact with Earth as well. All transmissions have ceased. Sweating suddenly in his space-suit, Vogel shouts into the microphone, jiggles controls, plugs in the fail-safe communications banks only to find that everything has failed; sand has invaded the crawler and holds them in a deadly blanket. "Impossible," Richardson says. "Since when is sand an insulator for radio waves?" Vogel shrugs. "It isn't a matter of insulation, dummy. It's a matter of total systems breakdown. I don't know why." They must be ten meters underneath the sand now. Entombed. Vogel pounds on the hatch, thinking that if they can get out of the crawler somehow they can dig their way to the surface through the loose sand, and then—and then what? Walk back ninety kilometers to the ship? Their suits carry thirty-six-hour breathing supplies. They would have to average two and a half kilometers an hour, over ragged cratered country, in order to get there in time; and with this storm raging their chances of surviving long enough to hike a single kilometer are dismal. Nor does Oxenshuer have a backup crawler in which he could come out to rescue them, even if he knew their plight; there is only the flimsy little one-man vehicle that they use for short-range geological field trips in the vicinity of the ship. "You know what?" Vogel says. "We're dead men, Bud." Richardson shakes his head vehemently. "Don't talk garbage. We'll wait out the storm, and then we'll get the hell out of here. Meanwhile we better just pray." There is no conviction in his voice, however. How will they know when the storm is over? Already they lie deep below the new surface of the Martian plain, and everything is snug and tranquil where they are. Tons of sand hold the crawler's hatch shut. There is no escape. Vogel is right: they are dead men. The only remaining question is one of time. Shall they wait for the crawler's air supply to exhaust itself, or shall they take some more immediate step to hasten the inevitable end, going out honorably and quickly and without pain? Here Oxenshuer's vision falters. He does not know how the trapped men chose to handle the choreography of their deaths. He knows only that whatever their decision was, it must have been reached without bitterness or panic, and that the manner of their departure was calm. The vision fades. He lies alone in the dark. The last of the drunkenness has burned itself from his mind.

"Come on," Matt said. "Let's do some wrestling."

It was a crisp winter morning, not cold, a day of clear, hard light. Matt took him downtown, and for the first time Oxenshuer entered one of the tall brick-faced buildings of the labyrinth streets. Inside was a large, bare gymnasium, unheated, with bleak yellow walls and threadbare purple mats on the floor. Will and Nick were already there. Their voices echoed in the cavernous room. Quickly Matt stripped down to his undershorts. He looked even bigger naked than clothed; his muscles were thick and rounded, his chest was formidably deep, his thighs were pillars. A dense covering of fair curly hair sprouted everywhere on him, even his back and shoulders. He stood at least two meters tall and must have weighed close to 110 kilos. Oxenshuer, tall but not nearly so tall as Matt, well built but at least 20 kilos lighter, felt himself badly outmatched. He was quick and agile, at any rate: perhaps those qualities would serve him. He tossed his clothing aside.

Matt looked him over closely. "Not bad," he said. "Could use a little more meat on the bones."

"Got to fatten him up some for the Feast, I guess," Will said. He grinned amiably. The three men laughed; the remark seemed less funny to Oxenshuer.

Matt signaled to Nick, who took a flask of wine from a locker and handed it to him. Uncorking it, Matt drank deeply and passed the flask to Oxenshuer. It was different from the usual table stuff: thicker, sweeter, almost a sacramental wine. Oxenshuer gulped it down. Then they went to the center mat.

They hunkered into crouches and circled one another tentatively, outstretched arms probing for an opening. Oxenshuer made the first move. He slipped in quickly, finding Matt surprisingly slow on his guard and unsophisticated in defensive technique. Nevertheless, the big man was able to break Oxenshuer's hold with one fierce toss of his body, shaking him off easily and sending him sprawling violently backward. Again they circled. Matt seemed willing to allow Oxenshuer every initiative. Warily Oxenshuer advanced, feinted toward Matt's shoulders, seized an arm instead; but Matt placidly ignored the gambit and somehow pivoted so that Oxenshuer was caught in the momentum of his own onslaught, thrown off balance, vulnerable to a bearhug. Matt forced him to the floor. For thirty seconds or so Oxenshuer stubbornly resisted him, arching his body; then Matt pinned him. They rolled apart and Nick proffered the wine again. Oxenshuer drank, gasping between pulls. "You've got good moves," Matt told him. But he took the second fall even more quickly, and the third with not very much greater effort. "Don't worry," Will murmured to Oxenshuer as they left the gym. "The day of the Feast, the saint will guide you against him."

Every night, now, he drinks heavily, until his face is flushed and his mind is dizzied. Matt, Will, and Nick are always close beside him, seeing to it that his cup never stays dry for long. The wine makes him hazy and groggy, and frequently he has visions as he lies in a stupor on his bed, recovering. He sees Claire Vogel's face glowing in the dark and the sight of her wrings his heart with love. He engages in long dreamlike imaginary dialogues with the Speaker on the nature of ecstatic communion. He sees himself dancing in the god-house with the other city-folk, dancing himself to exhaustion and ecstasy. He is even visited by St. Dionysus. The saint has a youthful and oddly innocent appearance, with a heavy belly, plump thighs, curling golden hair, a flowing golden beard; he looks like a rejuvenated Santa Claus. "Come," he says softly. "Let's go to the ocean." He takes Oxenshuer's hand and they drift through the silent dark streets, toward the desert, across the swirling dunes, floating in the night, until they reach a broad-bosomed sea, moonlight blazing on its surface like cold white fire. What sea is this? The saint says, "This is the sea that brought you to the world, the undying sea that carries every mortal into life. Why do you ever leave the sea? Here. Step into it with me." Oxenshuer enters. The water is warm, comforting, oddly viscous. He gives himself to it, ankle-deep, shin-deep, thigh-deep; he hears a low murmuring song rising from the gentle waves, and he feels all sorrow going from him, all pain, all sense of himself as a being apart from others. Bathers bob on the breast of the sea. Look: Dave Vogel is here, and Claire, and his parents, and his grandparents, and thousands more whom he does not know, millions, even, a horde stretching far out from shore, all the progeny of Adam, even Adam himself, yes, and Mother Eve, her soft pink body aglow in the water. "Rest," the saint whispers. "Drift. Float. Surrender. Sleep. Give yourself to the ocean, dear John." Oxenshuer asks if he will find God in this ocean. The saint replies, "God *is* the ocean. And God is within you. He always has been. The ocean is God. You are God. I am God. God is everywhere, John, and we are His indivisible atoms. God is everywhere. But before all else, God is within you."

What does the Speaker say? The Speaker speaks Freudian wisdom. Within us all, he says, there dwells a force, an entity—call it the unconscious; it's as good a name as any—that from its hiding place dominates and controls our lives, though its workings are mysterious and opaque to us. A god within our skulls. We have lost contact with that god, the Speaker says; we are unable to reach it or to comprehend its powers, and so we are divided against ourselves, cut off from the chief source of our strength and cut off, too, from one another: the god that is within me no longer has a way to reach the god that is within you, though you and I both came out of the same primordial ocean, out of that sea of divine unconsciousness in which all being is one. If we could tap that force, the Speaker says, if we could make contact with that hidden god, if we could make it rise into consciousness or allow ourselves to submerge into the realm of unconsciousness, the split in our souls would be healed and we would at last have full access to our godhood. Who knows what kind of creatures we would become then? We would speak, mind to mind. We would travel through space or time, merely by willing it. We would work miracles. The errors of the past could be undone; the patterns of old griefs could be rewoven. We might be able to do anything, the Speaker says, once we have reached that hidden god and transformed ourselves into the gods we were meant to be. Anything. Anything. Anything.

This is the dawn of the day of the Feast. All night long the drums and incantations have resounded through the city; he has been alone in the house, for not even the children were there; everyone was dancing in the plaza, and only he, the uninitiated, remained excluded from the revels. Much of the night he could not sleep. He thought of using wine to lull himself, but he feared the visions the wine might bring, and let the flask be. Now it is early morning, and he must have slept, for he finds himself fluttering up from slumber, but he does not remember having slipped down into it. He sits up. He hears footsteps, someone moving through the house. "John? You awake, John?" Matt's voice. "In here," Oxenshuer calls.

They enter his room: Matt, Will, Nick. Their robes are

spotted with splashes of red wine, and their faces are gaunt, eyes red-rimmed and unnaturally bright; plainly they have been up all night. Behind their fatigue, though, Oxenshuer perceives exhilaration. They are high, very high, almost in an ecstatic state already, and it is only the dawn of the day of the Feast. He sees that their fingers are trembling. Their bodies are tense with expectation.

"We've come for you," Matt says. "Here. Put this on."

He tosses Oxenshuer a robe similar to theirs. All this time Oxenshuer has continued to wear his mundane clothes in the city, making him a marked man, a conspicuous outsider. Naked, he gets out of bed and picks up his undershorts, but Matt shakes his head. Today, he says, only robes are worn. Oxenshuer nods and pulls the robe over his bare body. When he is robed he steps forward; Matt solemnly embraces him, a strong warm hug, and then Will and Nick do the same. The four men leave the house. The long shadows of dawn stretch across the avenue that leads to the labyrinth; the mountains beyond the city are tipped with red. Far ahead, where the avenue gives way to the narrower streets, a tongue of black smoke can be seen licking the sky. The reverberations of the music batter the sides of the buildings. Oxenshuer feels a strange onrush of confidence, and is certain he could negotiate the labyrinth unaided this morning; as they reach its outer border he is actually walking ahead of the others, but sudden confusion confounds him, an inability to distinguish one winding street from another comes over him, and he drops back in silence, allowing Matt to take the lead.

Ten minutes later they reach the plaza.

It presents a crowded, chaotic scene. All the city folk are there, some dancing, some singing, some beating on drums or blowing into trumpets, some lying sprawled in exhaustion. Despite the chill in the air, many robes hang open, and more than a few of the citizens have discarded their clothing entirely. Children run about, squealing and playing tag. Along the front of the dining hall a series of wine barrels has been installed, and the wine gushes freely from the spigots, drenching those who thrust cups forward or simply push their lips to the flow. To the rear, before the house of the Speaker, a wooden platform has sprouted, and the Speaker and the city elders sit enthroned upon it. A gigantic bonfire has been kindled in the center of the plaza, fed by logs from an immense woodpile—hauled no doubt from some storehouse in the labyrinth—that occupies some twenty square meters. The heat of this blaze is enormous, and it is the smoke from the bonfire that Oxenshuer was able to see from the city's edge.

His arrival in the plaza serves as a signal. Within moments, all is still. The music dies away; the dancing stops; the singers grow quiet; no one moves. Oxenshuer, flanked by his sponsors Nick and Will and preceded by his brother Matt, advances uneasily toward the throne of the Speaker. The old man rises and makes a gesture, evidently a blessing. "Dionysus receive you into His bosom," the Speaker says, his resonant voice traveling far across the plaza. "Drink, and let the saint heal your soul. Drink, and let the holy ocean engulf you. Drink. Drink."

"Drink," Matt says, and guides him toward the barrels. A girl of about fourteen, naked, sweat-shiny, wine-soaked, hands him a cup. Oxenshuer fills it and puts it to his lips. It is the thick, sweet wine, the sacramental wine, that he had had on the morning he had practiced wrestling with Matt. It slides easily down his throat; he reaches for more, and then for more when that is gone.

At a signal from the Speaker, the music begins again.

The frenzied dancing resumes. Three naked men hurl more logs on the fire and it blazes up ferociously, sending sparks nearly as high as the tip of the cross above the church. Nick and Will and Matt lead Oxenshuer into a circle of dancers who are moving in a whirling, dizzying step around the fire, shouting, chanting, stamping against the cobbles, flinging their arms aloft. At first Oxenshuer is put off by the uninhibited corybantic motions and finds himself self-conscious about imitating them, but as the wine reaches his brain he sheds all embarrassment, and prances with as much gusto as the others: he ceases to be a spectator of himself, and becomes fully a participant. Whirl. Stamp. Fling. Shout. Whirl. Stamp. Fling. Shout. The dance centrifuges his mind; pools of blood collect at the walls of his skull and flush the convolutions of his cerebellum as he spins. The heat of the fire makes his skin glow. He sings:

> Tell the saint to heat my heart
> Tell the saint to give me breath
> Tell the saint to quench my thirst.

Thirst. When he has been dancing so long that his breath is fire in his throat, he staggers out of the circle and helps himself freely at a spigot. His greed for the thick wine astonishes him. It is as if he has been parched for centuries, every cell of his body shrunken and withered, and only the wine can restore him.

Back to the circle again. His head throbs; his bare feet slap the cobbles; his arms claw the sky. This is the god whose name is music. This is the god whose soul is wine. There are ninety or a hundred people in the central circle of dancers now, and other circles have formed in the corners of the plaza, so that the entire square is a nest of dazzling interlocking vortices of motion. He is being drawn into these vortices, sucked out of himself; he is losing all sense of himself as a discrete individual entity.

Leaping shouting singing stamping
Rising climbing flying soaring
Melting joining loving blazing
Singing soaring joining loving

"Come," Matt murmurs. "It's time for us to do some wrestling."

He discovers that they have constructed a wrestling pit in the far corner of the plaza, over in front of the church. It is square, four low wooden borders about ten meters long on each side, filled with the coarse sand of the desert. The Speaker has shifted his lofty seat so that he now faces the pit; everyone else is crowded around the place of the wrestling, and all dancing has once again stopped. The crowd opens to admit Matt and Oxenshuer. Not far from the pit Matt shucks his robe; his powerful naked body glistens with sweat. Oxenshuer, after only a moment's hesitation, strips also. They advance toward the entrance of the pit. Before they enter, a boy brings them each a flask of wine. Oxenshuer, already feeling wobbly and hazy from drink, wonders what more wine will do to his physical coordination, but he takes the flask and drinks from it in great gulping swigs. In moments it is empty. A young girl offers him another. "Just take a few sips," Matt advises. "In honor of the god." Oxenshuer does as he is told. Matt is sipping from a second flask too; without warning, Matt grins and flings the contents of his flask over Oxenshuer. Instantly Oxenshuer retaliates. A great cheer goes up; both men are soaked with the sticky red wine. Matt laughs heartily and claps Oxenshuer on the back. They enter the wrestling pit.

> Wine in my heart today,
> Blood in my throat today,
> Fire in my soul today,
> All praise, O God, to thee.

They circle one another warily. Brother against brother. Romulus and Remus, Cain and Abel, Osiris and Set: the ancient ritual, the timeless conflict. Neither man offers. Oxenshuer feels heavy with wine, his brain clotted, and yet a strange lightness also possesses him; each time he puts his foot down against the sand the contact gives him a little jolt of ecstasy. He is excitingly aware of being alive, mobile, vigorous. The sensation grows and possesses him, and he rushes forward suddenly, seizes Matt, tries to force him down. They struggle in almost motionless rigidity. Matt will not fall, but his counterthrust is unavailing against Oxenshuer. They stand locked, body against sweat-slick, wine-drenched body, and after perhaps two minutes of intense tension they give up their holds by unvoiced agreement, backing away trembling from one another. They circle again. Brother. Brother. Abel. Cain. Oxenshuer crouches. Extends his hands, groping for a hold. Again they leap toward one another. Again they grapple and freeze. This time Matt's arms pass like bands around Oxenshuer, and he tries to lift Oxenshuer from the ground and hurl him down. Oxenshuer does not budge. Veins swell in Matt's forehead, and, Oxenshuer suspects, in his own. Faces grow crimson. Muscles throb with sustained effort. Matt gasps, loosens his grip, tries to step back; instantly Oxenshuer steps to one side of the bigger man, catches his arm, pulls him close. Once more they hug. Each in turn, they sway but do not topple. Wine and exertion blur Oxenshuer's vision; he is intoxicated with strain. Heaving, grabbing, twisting, shoving, he goes round and round the pit with Matt, until abruptly he experiences a dimming of perception, a sharp moment of blackout, and when his senses return to him he is stunned to find himself wrestling not with Matt but with Dave Vogel. Childhood friend, rival in love, comrade in space. Vogel, closer to him than any brother of the flesh, now here in the pit with him: thin, sandy hair, snub nose, heavy brows, thick-muscled shoulders. "Dave!" Oxenshuer cries. "Oh, Christ, Dave! Dave!" He throws his arms around the other man. Vogel gives him a mild smile and tumbles to the floor of the pit. "Dave!" Oxenshuer shouts, falling on him. "How did you get here, Dave?" He covers Vogel's body with his own. He embraces him with a terrible grip. He murmurs Vogel's name, whispering in wonder, and lets a thousand questions tumble out. Does Vogel reply? Oxenshuer is not certain. He thinks he hears answers, but they do not match the questions. Then Oxenshuer feels fingers tapping his back. "Okay, John," Will is saying. "You've pinned him fair and square. It's all over. Get up, man."

"Here, I'll give you a hand," says Nick.

In confusion Oxenshuer rises. Matt lies sprawled in the sand, gasping for breath, rubbing the side of his neck, nevertheless still grinning. "That was one hell of a press," Matt says. "That something you learned in college?"

"Do we wrestle another fall now?" Oxenshuer asks.

"No need. We go to the god-house now," Will tells him. They help Matt up. Flasks of wine are brought to them; Oxenshuer gulps greedily. The four of them leave the pit, pass through the opening crowd, and walk toward the church.

Oxenshuer has never been in here before. Except for a sort of altar at the far end, the huge building is wholly empty: no pews, no chairs, no chapels, no pulpit, no choir. A mysterious light filters through the stained-glass windows and suffuses the vast open interior space. The Speaker has already arrived; he stands before the altar. Oxenshuer, at a whispered command from Matt, kneels in front of him. Matt kneels to Oxenshuer's left; Nick and Will drop down behind them. Organ music, ghostly, ethereal, begins to filter from concealed grillwork. The congregation is assembling; Oxenshuer hears the rustle of people behind him, coughs, some murmuring. The familiar hymns soon echo through the church.

> I go to the god's house and his fire consumes me
> I cry the god's name and his thunder deafens me
> I take the god's cup and his wine dissolves me

Wine. The Speaker offers Oxenshuer a golden chalice. Oxenshuer sips. A different wine: cold, thin. Behind him a new hymn commences, one that he has never heard before, in a language he does not understand. Greek? The rhythms are angular and fierce; this is the music of the Bacchantes, this is an Orphic song, alien and frightening at first, then oddly comforting. Oxenshuer barely is conscious. He comprehends nothing. They are offering him communion. A wafer on a silver dish: dark bread, crisp, incised with an unfamiliar symbol. Take; eat. This is my body. This is my blood. More wine. Figures moving around him, other communicants coming forward. He is losing all sense of time and place. He is departing from the physical dimension and drifting across the breast of an ocean, a great warm sea, a gentle undulating sea that bears him easily and gladly. He is aware of light, warmth, hugeness, weightlessness; but he is aware of nothing tangible. The wine. The wafer. A drug in the wine, perhaps? He slides from the world and into the universe. This is my body. This is my blood. This is the experience of wholeness and unity. I take the god's cup and his wine dissolves me. How calm it is here. How empty. There's no one here, not even me. And everything radiates a pure warm light. I float. I go forth. I. I. I. John Oxenshuer. John Oxenshuer does not exist. John Oxenshuer is the universe. The universe is John Oxenshuer. This is the god whose soul is wine. This is the god whose name is music. This is the god who burns like fire. Sweet flame of oblivion. The cosmos is expanding like a balloon. Growing. Growing. Go, child, swim out to God. Jesus waits. The saint, the mad saint, the boozy old god who is a saint, will lead you to bliss, dear John. Make yourself whole. Make yourself into nothingness. I go to the god's house and his fire consumes me. Go. Go. Go. I cry the god's name and his thunder deafens me. *Dionysus! Dionysus!*

All things dissolve. All things become one.

This is Mars. Oxenshuer, running his ship on manual, lets it dance lightly down the final 500 meters to the touchdown site, touching up the yaw and pitch, moving serenely through the swirling red clouds that his rockets are kicking free. Contact light. Engine stop. Engine arm, off.

——All right, Houston, I've landed at Gulliver Base.

His signal streaks across space. Patiently he waits out the lag and gets his reply from Mission Control at last:

——Roger. Are you ready for systems checkout prior to EVA?

——Getting started on it right now, Houston.

He runs through his routines quickly, with the assurance born of total familiarity. All is well aboard the ship; its elegant mechanical brain ticks beautifully and flawlessly. Now Oxenshuer wriggles into his backpack, struggling a little with the cumbersome life-support system; putting it on without any fellow astronauts to help him is more of a chore than he expected, even under the light Martian gravity. He checks out his primary oxygen supply, his ventilating system, his water-support loop, his communications system. Helmeted and gloved and fully sealed, he exists now within a totally self-sufficient pocket universe. Unshipping his power shovel, he tests its compressed-air supply. All systems go.

——Do I have a go for cabin depressurization, Houston?

——You are go for cabin depress, John. It's all yours. Go for cabin depress.

He gives the signal and waits for the pressure to bleed down. Dials flutter. At last he can open the hatch. We have a go for EVA, John. He hoists his power shovel to his shoulder and makes his way carefully down the ladder. Boots bite into red sand. It is midday on Mars in this longitude, and the purple sky has a warm auburn glow. Oxenshuer approaches the burial mound. He is pleased to discover that he has relatively little excavating to do; the force of his rockets during the descent has stripped much of the overburden from his friends' tomb. Swiftly he sets the shovel in place and begins to cut away the remaining sand. Within minutes the glistening dome of the crawler is visible in several places. Now Oxenshuer works more delicately, scraping with care until he has revealed the entire dome. He flashes his light through it and sees the bodies of Vogel and Richardson. They are unhelmeted, and their suits are open: casual dress, the best outfit for dying. Vogel sits at the crawler's controls, Richardson lies just behind him on the floor of the vehicle. Their faces are dry, almost fleshless, but their features are still expressive, and Oxenshuer realizes that they must have died peaceful deaths, accepting the end in tranquility. Patiently he works to lift the crawler's dome. At length the catch yields and the dome swings upward. Climbing in, he slips his arms around Dave Vogel's body and draws it out of the spacesuit. So light: a mummy, an effigy. Vogel seems to have no weight at all. Easily Oxenshuer carries the parched corpse over to the ship. With Vogel in his arms he ascends the ladder. Within, he breaks out the flag-sheathed plastic container NASA has provided and tenderly wraps it around the body. He stows Vogel safely in the ship's hold. Then he returns to the crawler to get Bud Richardson. Within an hour the entire job is done.

———Mission accomplished, Houston.

The landing capsule plummets perfectly into the Pacific. The recovery ship, only three kilometers away, makes for the scene while the helicopters move into position over the bobbing spaceship. Frogmen come forth to secure the flotation collar: the old, old routine. In no time at all the hatch is open. Oxenshuer emerges. The helicopter closest to the capsule lowers its recovery basket; Oxenshuer disappears into the capsule, returning a moment later with Vogel's shrouded body, which he passes across to the swimmers. They load it into the basket and it goes up to the helicopter. Richardson's body follows, and then Oxenshuer himself.

The President is waiting on the deck of the recovery ship. With him are the two widows, black-garbed, dry-eyed, standing straight and firm. The President offers Oxenshuer a warm grin and grips his hand.

——A beautiful job, Captain Oxenshuer. The whole world is grateful to you.

——Thank you, sir.

Oxenshuer embraces the widows. Richardson's wife first: a hug and some soft murmurs of consolation. Then he draws Claire close, conscious of the television cameras. Chastely he squeezes her. Chastely he presses his cheek briefly to hers.

——I had to bring him back, Claire. I couldn't rest until I recovered those bodies.

——You didn't need to, John.

——I did it for you.

He smiles at her. Her eyes are bright and loving.

There is a ceremony on deck. The President bestows posthumous medals on Richardson and Vogel. Oxenshuer wonders whether the medals will be attached to the bodies, like morgue tags, but no, he gives them to the widows. Then Oxenshuer receives a medal for his dramatic return to Mars. The President makes a little speech. Oxenshuer pretends to listen, but his eyes are on Claire more often than not.

With Claire sitting beside him, he sets forth once more out of Los Angeles via the San Bernardino Freeway, east-ward through the plastic suburbs, through Alhambra and Azusa, past the Covina Hills Forest Lawn, through San Bernardino and Banning and Indio, out into the desert. It is a bright late-winter day, and recent rains have greened the hills and coaxed the cacti into bloom. He keeps a sharp watch for landmarks: flatlands, dry lakes.

——I think this is the place. In fact, I'm sure of it.

He leaves the freeway and guides the car northeastward. Yes, no doubt of it: there's the ancient lakebed, and there's his abandoned automobile, looking ancient also, rusted and corroded, its hood up, its wheels and engine stripped by scavengers long ago. He parks this car beside it, gets out, dons his backpack. He beckons to Claire.

——Let's go. We've got some hiking ahead of us.

She smiles timidly at him. She leaves the car and presses herself lightly against him, touching her lips to his. He begins to tremble.

——Claire. Oh, God, Claire.

——How far do we have to walk?

——Hours.

He gears his pace to hers. If necessary, they will camp overnight and go on into the city tomorrow, but he hopes they can get there before sundown. Claire is a strong hiker, and he is confident she can cover the distance in five or six hours, but there is always the possibility that he will fail to find the twin mesas. He has no compass points, no maps, nothing but his own intuitive sense of the city's location to guide him. They walk steadily northward. Neither of them says very much. Every half hour they pause to rest; he puts down his pack and she hands him the canteen. The air is mild and fragrant. Jackrabbits boldly accompany them. Blossoms are everywhere. Oxenshuer, transfigured by love, wants to leap and soar.

——We ought to be seeing those mesas soon.

——I hope so. I'm starting to get tired, John.

——We can stop and make camp if you like.

———No. No. Let's keep going. It can't be much farther, can it?

They keep going. Oxenshuer calculates they have covered twelve or thirteen kilometers already. Even allowing for some straying from course, they should be getting at least a glimpse of the mesas by this time, and it troubles him that they are not in view. If he fails to find them in the next half hour, he will make camp, for he wants to avoid hiking after sundown.

Suddenly they breast a rise in the desert and the mesas come into view, two steep wedges of rock, dark gray against the sand. The shadows of late afternoon partially cloak them, but there is no mistaking them.

———There they are, Claire. Out there.

———Can you see the city?

———Not from this distance. We've come around from the side, somehow. But we'll be there before very long.

At a faster pace, now, they head down the gentle slope and into the flats. The mesas dominate the scene. Oxenshuer's heart pounds, not entirely from the strain of carrying his pack. Ahead wait Matt and Jean, Will and Nick, the Speaker, the god-house, the labyrinth. They will welcome Claire as his woman; they will give them a small house on the edge of the city; they will initiate her into their rites. Soon. Soon. The mesas draw near.

———Where's the city, John?

———Between the mesas.

———I don't see it.

———You can't really see it from the front. All that's visible is the palisade, and when you get very close you can see some rooftops above it.

———But I don't even see the palisade, John. There's just an open space between the mesas.

———A shadow effect. The eye is easily tricked.

But it does seem odd to him. At twilight, yes, many deceptions are possible; nevertheless he has the clear impression from here that there is nothing but open space between the mesas. Can these be the wrong mesas? Hardly. Their shape is distinctive and unique; he could never confuse those two jutting slabs with other formations. The city, then? Where has the city gone? With each step he takes he grows more perturbed. He tries to hide his uneasiness from Claire, but she is tense, edgy, almost panicky now, repeatedly asking him what has happened, whether they are lost. He reassures her as best he can. This is the right place, he tells her. Perhaps it's an optical illusion that the city is invisible, or perhaps some other kind of illusion, the work of the city folk.

——Does that mean they might not want us, John? And they're hiding their city from us?

——I don't know, Claire.

——I'm frightened.

——Don't be. We'll have all the answers in just a few minutes.

When they are about 500 meters from the face of the mesas, Claire's control breaks. She whimpers and darts forward, sprinting through the cacti toward the opening between the mesas. He calls out to her, tells her to wait for him, but she runs on, vanishing into the deepening shadows. Hampered by his unwieldy pack, he stumbles after her, gasping for breath. He sees her disappear between the mesas. Weak and dizzy, he follows her path, and in a short while comes to the mouth of the canyon.

There is no city.

He does not see Claire.

He calls her name. Only mocking echoes respond. In wonder he penetrates the canyon, looking up at the steep sides of the mesas, remembering streets, avenues, houses.

——Claire?

No one. Nothing. And now night is coming. He picks his way over the rocky, uneven ground until he reaches the far end of the canyon, and looks back at the mesas, and outward at the desert, and he sees no one. The city has swallowed her and the city is gone.

——Claire! Claire!

Silence.

He drops his pack wearily, sits for a long while, finally lays out his bedroll. He slips into it but does not sleep; he waits out the night, and when dawn comes he searches again for Claire, but there is no trace of her. All right. All right. He yields. He will ask no questions. He shoulders his pack and begins the long trek back to the highway.

By mid-morning he reaches his car. He looks back at the desert, ablaze with noon light. Then he gets in and drives away.

He enters his apartment on Hollywood Boulevard. From here, so many months ago, he first set out for the desert; now all has come round to the beginning again. A thick layer of dust covers the cheap utilitarian furniture. The air is musty. All the blinds are drawn closed. He wanders aimlessly from hallway to livingroom, from livingroom to bedroom, from bedroom to kitchen, from kitchen to hallway. He kicks off his boots and sprawls out on the threadbare livingroom carpet, face down, eyes closed. So tired. So drained. I'll rest a bit.

"John?"

It is the Speaker's voice.

"Let me alone," Oxenshuer says. "I've lost her. I've lost you. I think I've lost myself."

"You're wrong. Come to us, John."

"I did. You weren't there."

"Come now. Can't you feel the city calling you? The Feast is over. It's time to settle down among us."

"I couldn't find you."

"You were still lost in dreams, then. Come now. Come. The saint calls you. Jesus calls you. Claire calls you."

"Claire?"

"Claire," he says.

Slowly Oxenshuer gets to his feet. He crosses the room and pulls the blinds open. This window faces Hollywood Boulevard; but, looking out, he sees only the red plains of Mars, eroded and cratered, glowing in purple noon light. Vogel and Richardson are out there, waving to him. Smiling. Beckoning. The faceplates of their helmets glitter by the cold gleam of the stars. Come on, they call to him. We're waiting for you. Oxenshuer returns their greeting and walks to another window. He sees a lifeless wasteland here too. Mars again, or is it only the Mojave Desert? He is unable to tell. All is dry, all is desolate, all is beautiful with the serene transcendent beauty of desolation. He sees Claire in the middle distance. Her back is to him; she is moving at a steady, confident pace toward the twin mesas. Between the mesas lies the City of the Word of God, golden and radiant in the warm sunlight. Oxenshuer nods. This is the right moment. He will go to her. He will go to the city. The Feast of St. Dionysus is over, and the city calls to him.

Bring us together. Lead us to the ocean.
Help us to swim. Give us to drink.

Wine in my heart today,
Blood in my throat today,
Fire in my soul today,

All praise, O God, to thee.

Oxenshuer runs in long loping strides. He sees the
mesas; he sees the city's palisade. The sound of far-off chanting throbs in his ears. "This way, brother!" Matt shouts.
"Hurry, John!" Claire cries. He runs. He stumbles, and recovers, and runs again. Wine in my heart today. Fire in my
soul today. "God is everywhere," the saint tells him. "But
before all else, God is within you." The desert is a sea, the
great warm cradling ocean, the undying mother-sea of all
things, and Oxenshuer enters it gladly, and drifts, and floats,
and lets it take hold of him and carry him wherever it will.

▾▴▾▴▾

SCHWARTZ
BETWEEN
THE
GALAXIES

*T*his much is reality: Schwartz sits comfortably co-cooned—passive, suspended—in a first-class passenger rack aboard a Japan Air Lines rocket, nine kilometers above the Coral Sea. And this much is fantasy: the same Schwartz has passage on a shining starship gliding silkily through the interstellar depths, en route at nine times the velocity of light from Betelgeuse IX to Rigel XXI, or maybe from Andromeda to the Lesser Magellanic.

There are no starships. Probably there never will be any. Here we are, a dozen decades after the flight of Apollo 11, and no human being goes anywhere except back and forth across the face of the little O, the Earth, for the planets are barren and the stars are beyond reach. That little O is too small for Schwartz. Too often it glazes for him; it turns to a nugget of dead porcelain; and lately he has formed the habit, when the world glazes, of taking refuge aboard that interstellar ship. So what JAL Flight 411 holds is merely his physical self, his shell, occupying a costly private cubicle on a slender 200-passenger vessel which, leaving Buenos Aires shortly after breakfast, has sliced westward along the Tropic of Capricorn for a couple of hours and will soon be landing at Papua's Torres Skyport. But his consciousness, his *anima*, the essential Schwartzness of him, soars between the galaxies.

What a starship it is! How marvelous its myriad passengers! Down its crowded corridors swarms a vast gaudy heterogeny of galactic creatures, natives of the worlds of Capella, Arcturus, Altair, Canopus, Polaris, Antares, beings both intelligent and articulate, methane-breathing or nitrogen-breathing or argon-breathing, spiny-skinned or skinless, many-armed or many-headed or altogether incorporeal, each a product of a distinct and distinctly unique and alien cultural heritage. Among these varied folk moves Schwartz, that superstar of anthropologists, that true heir to Kroeber and Morgan and Malinowski and Mead, delightedly devouring their delicious diversity. Whereas aboard this prosaic rocket, this planetlocked stratosphere-needle, one cannot tell the Canadians from the Portuguese, the Portuguese from the Romanians, the Romanians from the Irish, unless they open their mouths, and sometimes not always then.

In his reveries he confers with creatures from the Fomalhaut system about digital circumcision; he tapes the melodies of the Achernarnian eye-flute; he learns of the sneeze-magic of Acrux, the sleep-ecstasies of Aldebaran, the asteroid-sculptors of Thuban. Then a smiling JAL stewardess parts the curtain of his cubicle and peers in at him, jolting him from one reality to another. She is blue-eyed, frizzy-haired, straight-nosed, thin-lipped, bronze-skinned, a genetic mishmash, your standard twenty-first-century-model mongrel human, perhaps Melanesian-Swedish-Turkish-Bolivian, perhaps Polish-Berber-Tatar-Welsh. Cheap intercontinental transit has done its deadly work: all Earth is a crucible, all the gene pools have melted into one indistinguishable fluid. Schwartz wonders about the recessivity of those blue eyes and arrives at no satisfactory solution. She is beautiful, at any rate. Her name is Dawn—o sweet neutral nonculture-bound cognomen!—and they have played at a flirtation, he and she, Dawn and Schwartz, at occasional moments of this short flight. Twinkling, she says softly, "We're getting ready for our landing, Dr. Schwartz. Are your restrictors in polarity?"

"I never unfastened them."

"Good." The blue eyes, warm, interested, meet his. "I have a layover in Papua tonight," she says.

"That's nice."

"Let's have a drink while we're waiting for them to

unload the baggage," she suggests with cheerful bluntness. "All right?"

"I suppose," he says casually. "Why not?" Her availability bores him: somehow he enjoys the obsolete pleasures of the chase. Once such easiness in a woman like this would have excited him, but no longer. Schwartz is forty years old, tall, square-shouldered, sturdy, a showcase for the peasant genes of his rugged Irish mother. His close-cropped black hair is flecked with gray; many women find that interesting. One rarely sees gray hair now. He dresses simply but well, in sandals and Socratic tunic. Predictably, his physical attractiveness, both within his domestic sixness and without, has increased with his professional success. He is confident, sure of his powers, and he radiates an infectious assurance. This month alone eighty million people have heard his lectures.

She picks up the faint weariness in his voice. "You don't sound eager. Not interested?"

"Hardly that."

"What's wrong, then? Feeling sub, Professor?"

Schwartz shrugs. "Dreadfully sub. Body like dry bone. Mind like dead ashes." He smiles, full force, depriving his words of all their weight.

She registers mock anguish. "That sounds bad," she says. "That sounds awful!"

"I'm only quoting Chuang Tzu. Pay no attention to me. Actually, I feel fine, just a little stale."

"Too many skyports?"

He nods. "Too much of a sameness wherever I go." He thinks of a star-bright, top-deck bubble-dome where three boneless Spicans do a twining dance of propitiation to while away the slow hours of nine-light travel. "I'll be all right," he tells her. "It's a date."

Her hybrid face flows with relief and anticipation. "See you in Papua," she tells him, and winks, and moves jauntily down the aisle.

Papua. By cocktail time Schwartz will be in Port Moresby. Tonight he lectures at the University of Papua; yesterday it was Montevideo; the day after tomorrow it will be Bangkok. He is making the grand academic circuit. This is his year: he is very big, suddenly, in anthroplogical circles, since the publication of *The Mask Beneath the Skin.* From continent to continent he flashes, sharing his wisdom, Monday in Montreal, Tuesday Veracruz, Wednesday Montevideo, Thursday—Thursday? He crossed the international date line this morning, and he does not remember whether he has entered Thursday or Tuesday, though yesterday was surely Wednesday. Schwartz is certain only that this is July and the year is 2083, and there are moments when he is not even sure of that.

The JAL rocket enters the final phase of its landward plunge. Papua waits, sleek, vitrescent. The world has a glassy sheen again. He lets his spirit drift happily back to the gleaming starship making its swift way across the whirling constellations.

He found himself in the starship's busy lower-deck lounge, having a drink with his traveling companion, Pitkin, the Yale economist. Why Pitkin, that coarse, florid little man? With all of real and imaginary humanity to choose from, why had his unconscious elected to make him share this fantasy with such a boor?

"Look," Pitkin said, winking and leering. "There's your girlfriend."

The entry-iris had opened and the Antarean not-male had come in.

"Quit it," Schwartz snapped. "You know there's no such thing going on."

"Haven't you been chasing her for days?"

"She's not a 'her,' " Schwartz said.

Pitkin guffawed. "Such precision! Such scholarship! *She's* not a *her*, he says!" He gave Schwartz a broad nudge. "To you she's a she, friend, and don't try to kid me."

Schwartz had to admit there was some justice to Pitkin's vulgar innuendos. He did find the Antarean—a slim yellow-eyed ebony-skinned upright humanoid, sinuous and glossy, with tapering elongated limbs and a seal's fluid grace—powerfully attractive. Nor could he help thinking of the Antarean as feminine. That attitude was hopelessly culture-bound and species-bound, he knew; in fact the alien had cautioned him that terrestrial sexual distinctions were irrelevant in the Antares system, that if Schwartz insisted on thinking of "her" in genders, "she" could be considered only the negative of male, with no implication of biological femaleness.

He said patiently, "I've told you. The Antarean's neither male nor female as we understand those concepts. If we happen to perceive the Antarean as feminine, that's the result of our own cultural conditioning. If you want to believe that my interest in this being is sexual, go ahead, but I assure you that it's purely professional."

"Sure. You're only studying her."

"In a sense I am. And she's studying me. On her native world she has the status-frame of 'watcher-of-life,' which seems to translate into the Antarean equivalent of an anthropologist."

"How lovely for you both. She's your first alien and you're her first Jew."

"Stop calling her *her*," Schwartz hissed.

"But you've been doing it!"

Schwartz closed his eyes. "My grandmother told me

never to get mixed up with economists. Their thinking is muddy and their breath is bad, she said. She also warned me against Yale men. Perverts of the intellect, she called them. So here I am cooped up on an interstellar ship with 500 alien creatures and one fellow human, and he has to be an economist from Yale."

"Next trip travel with your grandmother instead."

"Go away," Schwartz said. "Stop lousing up my fantasies. Go peddle your dismal science somewhere else. You see those Delta Aurigans over there? Climb into their bottle and tell them all about the Gross Global Product." Schwartz smiled at the Antarean, who had purchased a drink, something that glittered an iridescent blue, and was approaching them. "Go *on*," Schwartz murmured.

"Don't worry," Pitkin said. "I wouldn't want to crowd you." He vanished into the motley crowd.

The Antarean said, "The Capellans are dancing, Schwartz."

"I'd like to see that. Too damned noisy in here anyway." Schwartz stared into the alien's vertical-slitted citreous eyes. Cat's eyes, he thought. Panther's eyes. The Antarean's gaze was focused, as usual, on Schwartz's mouth: other worlds, other customs. He felt a strange, unsettling tremor of desire. Desire for what, though? It was a sensation of pure need, nonspecific, certainly nonsexual. "I think I'll take a look. Will you come with me?"

The Papua rocket has landed. Schwartz, leaning across the narrow table in the skyport's lounge, says to the stewardess in a low, intense tone, "My life was in crisis. All my values were becoming meaningless. I was discovering that my chosen profession was empty, foolish, as useless as—as playing chess."

"How awful," Dawn whispers gently.

"You can see why. You go all over the world, you see a thousand skyports a year. Everything the same everywhere. The same clothes, the same slang, the same magazines, the same styles of architecture and decor."

"Yes."

"International homogeneity. Worldwide uniformity. Can you understand what it's like to be an anthropologist in a world where there are no primitives left, Dawn? Here we sit on the island of Papua—you know, head-hunters, animism, body-paint, the drums at sunset, the bone through the nose—and look at the Papuans in their business robes all around us. Listen to them exchanging stock-market tips, talking baseball, recommending restaurants in Paris and barbers in Johannesburg. It's no different anywhere else. In a single century we've transformed the planet into one huge sophisticated plastic western industrial state. The TV relay satellites, the two-hour intercontinental rockets, the breakdown of religious exclusivism and genetic taboo, have mongrelized every culture, don't you see? You visit the Zuni and they have plastic African masks on the wall. You visit the Bushmen and they have Japanese-made Hopi-motif ashtrays. It's all just so much interior decoration, and underneath the carefully selected primitive motifs there's the same universal pseudo-American sensibility, whether you're in the Kalahari or the Amazon rain-forest. Do you comprehend what's happened, Dawn?"

"It's such a terrible loss," she says sadly. She is trying very hard to be sympathetic, but he senses she is waiting for him to finish his sermon and invite her to share his hotel room. He *will* invite her; but there is no stopping him once he has launched into his one great theme.

"Cultural diversity is gone from the world," he says. "Religion is dead; true poetry is dead; inventiveness is dead;

individuality is dead. Poetry. Listen to this." In a high monotone he chants:

> *In beauty I walk*
> *With beauty before me I walk*
> *With beauty behind me I walk*
> *With beauty above me I walk*
> *With beauty above and about me I walk*
> *It is finished in beauty*
> *It is finished in beauty*

He has begun to perspire heavily. His chanting has created an odd sphere of silence in his immediate vicinity; heads are turning, eyes are squinting. "Navaho," he says. "The Night Way, a nine-day chant, a vision, a spell. Where are the Navaho now? Go to Arizona and they'll chant for you, yes, for a price, but they don't know what the words mean, and chances are the singers are only one-fourth Navaho, or one-eighth, or maybe just Hopi hired to dress in Navaho costumes, because the real Navaho, if any are left, are off in Mexico City hired to be Aztecs. So much is gone. Listen." He chants again, more piercingly even than before:

> The animal runs, it passes, it dies. And it is the great cold.
> *It is the great cold of the night, it is the dark.*
> The bird flies, it passes, it dies. And it is—

"JAL FLIGHT 411 BAGGAGE IS NOW UNLOADING ON CONCOURSE FOUR," a mighty mechanical voice cries.

—the great cold.
It is the great cold of the night, it is the dark.

"JAL FLIGHT 411 BAGGAGE . . ."

The fish flees, it passes, it dies. And—

"People are staring," Dawn says uncomfortably.
"—ON CONCOURSE FOUR."
"Let them stare. Do them some good. That's a Pygmy chant, from Gabon, in equatorial Africa. Pygmies? There are no more Pygmies. Everybody's two meters tall. And what do we sing? Listen. Listen." He gestures fiercely at the cloud of tiny golden loudspeakers floating near the ceiling. A mush of music comes from them: the current popular favorite. Savagely he mouths words: *"Star . . . far . . . here . . . hear.* Playing in every skyport right now, all over the world." She smiles thinly. Her hand reaches toward his, covers it, presses against the knuckles. He is dizzy. The crowd, the eyes, the music, the drink. The plastic. Everything shines. Porcelain. Porcelain. The planet vitrifies. "Tom?" she asks uneasily. "Is anything the matter?" He laughs, blinks, coughs, shivers. He hears her calling for help, and then he feels his soul swooping outward, toward the galactic blackness.

With the Antarean not-male beside him, Schwartz peered through the viewport, staring in awe and fascination at the seductive vision of the Capellans coiling and recoiling outside the ship. Not all the passengers on this voyage had cozy staterooms like his. The Capellans were too big to come on board; and in any case they preferred never to let themselves be enclosed inside metal walls. They traveled just alongside the starship, basking like slippery whales in the piquant radiations of space. So long as they kept within twenty meters of the hull they would be inside the effective field of the Rabinowitz Drive, which swept ship and contents and associated fellow travelers toward Rigel, or the Lesser Magellanic, or was it one of the Pleiades toward which they were bound at a cool nine lights?

He watched the Capellans moving beyond the shadow of the ship in tracks of shining white. Blue, glossy green, and velvet black, they coiled and swam, and every track was a flash of golden fire. "They have a dangerous beauty," Schwartz whispered. "Do you hear them calling? I do."

"What do they say?"

"They say, *'Come to me, come to me, come to me!'*"

"Go to them, then," said the Antarean simply. "Step through the hatch."

"And perish?"

"And enter into your next transition. Poor Schwartz! Do you love your present body so?"

"My present body isn't so bad. Do you think I'm likely to get another one some day?"

"No?"

"No," Schwartz said. "This one is all I get. Isn't it that way with you?"

"At the Time of Openings I receive my next housing. That will be fifty years from now. What you see is the fifth form I have been given to wear."

"Will the next be as beautiful as this?"

"All forms are beautiful," the Antarean said. "You find me attractive?"

"Of course."

A slitted wink. A bobbing nod toward the viewport. "As attractive as *those?*"

Schwartz laughed. "Yes. In a different way."

Coquettishly the Antarean said, "If I were out there, you would walk though the hatch into space?"

"I might. If they gave me a spacesuit and taught me how to use it."

"But not otherwise? Suppose I were out there right now. I could live in space five, ten, maybe fifteen minutes. I am there and I say, '*Come to me, Schwartz, come to me!*' What do you do?"·

"I don't think I'm all that much self-destructive."

"To die for love, though! To make a transition for the sake of beauty."

"No. Sorry."

The Antarean pointed toward the undulating Capellans. "If *they* asked you, you would go."

"They are asking me," he said.

"And you refuse the invitation?"

"So far. So far."

The Antarean laughed an Antarean laugh, a thick silvery snort. "Our voyage will last many weeks more. One of these days, I think, you will go to them."

"You were unconscious at least five minutes," Dawn says. "You gave everyone a scare. Are you sure you ought to go through with tonight's lecture?"

Nodding, Schwartz says, "I'll be all right. I'm a little tired, is all. Too many time-zones this week." They stand on the terrace of his hotel room. Night is coming on, already, here in late afternoon: it is midwinter in the Southern Hemisphere, though the fragrance of tropic blossoms perfumes the air. The first few stars have appeared. He has never really known which star is which. That bright one, he thinks, could be Rigel, and that one Sirius, and perhaps this is Deneb over there. And this? Can this be red Antares, in the heart of the Scorpion, or is it only Mars? Because of his collapse at the skyport he has been able to beg off the customary faculty reception and the formal dinner; pleading the need for rest, he has arranged to have a simple snack at his hotel room, *a deux*. In two hours they will come for him and take him to the University to speak. Dawn watches him closely. Perhaps she is worried about his health, perhaps she is only waiting for him to make his move toward her. There's time for all that later, he figures. He would rather talk now. Warming up for the audience, he seizes his earlier thread:

"For a long time I didn't understand what had taken place. I grew up insular, cut off from reality, a New York boy, bright mind and a library card. I read all the anthropological classics, *Patterns of Culture* and *Coming of Age in Samoa* and *Life of a South African Tribe* and the rest, and I dreamed of field trips, collecting myths and grammars and folkways and artifacts and all that, until when I was twenty-five I finally got out into the field and started to discover I had gone into a dead science. We have only one worldwide culture now, with local variants but no basic divergences: there's nothing primitive left on Earth, *and there are no other planets*. Not inhabited ones. I can't go to Mars or Venus or Saturn and study the natives. What natives? And we can't reach the stars. All I have to work with is Earth. I was thirty years old when the whole thing clicked together for me and I knew I had wasted my life."

She says, "But surely there was something for you to study on Earth."

"One culture, rootless and homogeneous. That's work for a sociologist, not for me. I'm a romantic, I'm an exotic, I want strangeness, difference. Look, we can never have any real perspective on our own time and lives. The sociologists try to attain it, but all they get is a mound of raw indigestible data. Insight comes later—two, five, ten generations later. But one way we've always been able to learn about ourselves is by studying alien cultures, studying them *completely*, and defining ourselves by measuring what they are that we aren't. The cultures have to be isolated, though. The anthropologist himself corrupts that isolation in the Heisenberg sense when he comes around with his camera and scanners and starts asking questions, but we can compensate, more or less, for the inevitable damage a lone observer causes. We can't compensate when our whole culture collides with another and absorbs and obliterates it. Which we technological-mechanical people now have done everywhere. One day I woke up and saw there were no alien cultures left. Hah! Crushing revelation! Schwartz's occupation is gone!"

"What did you do?"

"For years I was in an absolute funk. I taught, I studied, I went through the motions, knowing it was all meaningless. All I was doing was looking at records of vanished cultures left by earlier observers and trying to cudgel new meanings. Secondary sources, stale findings: I was an evaluator of dry bones, not a gatherer of evidence. Paleontology. Dinosaurs are interesting, but what do they tell you about the contemporary world and the meaning of its patterns? Dry bones, Dawn, dry bones. Despair. And then a clue. I had this Nigerian student, this Ibo—well, basically an Ibo, but she's got some Israeli in her and I think Chinese—and we grew very close, she was as close to me as anybody in my own sixness, and I told her my troubles. I'm going to give it all up, I said, because it isn't what I expected it to be. She laughed at me and said, What right do you have to be upset because the world doesn't live up to your expectations? Reshape your life, Tom; you can't reshape the world. I said, But how? And she said, Look inward, find the primitive in yourself, see what made you what you are, what made today's culture what it is, see how these alien streams have flowed together. Nothing's been lost here, only merged. Which made me think. Which gave me a new way of looking at things. Which sent me on an inward quest. It took me three years to grasp the patterns, to come to an understanding of what our planet has become, and only after I accepted the planet——"

It seems to him that he has been talking forever. Talking. Talking. But he can no longer hear his own voice. There is only a distant buzz.

"After I accepted——"

A distant buzz.

"What was I saying?" he asks.

"After you accepted the planet——"

"After I accepted the planet," he says, "that I could begin——" *Buzz. Buzz.* "That I could begin to accept myself."

He was drawn toward the Spicans too, not so much for themselves—they were oblique, elliptical characters, self-contained and self-satisfied, hard to approach—as for the apparently psychedelic drug they took in some sacramental way before the beginning of each of their interminable ritual dances. Each time he had watched them take the drug, they had seemingly made a point of extending it toward him, as if inviting him, as if tempting him, before popping it into their mouths. He felt baited; he felt pulled.

There were three Spicans on board, slender creatures two and a half meters long, with flexible cylindrical bodies and small stubby limbs. Their skins were reptilian, dry and smooth, deep green with yellow bands, but their eyes were weirdly human, large liquid-brown eyes, sad Levantine eyes, the eyes of unfortunate medieval travelers transformed by enchantment into serpents. Schwartz had spoken with them several times. They understood English well enough—all galactic races did; Schwartz imagined it would become the interstellar *lingua franca* as it had on Earth—but the construction of their vocal organs was such that they had no way of speaking it, and they relied instead on small translating machines hung round their necks that converted their soft whispered hisses into amber words pulsing across a screen.

Cautiously, the third or fourth time he spoke with them, he expressed polite interest in their drug. They told him it enabled them to make contact with the central forces of the universe. He replied that there were such drugs on Earth, too, and that he used them frequently, that they gave him great insight into the workings of the cosmos. They showed some curiosity, perhaps even intense curiosity: reading their eyes was difficult and the tone of their voices gave no clues. He took his elegant leather-bound drug-case from his pouch and showed them what he had: learitonin, psilocerebrin, siddharthin, and acid-57. He described the effects of each and suggested an exchange, any of his for an equivalent dose of the shriveled orange fungoid they nibbled. They conferred. Yes, they said, we will do this. But not now. Not until the proper moment. Schwartz knew better than to ask them when that would be. He thanked them and put his drugs away.

Pitkin, who had watched the interchange from the far side of the lounge, came striding fiercely toward him as the Spicans glided off. "What are you up to now?" he demanded.

"How about minding your own business?" Schwartz said amiably.

"You're trading pills with those snakes, aren't you?"

"Let's call it field research."

"Research? Research? What are you going to do, trip on that orange stuff of theirs?"

"I might," Schwartz said.

"How do you know what its effects on the human metabolism might be? You could end up blind or paralyzed or crazy or——"

"——or illuminated," Schwartz said. "Those are the risks one takes in the field. The early anthropologists who unhesitatingly sampled peyote and yage and ololiuqui accepted those risks, and——"

"But those were drugs that *humans* were using. You have no way of telling how—, oh, what's the use, Schwartz? Research, he calls it. Research." Pitkin sneered. "*Junkie!*"

Schwartz matched him sneer for sneer. "*Economist!*"

The house is a decent one tonight, close to three thousand, every seat in the University's great horseshoe-shaped auditorium taken, and a video relay besides, beaming his lecture to all of Papua and half of Indonesia. Schwartz stands on the dais like a demigod under a brilliant no-glare spotlight. Despite his earlier weariness he is in good form now, gestures broad and forceful, eyes commanding, voice deep and resonant, words flowing freely. "Only one planet," he says, "one small and crowded planet, on which all cultures converge to a drab and depressing sameness. How sad that is! How tiny we make ourselves, when we make ourselves to resemble one another!" He flings his arms upward. "Look to the stars, the unattainable stars! Imagine, if you can, the millions of worlds that orbit those blazing suns beyond the night's darkness! Speculate with me on other peoples, other ways, other gods. Beings of every imaginable form, alien in appearance but not grotesque, not hideous, for all life is beautiful: beings that breathe gases strange to us, beings of immense size, beings of many limbs or of none, beings to whom death is a divine culmination of existence, beings who never die, beings who bring forth their young a thousand at a time, beings who do not reproduce—all the infinite possibilities of the infinite universe!

"Perhaps on each of those worlds it is as it has become here: one intelligent species, one culture, the eternal convergence. But the many worlds together offer a vast spectrum of variety. And now: share this vision with me! I see a ship voyaging from star to star, a spaceliner of the future, and aboard that ship is a sampling of many species, many cultures, a random scoop out of the galaxy's fantastic diversity. That ship is like a little cosmos, a small world, enclosed, sealed. How exciting to be aboard it, to encounter in that little compass such richness of cultural variation! Now our own world was once like that starship, a little cosmos, bearing with it all the thousands of Earthborn cultures, Hopi and Eskimo and Aztec and Kwakiutl and Arapesh and Orokolo and all the rest. In the course of our voyage we have come to resemble one another too much, and it has impoverished the lives of all of us, because—" He falters suddenly. He feels faint, and grasps the sides of the lectern. "Because

—" The spotlight, he thinks. In my eyes. Not supposed to glare like that, but it's blinding. Got to have them move it. "In the course—the course of our voyage—" What's happening? Breaking into a sweat, now. Pain in my chest. My heart? Wait, slow up, catch your breath. That light in my eyes——

"Tell me," Schwartz said earnestly, "what it's like to know you'll have ten successive bodies and live more than a thousand years."

"First tell me," said the Antarean, "what it's like to know you'll live ninety years or less, and perish forever."

Somehow he continues. The pain in his chest grows more intense, he cannot focus his eyes; he believes he will lose consciousness at any moment and may even have lost it already at least once, and yet he continues. Clinging to the lectern, he outlines the program he developed in *The Mask Beneath the Skin*. A rebirth of tribalism without a revival of ugly nationalism. The quest for a renewed sense of kinship with the past. A sharp reduction in non-essential travel, especially tourism. Heavy taxation of exported artifacts, including films and video shows. An attempt to create independent cultural units on Earth once again while maintaining present levels of economic and political interdependence. Relinquishment of materialistic technological-industrial values. New searches for fundamental meanings. An ethnic revival, before it is too late, among those cultures of mankind that have only recently shed their traditional folkways. (He repeats and embellishes this point particularly, for the benefit of the Papuans before him, the great-grandchildren of cannibals.)

The discomfort and confusion come and go as he unreels his themes. He builds and builds, crying out passionately for an end to the homogenization of Earth, and gradually the physical symptoms leave him, all but a faint vertigo. But a different malaise seizes him as he nears his peroration. His voice becomes, to him, a far-off quacking, meaningless and foolish. He has said all this a thousand times, always to great ovations, but who listens? Who listens? Everything seems hollow tonight, mechanical, absurd. An ethnic revival? Shall these people before him revert to their loincloths and their pig-roasts? His starship is a fantasy; his dream of a diverse Earth is mere silliness. What is, will be. And yet he pushes on toward his conclusion. He takes his audience back to that starship, he creates a horde of fanciful beings for them, he completes the metaphor by sketching the structures of half a dozen vanished "primitive" cultures of Earth, he chants the chants of the Navaho, the Gabon Pygmies, the Ashanti, the Mundugumor. It is over. Cascades of applause engulf him. He holds his place until members of the sponsoring committee come to him and help him down: they have perceived his distress. "It's nothing," he gasps. "The lights—too bright—" Dawn is at his side. She hands him a drink, something cool. Two of the sponsors begin to speak of a reception for him in the Green Room. "Fine," Schwartz says. "Glad to." Dawn murmurs a protest. He shakes her off. "My obligation," he tells her. "Meet community leaders. Faculty people. I'm feeling better now. Honestly." Swaying, trembling, he lets them lead him away.

"A Jew," the Antarean said. "You call yourself a Jew, but what is this exactly? A clan, a sept, a moiety, a tribe, a nation, what? Can you explain?"

"You understand what a religion is?"

"Of course."

"Judaism—Jewishness—it's one of Earth's major religions."

"You are therefore a priest?"

"Not at all. I don't even practice Judaism. But my ancestors did, and therefore I consider myself Jewish, even though—"

"It is an hereditary religion, then," the Antarean said, "that does not require its members to observe its rites?"

"In a sense," said Schwartz desperately. "More an hereditary cultural subgroup, actually, evolving out of a common religious outlook no longer relevant."

"Ah. And the cultural traits of Jewishness that define it and separate you from the majority of humankind are—?"

"Well—" Schwartz hesitated. "There's a complicated dietary code, a rite of circumcision for newborn males, a rite of passage for male adolescents, a language of scripture, a vernacular language that Jews all around the world more or less understand, and plenty more, including a certain intangible sense of clannishness and certain attitudes, such as a peculiar self-deprecating style of humor—"

"You observe the dietary code? You understand the language of scripture?"

"Not exactly," Schwartz admitted. "In fact I don't do anything that's specifically Jewish except think of myself as a Jew and adopt many of the characteristically Jewish personality modes, which however are not uniquely Jewish any longer—They can be traced among Italians, for example, and to some extent among Greeks. I'm speaking of Italians and Greeks of the late twentieth century, of course. Nowadays—"

It was all becoming a terrible muddle. "Nowadays——"

"It would seem," said the Antarean, "that you are a Jew only because your maternal and paternal gene-givers were Jews, and they——"

"No, not quite. Not my mother, just my father, and he was Jewish only on his father's side, but even my grandfather never observed the customs, and——"

"I think this has grown too confusing," said the Antarean. "I withdraw the entire inquiry. Let us speak instead of my own traditions. The Time of Openings, for example, may be understood as——"

In the Green Room some eighty or a hundred distinguished Papuans press toward him, offering congratulations. "Absolutely right," they say. "A global catastrophe." "Our last chance to save our culture." Their skins are chocolate-tinted but their faces betray the genetic mishmash that is their ancestry: perhaps they call themselves Arapesh, Mundugumor, Tchambuli, Mafulu, in the way that he calls himself a Jew, but they have been liberally larded with chromosomes contributed by Chinese, Japanese, Europeans, Africans, everything. They dress in International Contemporary. They speak slangy, lively English. Schwartz feels seasick. "You look dazed," Dawn whispers. He smiles bravely. Body like dry bone. Mind like dead ashes. He is introduced to a tribal chieftain, tall, gray-haired, who looks and speaks like a professor, a lawyer, a banker. What, will these people return to the hills for the ceremony of the yam harvest? Will newborn girl-children be abandoned, cords uncut, skins unwashed, if their fathers do not need more girls? Will boys entering manhood submit to the expensive services of the initiator who scarifies them with the teeth of crocodiles? The crocodiles are gone The shamans have become stockbrokers.

Suddenly he cannot breathe.

"Get me out of here," Schwartz mutters hoarsely, choking.

Dawn, with stewardess efficiency, chops a path for him through the mob. The sponsors, concerned, rush to his aid. He is floated swiftly back to the hotel in a glistening little bubble-car. Dawn helps him to bed. Reviving, he reaches for her.

"You don't have to," she says. "You've had a rough day."

He persists. He embraces her and takes her, quickly, fiercely, and they move together for a few minutes and it ends and he sinks back, exhausted, stupefied. She gets a cool cloth and pats his forehead, and urges him to rest. "Bring me my drugs," he says. He wants siddharthin, but she misunderstands, probably deliberately, and offers him something blue and bulky, a sleeping pill, and, too weary to object, he takes it. Even so, it seems to be hours before sleep comes.

He dreams he is at the skyport, boarding the rocket for Bangkok, and instantly he is debarking at Bangkok—just like Port Moresby, only more humid—and he delivers his speech to a horde of enthusiastic Thais, while rockets flicker about him, carrying him to skyport after skyport, and the Thais blur and become Japanese, who are transformed into Mongols, who become Uighurs, who become Iranians, who become Sudanese, who become Zambians, who become Chileans, and all look alike, all look alike, all look alike.

The Spicans hovered above him, weaving, bobbing, swaying like cobras about to strike. But their eyes, warm and liquid, were sympathetic: loving, even. He felt the glow of their compassion. If they had had the sort of musculature that enabled them to smile, they would be smiling tenderly, he knew.

One of the aliens leaned close. The little translating device dangled toward Schwartz like a holy medallion. He narrowed his eyes, concentrating as intently as he could on the amber words flashing quickly across the screen.

". . . has come. We shall. . . ."

"Again, please," Schwartz said. "I missed some of what you were saying."

"The moment . . . has come. We shall . . . make the exchange of sacraments now."

"Sacraments?"

"Drugs."

"Drugs, yes. Yes. Of course." Schwartz groped in his pouch. He felt the cool smooth leather skin of his drug-case. Leather? Snakeskin, maybe. Anyway. He drew it forth. "Here," he said. "Siddharthin, learitonin, psilocerebrin, acid-57. Take your pick." The Spicans selected three small blue siddharthins. "Very good," Schwartz said. "The most transcendental of all. And now——"

The longest of the aliens proffered a ball of dried orange fungus the size of Schwartz's thumbnail.

"It is an equivalent dose. We give it to you."

"Equivalent to all three of my tablets, or to one?"

"Equivalent. It will give you peace."

Schwartz smiled. There was a time for asking questions, and a time for unhesitating action. He took the fungus and reached for a glass of water.

"*Wait!*" Pitkin cried, appearing suddenly. "What are you——"

"Too late," Schwartz said serenely, and swallowed the Spican drug in one joyous gulp.

The nightmares go on and on. He circles the Earth like the Flying Dutchman, like the Wandering Jew, skyport to skyport to skyport, an unending voyage from nowhere to nowhere. Obliging committees meet him and convey him to his hotel. Sometimes the committee members are contemporary types, indistinguishable from one another, with standard faces, standard clothing, the all-purpose new-model hybrid unihuman, and sometimes they are consciously ethnic, elaborately decked out in feathers and paint and tribal emblems, but their faces, too, are standard behind the gaudy regalia, their slang is the slang of Uganda and Tierra del Fuego and Nepal, and it seems to Schwartz that these masqueraders are, if anything, less authentic, less honest, than the other sort, who at least are true representatives of their era. So it is hopeless either way. He lashes at his pillow, he groans, he wakens. Instantly Dawn's arms enfold him. He sobs incoherent phrases into her clavicle and she murmurs soothing sounds against his forehead. He is having some sort of breakdown, he realizes: a new crisis of values, a shattering of the philosophical synthesis that has allowed him to get through the last few years. He is bound to the wheel; he spins, he spins, he spins, traversing the continents, getting nowhere. There is no place to go. No. There is one, just one, a place where he will find peace, where the universe will be as he needs it to be. Go there, Schwartz. Go and stay as long as you can. "Is there anything I can *do?*" Dawn asks. He shivers and shakes his head. "Take this," she says, and gives him some sort of pill. Another tranquilizer. All right. All right. The world has turned to porcelain. His skin feels like a plastic coating. Away, away, to the ship. To the ship! "So long," Schwartz says.

Outside the ship the Capellans twist and spin in their ritual dance as, weightless and without mass, they are swept toward the rim of the galaxy at nine times the velocity of light. They move with a grace that is astonishing for creatures of such tremendous bulk. A dazzling light that emanates from the center of the universe strikes their glossy skin and, rebounding, resonates all up and down the spectrum, splintering into brilliant streamers of ultrared, infraviolet, exoyellow. All the cosmos glows and shimmers. A single perfect note of music comes out of the remote distance and, growing closer, swells in an infinite crescendo. Schwartz trembles at the beauty of all he perceives.

Beside him stands the seal-slick Antarean. She—definitely *she*, no doubt of it, *she*—plucks at his arm and whispers, "Will you go to them?"

"Yes. Yes, of course."

"So will I. Wherever you go."

"Now," Schwartz says. He reaches for the lever that opens the hatch. He pulls down. The side of the starship swings open.

The Antarean looks deep into his eyes and says blissfully, "I have never told you my name. My name is Dawn."

Together they float through the hatch into space.

The blackness receives them gently. There is no chill, no pressure at the lungs, no discomfort at all. He is surrounded by luminous surges, by throbbing mantles of pure color, as though he has entered the heart of an aurora. He and Dawn swim toward the Capellans, and the huge beings welcome them with deep, glad, booming cries. Dawn joins the dance at once, moving her sinuous limbs with extravagant ease; Schwartz will do the same in a moment, but first he turns to face the starship, hanging in space close by him like a vast coppery needle, and in a voice that could shake universes he calls, "Come, friends! Come, all of you! Come dance with us!" And they come, pouring through the hatch, the Spicans first, then all the rest, the infinite multitude of beings, the travelers from Fomalhaut and Achernar and Acrux and Aldebaran, from Thuban and Arcturus and Altair, from Polaris and Canopus and Sirius and Rigel, hundreds of star-creatures spilling happily out of the vessel, bursting forth, all of them, even Pitkin, poor little Pitkin, everyone joining hands and tentacles and tendrils and whatever, forming a great ring of light across space, creating union out of diversity while preserving diversity within union, everyone locked in a cosmic harmony, everyone dancing. Dancing. Dancing.

▼▲▼▲▼

TRIPS

Does this path have a heart? All paths are the same: they lead nowhere. They are paths going through the bush, or into the bush. In my own life I could say I have traversed long, long paths, but I am not anywhere. . . . Does this path have a heart? If it does, the path is good; if it doesn't, it is of no use. Both paths lead nowhere; but one has a heart, the other doesn't. One makes for a joyful journey; as long as you follow it, you are one with it. The other will make you curse your life.

—The Teachings of Don Juan

1.

*T*he second place you come to—the first having proved unsatisfactory, for one reason and another—is a city which could almost be San Francisco. Perhaps it is, sitting out there on the peninsula between the ocean and the bay, white buildings clambering over improbably steep hills. It occupies the place in your psychic space that San Francisco has always occupied, although you don't really know yet what this city calls itself. Perhaps you'll find out before long.

You go forward. What you feel first is the strangeness of the familiar, and then the utter heartless familiarity of the strange. For example the automobiles, and there are plenty of them, are all halftracks: low sleek sexy sedans that have the flashy Detroit styling, the usual chrome, the usual streamlining, the low-raked windows all agleam, but there are only two wheels, both of them in front, with a pair of tread-belts circling endlessly in back. Is this good design for city use? Who knows? Somebody evidently thinks so, here. And then the newspapers: the format is the same, narrow columns, gaudy screaming headlines, miles of black type on coarse grayish-white paper, but the names and the places have been changed. You scan the front page of a newspaper in the window of a curbside vending machine. Big photo of Chairman DeGrasse, serving as host at a reception for the Patagonian Ambassador. An account of the tribal massacres in the highlands of Dzungaria. Details of the solitude epidemic that is devastating Persepolis. When the halftracks stall on the hillsides, which is often, the other drivers ring silvery chimes, politely venting their impatience. Men who look like Navahos chant what sound like sutras in the intersections. The traffic lights are blue and orange. Clothing tends toward the prosaic, grays and dark blues, but the cut and slope of men's jackets has an angular, formal, eighteenth-century look, verging on pomposity. You pick up a bright coin that lies in the street; it is vaguely metallic but rubbery, as if you could compress it between your fingers, and its thick edges bear incuse lettering: TO GOD WE OWE OUR SWORDS. On the next block a squat two-story building is ablaze, and agitated clerks do a desperate dance. The fire engine is glossy green and its pump looks like a diabolical cannon embellished with sweeping flanges; it spouts a glistening yellow foam that eats the flames and, oxidizing, runs off down the gutter, a trickle of sluggish blue fluid. Everyone wears eyeglasses here, *everyone*. At a sidewalk cafe, pale waitresses offer mugs of boiiing-hot milk into which the silent tight-faced patrons put cinnamon, mustard, and what seems to be Tabasco sauce. You offer your coin and try a sample, imitating what they do, and everyone bursts into laughter. The girl behind the counter pushes a thick stack of paper currency at you by way of change: UNITED FEDERAL COLUMBIAN REPUBLIC, each bill declares. GOOD FOR ONE EXCHANGE. Illegible signatures. Portrait of early leader of the republic, so famous that they give him no label of identification, bewigged, wall-eyed, ecstatic. You sip your milk, blowing gently. A light scum begins to form on its speckled surface. Sirens start to wail. About you, the other milk-drinkers stir uneasily. A parade is coming. Trumpets, drums, far-off chanting. Look! Four naked boys carry an open brocaded litter on which there sits an immense block of ice, a great frosted cube, mysterious, impenetrable. "Patagonia!" the onlookers cry sadly. The word is wrenched from them: "Patagonia!" Next, marching by himself, a mitred bishop advances, all in green, curtseying to the crowd, tossing hearty blessings as though they were flowers. "Forget your sins! Cancel your debts! All is made new! All is good!" You shiver and peer intently into his eyes as he passes you, hoping that he will single you out for an embrace. He is terribly tall but white-haired and fragile, somehow, despite his agility and energy. He reminds you of Norman, your wife's older brother, and perhaps he *is* Norman, the Norman of this place, and you wonder if he can give you news of Elizabeth, the Elizabeth of this place, but you say nothing and he goes by. And then comes a tremendous wooden scaffold on wheels, a true juggernaut, at the summit of which rests a polished statue carved out of gleaming black stone: a human figure, male, plump, arms intricately folded, face complacent. The statue emanates a sense of vast Sumerian calm. The face is that of Chairman DeGrasse. "He'll die in the first blizzard," murmurs a man to your left. Another, turning suddenly, says with great force, "No, it's going to be done the proper way. He'll last until the time of the accidents, just as he's supposed to. I'll bet on that." Instantly they are nose to nose, glaring, and then they are wagering—a tense complicated ritual involving slapping of palms, interchanges of slips of paper, formal voiding of spittle, hysterical appeals to witnesses. The emotional climate here seems a trifle too intense. You decide to move along. Warily you leave the cafe, looking in all directions.

2.

Before you began your travels you were told how essential it was to define your intended role. Were you going to be a tourist, or an explorer, or an infiltrator? Those are the choices that confront anyone arriving at a new place. Each bears its special risks.

To opt for being a tourist is to choose the easiest but most contemptible path; ultimately it's the most dangerous one, too, in a certain sense. You have to accept the built-in epithets that go with the part: they will think of you as a *foolish* tourist, an *ignorant* tourist, a *vulgar* tourist, a *mere* tourist. Do you want to be considered mere? Are you able to accept that? Is that really your preferred self-image—baffled, bewildered, led about by the nose? You'll sign up for packaged tours, you'll carry guidebooks and cameras, you'll go to the cathedral and the museums and the marketplace, and you'll remain always on the outside of things, seeing a great deal, experiencing nothing. What a waste! You will be diminished by the very traveling that you thought would expand you. Tourism hollows and parches you. All places become one: a hotel, a smiling, swarthy, sunglassed guide, a bus, a plaza, a fountain, a marketplace, a museum, a cathedral. You are transformed into a feeble shriveled thing made out of glued-together travel folders; you are naked but for your visas; the sum of your life's adventures is a box of left-over small change from many indistinguishable lands.

To be an explorer is to make the *macho* choice. You swagger in, bent on conquest, for isn't any discovery a kind of conquest? Your existential position, like that of any mere tourist, lies outside the heart of things, but you are unashamed of that; and while tourists are essentially passive the explorer's role is active; an explorer intends to grasp that heart, take possession, squeeze. In the explorer's role you consciously cloak yourself in the trappings of power: self-assurance, thick bankroll, stack of credit cards. You capitalize on the glamor of being a stranger. Your curiosity is invincible; you ask unabashed questions about the most intimate things, never for an instant relinquishing eye-contact. You open locked doors and flash bright lights into curtained rooms. You are Magellan; you are Malinowski; you are Captain Cook. You will gain much, but—ah, here is the price!— you will always be feared and hated, you will never be permitted to attain the true core. Nor is superficiality the worst peril. Remember that Magellan and Captain Cook left their bones on tropic beaches. Sometimes the natives lose patience with explorers.

The infiltrator, though? His is at once the most difficult role and the most rewarding one. Will it be yours? Consider. You'll have to get right with it when you reach your destination, instantly learn the regulations, find your way around like an old hand, discover the location of shops and freeways and hotels, figure out the units of currency, the rules of social intercourse—all of this knowledge mastered surreptitiously, through observation alone, while moving about silently, camouflaged, *never asking for help*. You must become a part of the world you have entered, and the way to do it is to encourage a general assumption that you already are a part of it, have always been a part of it. Wherever you land, you need to recognize that life has been going on for millions of years, life goes on there steadily, with you or without you; you are the intrusive one, and if you don't want to feel intrusive you'd better learn fast how to fit in. Of course it isn't easy. The infiltrator doesn't have the privilege of buying stability by acting dumb. You won't be able to say, "How much does it cost to ride on the cable-car?" You won't be able to say, "I'm from somewhere else, and this is the kind of money I carry, dollars quarters pennies halves nickels, is any of it legal tender here?" You don't dare identify yourself in any way as an outsider. If you don't get the idioms or the accent right, you can tell them you grew up out of town, but that's as much as you can reveal. The truth is your eternal secret, even when you're in trouble, *especially* when you're in trouble. When your back's to the wall you won't have time to say, "Look, I wasn't born in this universe at all, you see, I came zipping in from some other place, so pardon me, forgive me, excuse me, pity me." No, no, no, you can't do that. They won't believe you, and even if they do, they'll make it all the worse for you once they know. If you want to infiltrate, Cameron, you've got to fake it all the way. Jaunty smile; steely, even gaze. And you have to infiltrate. You know that, don't you? You don't really have any choice.

Infiltrating has its dangers too. The rough part comes when they find you out, and they always will find you out. Then they'll react bitterly against your deception; they'll lash out in blind rage. If you're lucky, you'll be gone before they learn your sweaty little secret. Before they discover the discarded phrasebook hidden in the boarding-house room, before they stumble on the torn-off pages of your private journal. They'll find you out. They always do. But by then you'll be somewhere else, you hope, beyond the reach of their anger and their sorrow, beyond their reach, beyond their reach.

3.

Suppose I show you, for Exhibit A, Cameron reacting to an extraordinary situation. You can test your own resilience by trying to picture yourself in his position. There has been a sensation in Cameron's mind very much like that of the extinction of the cosmos: a thunderclap, everything going black, a blankness, a total absence. Followed by the return of light, flowing inward upon him like high tide on the celestial shore, a surging stream of brightness moving with inexorable certainty. He stands flatfooted, dumbfounded, high on a bare hillside in warm early-hour sunlight. The house— redwood timbers, picture window, driftwood sculptures, paintings, books, records, refrigerator, gallon jugs of red wine, carpets, tiles, avocado plants in wooden tubs, carport, car, driveway—is gone. The neighboring houses are gone. The winding street is gone. The eucalyptus forest that ought to be behind him, rising toward the crest of the hill, is gone. Downslope there is no Oakland, there is no Berkeley, only a scattering of crude squatters' shacks running raggedly along unpaved switchbacks toward the pure blue bay. Across the water there is no Bay Bridge; on the far shore there is no San Francisco. The Golden Gate Bridge does not span the gap between the city and the Marin headland. Cameron is astonished, not that he didn't expect something like this, but that the transformation is so complete, so absolute. If you don't want your world any more, the old man had said, you can just drop it, can't you? Let go of it, let it drop. Can't you? Of course you can. And so Cameron has let go of it. He's in another place entirely, now. Wherever this place is, it isn't home. The sprawling Bay Area cities and towns aren't here, never were. Goodbye, San Leandro, San Mateo, El

Cerrito, Walnut Creek. He sees a landscape of gentle bare hills, rolling meadows, the dry brown grass of summer; the scarring hand of man is evident only occasionally. He begins to adapt. This is what he must have wanted, after all; and though he has been jarred by the shock of transition he is recovering quickly; he is settling in; he feels already that he could belong here. He will explore this unfamiliar world, and if he finds it good he will discover a niche for himself. The air is sweet. The sky is cloudless. Has he really gone to some new place, or is he still in the old place and has everything else that was there simply gone away? Easy. He has gone. Everything else has gone. The cosmos has entered into a transitional phase. Nothing's stable any more. From this moment onward, Cameron's existence is a conditional matter, subject to ready alteration. What did the old man say? Go wherever you like. Define your world as you would like it to be, and go there, and if you discover that you don't care for this or don't need that, why, go somewhere else. It's all trips, this universe. What else is there? There isn't anything but trips. Just trips. So here you are, friend. New frameworks! New patterns! New!

4.

There is a sound to his left, the crackling of dry brush under foot, and Cameron turns, looking straight into the morning sun, and sees a man on horseback approaching him. He is tall, slender, about Cameron's own height and build, it seems, but perhaps a shade broader through the shoulders. His hair, like Cameron's, is golden, but it is much longer, descending in a straight flow to his shoulders and tumbling onto his chest. He has a soft full curling beard, untrimmed but tidy. He wears a wide-brimmed hat, buckskin chaps, and a light fringed jacket of tawny leather. Because of the sunlight Cameron has difficulty at first making out his features, but after a moment his eyes adjust and he sees that the other's face is very much like his own, thin lips, jutting high-bridged nose, clefted chin, cool blue eyes below heavy brows. Of course. Your face is my face. You and I, I and you, drawn to the same place at the same time across the many worlds. Cameron had not expected this, but now that it has happened it seems to have been inevitable.

They look at each other. Neither speaks. During that silent moment Cameron invents a scene for them. He imagines the other dismounting, inspecting him in wonder, walking around him, peering into his face, studying it, frowning, shaking his head, finally grinning and saying:

——I'll be damned. I never knew I had a twin brother. But here you are. It's just like looking in the mirror.

——We aren't twins.

——We've got the same face. Same everything. Trim away a little hair and nobody could tell me from you, you from me. If we aren't twins, what are we?

——We're closer than brothers.

——I don't follow your meaning, friend.

——This is how it is: I'm you. You're me. One soul, one identity. What's your name?

——Cameron.

——Of course. First name?

——Kit.

——That's short for Christopher, isn't it? My name is Cameron too. Chris. Short for Christopher. I tell you, we're one and the same person, out of two different worlds. Closer than brothers. Closer than anything.

None of this is said, however. Instead the man in the leather clothing rides slowly toward Cameron, pauses, gives him a long incurious stare, and says simply, "Morning. Nice day." And continues onward.

"Wait," Cameron says.

The man halts. Looks back. "What?"

Never ask for help. Fake it all the way. Jaunty smile, steely even gaze.

Yes. Cameron remembers all that. Somehow, though, infiltration seems easier to bring off in a city. You can blend into the background there. More difficult here, exposed as you are against the stark unpeopled landscape.

Cameron says, as casually as he can, using what he hopes is a colorless neutral accent, "I've been traveling out from inland. Came a long way."

"Umm. Didn't think you were from around here. Your clothes."

"Inland clothes."

"The way you talk. Different. So?"

"New to these parts. Wondered if you could tell me a place I could hire a room till I got settled."

"You come all this way on foot?"

"Had a mule. Lost him back in the valley. Lost everything I had with me."

"Umm. Indians cutting up again. You give them a little gin, they go crazy." The other smiles faintly; then the smile fades and he retreats into impassivity, sitting motionless with hands on thighs, face a mask of patience that seems merely to be a thin covering for impatience or worse.

—Indians?—

"They gave me a rough time," Cameron says, getting into the fantasy of it.

"Umm."

"Cleaned me out; let me go."

"Umm. Umm."

Cameron feels his sense of a shared identity with this man lessening. There is no way of engaging him. I am you, you are I, and yet you take no notice of the strange fact that I wear your face and body, you seem to show no interest in me at all. Or else you hide your interest amazingly well.

Cameron says, "You know where I can get lodging?"

"Nothing much around here. Not many settlers this side of the bay, I guess."

"I'm strong. I can do most any kind of work. Maybe you could use——"

"Umm. No." Cold dismissal glitters in the frosty eyes. Cameron wonders how often people in the world of his former life saw such a look in his own. A tug on the reins. Your time is up, stranger. The horse swings around and begins picking its way daintily along the path.

Desperately Cameron calls, "One thing more!"

"Umm?"

"Is your name Cameron?"

A flicker of interest. "Might be."

"Christopher Cameron. Kit. Chris. That you?"

"Kit." The other's eyes drill into his own. The mouth compresses until the lips are invisible: not a scowl but a speculative, pensive movement. There is tension in the way the other man grasps his reins. For the first time Cameron feels that he has made contact. "Kit Cameron, yes. Why?"

"Your wife," Cameron says. "Her name Elizabeth?"

The tension increases. The other Cameron is cloaked in

explosive silence. Something terrible is building within him. Then, unexpectedly, the tension snaps. The other man spits, scowls, slumps in his saddle. "My woman's dead," he mutters. "Say, who the hell are you? What do you want with me?"

"I'm—I'm," Cameron falters. He is overwhelmed by fear and pity. A bad start, a lamentable start. He trembles. He had not thought it would be anything like this. With an effort he masters himself. Fiercely he says, "I've got to know. Was her name Elizabeth?" For an answer the horseman whacks his heels savagely against his mount's ribs and gallops away, fleeing as though he has had an encounter with Satan.

5.

Go, the old man said. You know the score. This is how it is: everything's random, nothing's fixed unless we want it to be, and even then the system isn't as stable as we think it is. So go. Go. Go, he said, and, of course, hearing something like that, Cameron went. What else could he do, once he had his freedom, but abandon his native universe and try a different one? Notice that I didn't say a better one, just a different one. Or two or three or five different ones. It was a gamble, certainly. He might lose everything that mattered to him, and gain nothing worth having. But what of it? Every day is full of gambles like that: you stake your life whenever you open a door. You never know what's heading your way, not ever, and still you choose to play the game. How can a man be expected to become all he's capable of becoming if he spends his whole life pacing up and down the same courtyard? Go. Make your voyages. Time forks, again

and again and again. New universes split off at each instant
of decision. Left turn, right turn, honk your horn, jump the
traffic light, hit your gas, hit your brake, every action
spawns whole galaxies of possibility. We move through a
soup of infinities. If repressing a sneeze generates an alternative continuum, what, then, are the consequences of the
truly major acts, the assassinations and inseminations, the
conversions, the renunciations? Go. And as you travel, mull
these thoughts constantly. Part of the game is discerning the
precipitating factors that shaped the worlds you visit. What's
the story here? Dirt roads, donkey-carts, hand-sewn clothes.
No Industrial Revolution, is that it? The steam-engine
man—what was his name, Savery, Newcomen, Watt?—
smothered in his cradle? No mines, no factories, no assembly
lines, no dark Satanic mills. That must be it. The air is so
pure here: you can tell by that, it's a simpler era. Very good,
Cameron. You see the patterns swiftly. But now try somewhere else. Your own self has rejected you here; besides, this
place has no Elizabeth. Close your eyes. Summon the light-
ning.

6.

The parade has reached a disturbing level of frenzy.
Marchers and floats now occupy the side streets as well
as the main boulevard, and there is no way to escape
from their demonic enthusiasm. Streamers cascade from office windows and gigantic photographs of Chairman De-
Grasse have sprouted on every wall, suddenly, like dark in-
festations of lichen. A boy presses close against Cameron,
extends a clenched fist, opens his fingers: on his palm rests a

glittering jeweled case, egg-shaped, thumbnail-sized. "Spores from Patagonia," he says. "Let me have ten exchanges and they're yours." Politely Cameron declines. A woman in a blue and orange frock tugs at his arm and says urgently, "All the rumors are true, you know. They've just been confirmed. What are you going to do about that? What are you going to *do?*" Cameron shrugs and smiles and disengages himself. A man with gleaming buttons asks, "Are you enjoying the festival? I've sold everything and I'm going to move to the highway next Godsday." Cameron nods and murmurs congratulations, hoping congratulations are in order. He turns a corner and confronts, once more, the bishop who looks like Elizabeth's brother, who *is*, he concludes, indeed Elizabeth's brother. "Forget your sins!" he is crying still. "Cancel your debts!" Cameron thrusts his head between two plump girls at the curb and attempts to call to him, but his voice fails, nothing coming forth but a hoarse wordless rasp, and the bishop moves on. Moving on is a good idea, Cameron tells himself. This place exhausts him. He has come to it too soon, and its manic tonality is more than he wants to handle. He finds a quiet alleyway and presses his cheek against a cool brick wall, and stands there breathing deeply until he is calm enough to depart. All right. Onward.

7.

Empty grasslands spread to the horizon. This could be the Gobi steppe. Cameron sees neither cities nor towns nor even villages, just six or seven squat black tents pitched in a loose circle in the saddle between two low gray-green hummocks, a few hundred yards from where he stands. He looks beyond, across the gently folded land, and spies dark animal figures at the limits of his range of vision: about a dozen horses, close together, muzzle to muzzle, flank to flank, horses with riders. Or perhaps they are a congregation of centaurs. Anything is possible. He decides, though, that they are Indians, a war party of young braves, maybe, camping in these desolate plains. They see him. Quite likely they saw him some while before he noticed them. Casually they break out of their grouping, wheel, ride in his direction.

He awaits them. Why should he flee? Where could he hide? Their pace accelerates from trot to canter, from canter to wild gallop; now they plunge toward him with fluid ferocity and a terrifying eagerness. They wear open leather jackets and rough rawhide leggings; they carry lances, bows, battle-axes, long curved swords; they ride small, agile horses, hardly more than ponies, tireless packets of energy. They surround him, pulling up, the fierce little steeds rearing and whinnying; they peer at him, point, laugh, exchange harsh derisive comments in a mysterious language. Then, solemnly, they begin to ride slowly in a wide circle around him. They are flat-faced, small-nosed, bearded, with broad, prominent cheekbones; the crowns of their heads are shaven but long black hair streams down over their ears and the napes of their necks. Heavy folds in the upper lids give their eyes a slanted look. Their skins are copper-colored but with an underlying golden tinge, as though these are not Indians at all, but— what? Japanese? A samurai corps? No, probably not Japanese. But not Indians either.

They continue to circle him, gradually moving more swiftly. They chatter to one another and occasionally hurl what sound like questions at him. They seem fascinated by him, but also contemptuous. In a sudden demonstration of horsemanship one of them cuts from the circular formation and, goading his horse to an instant gallop, streaks past Cameron, leaning down to jab a finger into his forearm. Then another does it, and another, streaking back and forth across the circle, poking him, plucking at his hair, tweaking him, nearly running him down. They draw their swords and swish them through the air just above his head. They menace him, or pretend to, with their lances. Throughout it all they laugh. He stands perfectly still. This ordeal, he suspects, is a test of his courage. Which he passes, eventually. The lunatic galloping ceases; they rein in, and several of them dismount.

They are little men, chest-high to him but thicker through the chest and shoulders than he is. One unships a leather pouch and offers it to him with an unmistakable gesture: take, drink. Cameron sips cautiously. It is a thick grayish fluid, both sweet and sour. Fermented milk? He gags, winces, forces himself to sip again; they watch him closely. The second taste isn't so bad. He takes a third more willingly and gravely returns the pouch. The warriors laugh, not derisively now but more in applause, and the man who had given him the pouch slaps Cameron's shoulder admiringly. He tosses the pouch back to Cameron. Then he leaps to his saddle, and abruptly they all take off. Mongols, Cameron realizes. The sons of Genghis Khan, riding to the horizon. A worldwide empire? Yes, and this must be the wild west for them, the frontier, where the young men enact their rites of passage. Back in Europe, after seven centuries of Mongol dominance, they have become citified, domesticated, sippers of wine, theatergoers, cultivators of gardens, but here they follow the ways of their all-conquering forefathers. Cameron shrugs. Nothing for him here. He takes a last sip of the milk and drops the pouch into the tall grass. Onward.

8.

No grass grows here. He sees the stumps of buildings, the blackened trunks of dead trees, mounds of broken tile and brick. The smell of death is in the air. All the bridges are down. Fog rolls in off the bay, dense and greasy, and becomes a screen on which images come alive. These ruins are inhabited. Figures move about. They are the living dead. Looking into the thick mist he sees a vision of the shock wave, he recoils as alpha particles shower his skin. He beholds the survivors emerging from their shattered houses, straggling into the smoldering streets, naked, stunned, their bodies charred, their eyes glazed, some of them with their hair on fire. The walking dead. No one speaks. No one asks why this has happened. He is watching a silent movie. The apocalyptic fire has touched the ground here; the land itself is burning. Blue phosphorescent flames rise from the earth. The final judgment, the day of wrath. Now he hears a dread music beginning, a dead-march, all 'cellos and basses, the dark notes coming at wide intervals: ooom ooom ooom ooom ooom. And then the tempo picks up, the music becomes a danse macabre, syncopated, lively, the timbre still dark, the rhythms funereal: ooom ooom ooom-de-ooom de-ooom de-ooom de-ooom-de-ooom, jerky, chaotic, wildly gay. The distorted melody of the Ode to Joy lurks somewhere in the ragged strands of sound. The dying victims stretch their fleshless hands toward him. He shakes his head. What service can I do for you? Guilt assails him. He is a tourist in the land of their grief. Their eyes reproach him. He would embrace them, but he fears they will crumble at his touch, and he lets the procession go past him without doing anything to cross the gulf between himself and them. "Elizabeth?" he murmurs. "Norman?" They have no faces, only eyes. "What can I do? I can't do anything for you." Not even tears will come. He looks away. Though I speak with the tongues of men and of angels, and have not charity, I am become as sounding brass, or a tinkling cymbal. And though I have the gift of prophecy, and understand all mysteries, and all knowledge; and though I have all faith, so that I could remove mountains, and have not charity, I am nothing. But this world is beyond the reach of love. He looks away. The sun appears. The fog burns off. The visions fade. He sees only the dead land, the ashes, the ruins. All right. Here we have no continuing city, but we seek one to come. Onward. Onward.

9.

And now, after this series of brief, disconcerting intermediate stops, Cameron has come to a city that is San Francisco beyond doubt, not some other city on San Francisco's site but a true San Francisco, a recognizable San Francisco. He pops into it atop Russian Hill, at the very crest, on a dazzling, brilliant, cloudless day. To his left, below, lies Fisherman's Wharf; ahead of him rises the Coit Tower; yes, and he can see the Ferry Building and the Bay Bridge. Familiar landmarks—but how strange all the rest seems! Where is the eye-stabbing Transamerica pyramid? Where is the colossal somber stalk of the Bank of America? The strangeness, he realizes, derives not so much from substitutions as from absences. The big Embarcadero developments are not there, nor the Chinatown Holiday Inn, nor the miserable tentacles of the elevated freeways, nor, apparently, anything else that was constructed in the last twenty years. This is the old short-shanked San Francisco of his boyhood, a sparkling miniature city, unManhattanized, skylineless. Surely he has returned to the place he knew in the sleepy 1950s, the tranquil Eisenhower years.

He heads downhill, searching for a newspaper box. He find one at the corner of Hyde and North Point, a bright-yellow metal rectangle. San Francisco *Chronicle,* ten cents? Is that the right price for 1954? One Roosevelt dime goes into the slot. The paper, he finds, is dated Tuesday, August 19, 1975. In what Cameron still thinks of, with some irony now, as the real world, the world that has been receding rapidly from his all day in a series of discontinuous jumps, it is also Tuesday, the 19th of August, 1975. So he has not gone backward in time at all; he has come to a San Francisco where time has seemingly been standing still. Why? In vertigo he eyes the front page.

A three-column headline declares:

FUEHRER ARRIVES IN WASHINGTON

Under it, to the left, a photograph of three men, smiling broadly, positively beaming at one another. The caption identifies them as President Kennedy, Fuehrer Goering, and Ambassador Togarashi of Japan, meeting in the White House rose garden. Cameron closes his eyes. Using no data other than the headline and the caption, he attempts to concoct a plausible speculation. This is a world, he decides, in which the Axis must have won the war. The United States is a German fiefdom. There are no high-rise buildings in San Francisco because the American economy, shattered by defeat, has not yet in thirty years of peace returned to a level where it can afford to erect them, or perhaps because American venture capital, prodded by the financial ministers of the Third Reich—(Hjalmar Schacht? The name drifts out of the swampy recesses of memory)—now tends to flow toward Europe. But how could it have happened? Cameron remembers the war years clearly, the tremendous surge of patriotism, the vast mobilization, the great national effort. Rosie the Riveter. Lucky Strike Green Goes To War. Let's Remember Pearl Harbor, As We Did The Alamo. He doesn't see any way the Germans might have brought America to her knees. Except one. The bomb, he thinks, the bomb, the Nazis get the bomb in 1940 and Wernher von Braun invents a transatlantic rocket and New York and Washington are nuked one night and that's it, we've been pushed beyond the resources of patriotism; we cave in and surrender within a week. And so——

He studies the photograph. President Kennedy, grinning, standing between Reichsfuehrer Goering and a suave youthful-looking Japanese. Kennedy? Ted? No, this is Jack, the very same Jack who, looking jowly, heavy bags under his eyes, deep creases in his face—he must be almost sixty years old, nearing the end of what is probably his second term of office. Jacqueline waiting none too patiently for him upstairs. Get done with your Japs and Nazis, love, and let's have a few drinkies together before the concert. Yes. John-John and Caroline somewhere on the premises too, the nation's darlings, models for young people everywhere. Yes. And Goering? Indeed, the very same Goering who . . . . Well into his eighties, monstrously fat, chin upon chin, multitudes of chins, vast bemedaled bosom, little mischievous eyes glittering with a long lifetime's cheery recollections of gratified lusts. How happy he looks! And how amiable! It was always impossible to hate Goering the way one loathed Goebbels, say, or Himmler or Streicher; Goering had charm, the outrageous charm of a monstre sacré, of a Nero, of a Caligula, and here he is alive in the 1970s, a mountain of immortal flesh, having survived Adolf to become—Cameron assumes—second Fuehrer and to be received in pomp at the White House, no less. Perhaps a state banquet tomorrow night, rollmops, sauerbraten, kassler rippchen, koenigsberger klopse, washed down with flagons of Bernkasteler Doktor '69, Schloss Johannisberg '71, or does the Fuehrer prefer beer? We have the finest lagers on tap, Löwenbrau, Würzburger Hofbrau——

But wait. Something rings false in Cameron's historical construct. He is unable to find in John F. Kennedy those depths of opportunism that would allow him to serve as puppet President of a Nazi-ruled America, taking orders from some slick-haired hard-eyed gauleiter and hopping obediently when the Fuehrer comes to town. Bomb or no bomb, there would have been a diehard underground resistance movement, decades of guerrilla warfare, bitter hatred of the German oppressor and of all collaborators. No surrender, then. The Axis has won the war, but the United States has retained its autonomy. Cameron revises his speculations. Suppose, he tells himself, Hitler in this universe did not break his pact with Stalin and invade Russia in the summer of 1941, but led his forces across the Channel instead to wipe out Britain. And the Japanese left Pearl Harbor alone, so the United States never was drawn into the war, which was over in fairly short order—say, by September of 1942. The Germans now rule Europe from Cornwall to the Urals and the Japanese have the whole Pacific west of Hawaii; the United States, lost in dreamy neutrality, is an isolated nation, a giant Portugal, economically stagnant, largely cut off from world trade. There are no skyscrapers in San Francisco because no one sees reason to build anything in this country. Yes? Is this how it is?

He seats himself on the stoop of a house and explores his newspaper. This world has a stock market, albeit a sluggish one: the Dow-Jones Industrials stand at 354.61. Some of the listings are familiar—IBM, AT&T, General Motors—but many are not. Litton, Syntex, and Polaroid all are missing; so is Xerox, but he finds its primordial predecessor, Haloid, in the quotations. There are two baseball leagues, each with eight clubs; the Boston Braves have moved to Milwaukee but otherwise the table of teams could have come straight out of the 1940s. Brooklyn is leading in the National League, Philadelphia in the American. In the news section he finds recognizable names: New York has a Senator Rockefeller, Massachusetts has a Senator Kennedy. (Robert, apparently. He is currently in Italy. Yesterday he toured the majestic Tomb of Mussolini near the Colosseum, today he has an audience with Pope Benedict.) An airline advertisement invites San Franciscans to go to New York via TWA's glorious new Starliners, now only twelve hours with only a brief stop in Chicago. The accompanying sketch indicates that they have about reached the DC-4 level here, or is that a DC-6, with all those propellers? The foreign news is tame and sketchy: not a word about Israel vs. the Arabs, the squabbling republics of Africa, the People's Republic of China, or the war in South America. Cameron assumes that the only surviving Jews are those of New York and Los Angeles, that Africa is one immense German colonial tract with a few patches under Italian rule, that China is governed by the Japanese, not by the heirs of Chairman Mao, and that the South American nations are torpid and unaggressive. Yes? Reading this newspaper is the strangest experience this voyage has given him so far, for the pages *look* right, the tone of the writing *feels* right, there is the insistent texture of unarguable reality about the whole paper, and yet everything is subtly off, everything has undergone a slight shift along the spectrum of events. The newspaper has the quality of a dream, but he has never known a dream to have such overwhelming substantive density.

He folds the paper under his arm and strolls toward the bay. A block from the waterfront he finds a branch of the Bank of America—some things withstand all permutations—and goes inside to change some money. There are risks, but he is curious. The teller unhesitatingly takes his five-dollar bill and hands him four singles and a little stack of coins. The singles are unremarkable, and Lincoln, Jefferson, and Washington occupy their familiar places on the cent, nickel, and quarter; but the dime shows Ben Franklin and the fifty-cent piece bears the features of a hearty-looking man, youngish, full-faced, bushy-haired, whom Cameron is unable to identify at all.

On the next corner eastward he comes to a public library. Now he can confirm his guesses. An almanac! Yes, and how odd the list of Presidents looks. Roosevelt, he learns, retired in poor health in 1940, and that, so far as he can discover, is the point of divergence between this world and his. The rest follows predictably enough. Wendell Willkie, defeating John Nance Garner in the 1940 election, maintains a policy of strict neutrality while—yes, it was as he had imagined—the Germans and Japanese quickly conquer most of the world. Willkie dies in office during the 1944 Presidential campaign—Aha! That's Willkie on the half dollar!—and is briefly succeeded by Vice President McNary, who does not want the Presidency; a hastily recalled Republican convention nominates Robert Taft. Two terms then for Taft, who beats James Byrnes, and two for Thomas Dewey, and then in 1960 the long Republican era is ended at last by Senator Lyndon Johnson of Texas. Johnson's running mate—it is an amusing reversal, Cameron thinks—is Senator John F. Kennedy of Massachusetts. After the traditional two terms, Johnson steps down and Vice President Kennedy wins the 1968 Presidential election. He has been reelected in 1972, naturally; in this placid world incumbents always win. There is, of course, no UN here, there has been no Korean War, no movement of colonial liberation, no exploration of space. The almanac tells Cameron that Hitler lived until 1960, Mussolini until 1958. The world seems to have adapted remarkably readily to Axis rule, although a German army of occupation is still stationed in England.

He is tempted to go on and on, comparing histories, learning the transmuted destinies of such figures as Hubert Humphrey, Dwight Eisenhower, Harry Truman, Nikita Khruschchev, Lee Harvey Oswald, Juan Peron. But suddenly a more intimate curiosity flowers in him. In a hallway alcove he consults the telephone book. There is one directory covering both Alameda and Contra Costa counties, and it is a much more slender volume than the directory which in his world covers Oakland alone. There are two dozen Cameron listings, but none at his address, and no Christophers or Elizabeths or any plausible permutations of those names. On a hunch he looks in the San Francisco book. Nothing promising there either; but then he checks Elizabeth under her maiden name, Dudley, and yes, there is an Elizabeth Dudley at the familiar old address on Laguna. The discovery causes him to tremble. He rummages in his pocket, finds his Ben Franklin dime, drops it in the slot. He listens. There's the dial tone. He makes the call.

10.

The apartment, what he can see of it by peering past her shoulder, looks much as he remembers it: well-worn couches and chairs upholstered in burgundy and dark green, stark whitewashed walls, elaborate sculptures—her own—of gray driftwood, huge ferns in hanging containers. To behold these objects in these surroundings wrenches powerfully at his sense of time and place and afflicts him with an almost unbearable nostalgia. The last time he was here, if indeed he has ever been "here" in any sense, was in 1969; but the memories are vivid, and what he sees corresponds so closely to what he recalls that he feels transported to that earlier era. She stands in the doorway, studying him with cool curiosity tinged with unmistakable suspicion. She wears unexpectedly ordinary clothes, a loose-fitting embroidered white blouse and a short, pleated blue skirt, and her golden hair looks dull and carelessly combed, but surely she is the same woman from whom he parted this morning, the same woman with whom he has shared his life these past seven years, a beautiful woman, a tall woman, nearly as tall as he—on some occasions taller, it has seemed—with a serene smile and steady green eyes and smooth, taut skin. "Yes?" she says uncertainly. "Are you the man who phoned?"

"Yes. Chris Cameron." He searches her face for some flicker of recognition. "You don't know me? Not at all?"

"Not at all. Should I know you?"

"Perhaps. Probably not. It's hard to say."

"Have we once met? Is that it?"

"I'm not sure how I'm going to explain my relationship to you."

"So you said when you called. Your *relationship* to me? How can strangers have had a relationship?"

"It's complicated. May I come in?"

She laughs nervously, as though caught in some embarrassing faux pas. "Of course," she says, not without giving him a quick appraisal, making a rapid estimate of risk. The apartment is in fact almost exactly as he knew it, except that there is no stereo phonograph, only a bulky archaic Victrola, and her record collection is surprisingly scanty, and there are rather fewer books than his Elizabeth would have had. They confront one another stiffly. He is as uneasy over this encounter as she is, and finally it is she who seeks some kind of social lubricant, suggesting that they have a little wine. She offers him red or white.

"Red, please," he says.

She goes to a low sideboard and takes out two cheap, clumsy-looking tumblers. Then, effortlessly, she lifts a gallon jug of wine from the floor and begins to unscrew its cap. "You were awfully mysterious on the phone," she says, "and you're still being mysterious now. What brings you here? Do we have mutual friends?"

"I think it wouldn't be untruthful to say that we do. At least in a manner of speaking."

"Your own manner of speaking is remarkably roundabout, Mr. Cameron."

"I can't help that right now. And call me Chris, please." As she pours the wine he watches her closely, thinking of that other Elizabeth, *his* Elizabeth, thinking how well he knows her body, the supple play of muscles in her back, the sleek texture of her skin, the firmness of her flesh, and he flashes instantly to their strange, absurdly romantic meeting years ago, that June when he had gone off alone into the Sierra high country for a week of backpacking and, following heaps of stones that he had wrongly taken to be trail-markers, had come to a place well off the path, a private place, a cool dark glacial lake rimmed by brilliant patches of late-lying snow, and had begun to make camp, and had become suddenly aware of someone else's pack thirty yards away, and a pile of discarded clothing on the shore, and then had seen her, swimming just beyond a pine-tipped point, heading toward land, rising like Venus from the water, naked, noticing him, startled by his presence, apprehensive for a moment but then immediately making the best of it, relaxing, smiling, standing unashamed shin-deep in the chilly shallows and inviting him to join her for a swim. These recollections of that first contact and all that ensued excite him terribly, for this person before him is at once the Elizabeth he loves, familiar, joined to him by the bond of shared experience, and also someone new, a complete stranger, from whom he can draw fresh inputs, that jolting gift of novelty which his Elizabeth can never again offer him. He stares at her shoulders and back with fierce, intense hunger; she turns toward him with the glasses of wine in her hands, and, before he can mask that wild gleam of desire, she receives it with full force. The impact is immediate. She recoils. She is not the Elizabeth of the Sierra lake; she seems unable to handle such a level of unexpected erotic voltage. Jerkily she thrusts the wine at him, her hands shaking so that she spills a little on her sleeve. He takes the glass and backs away, a bit dazed by his own frenzied upwelling of emotion. With an effort he calms himself. There is a long moment of awkward silence while they drink. The psychic atmosphere grows less torrid; a certain mood of remote, businesslike courtesy develops between them.

After the second glass of wine she says, "Now. How do you know me and what do you want from me?"

Briefly he closes his eyes. What can he tell her? How can he explain? He has rehearsed no strategies. Already he has managed to alarm her with a single unguarded glance; what effect would a confession of apparent madness have? But he has never used strategies with Elizabeth, has never resorted to any tactics except the tactic of utter candidness. And this is Elizabeth. Slowly he says, "In another existence you and I are married, Elizabeth. We live in the Oakland hills and we're extraordinarily happy together."

"Another existence?"

"In a world apart from this, a world where history took a different course a generation ago, where the Axis lost the war, where John Kennedy was President in 1963 and was killed by an assassin, where you and I met beside a lake in the Sierra and fell in love. There's an infinity of worlds, Elizabeth, side by side, worlds in which all possible variations of every possible event take place. Worlds in which you and I are married happily, in which you and I have been married and divorced, in which you and I don't exist, in which you exist and I don't, in which we meet and loathe one another, in which—in which—do you see, Elizabeth, there's a world for everything, and I've been traveling from world to world. I've seen nothing but wilderness where San Francisco ought to be, and I've met Mongol horsemen in the East Bay hills, and I've seen this whole area devastated by atomic warfare, and—does this sound insane to you, Elizabeth?"

"Just a little." She smiles. The old Elizabeth, cool, judicious, performing one of her specialties, the conditional acceptance of the unbelievable for the sake of some amusing conversation. "But go on. You've been jumping from world to world. I won't even bother to ask you how. What are you running away from?"

"I've never seen it that way. I'm running *toward*."

"Toward what?"

"An infinity of worlds. An endless range of possible experience."

"That's a lot to swallow. Isn't one world enough for you to explore?"

"Evidently not."

"You had all infinity," she says. "Yet you chose to come to me. Presumably I'm the one point of familiarity for you in this otherwise strange world. Why come here? What's the point of your wanderings, if you seek the familiar? If all you wanted to do was find your way back to your Elizabeth, why did you leave her in the first place? Are you as happy with her as you claim to be?"

"I can be happy with her and still desire her in other guises."

"You sound driven."

"No," he says. "No more driven than Faust. I believe in searching as a way of life. Not searching *for*, just searching. And it's impossible to stop. To stop is to die, Elizabeth. Look at Faust, going on and on, going to Helen of Troy herself, experiencing everything the world has to offer, and always seeking more. When Faust finally cries out, *This is it, this is what I've been looking for, this is where I choose to stop*, Mephistopheles wins his bet."

"But that was Faust's moment of supreme happiness."

"True. When he attains it, though, he loses his soul to the devil, remember?"

"So you go on, on and on, world after world, seeking you know not what, just seeking, unable to stop. And yet you claim you're not driven."

He shakes his head. "Machines are driven. Animals are driven. I'm an autonomous human being operating out of free will. I don't make this journey because I have to, but because I want to."

"Or because you think you ought to want to."

"I'm motivated by feelings, not by intellectual calculations and preconceptions."

"That sounds very carefully thought out," she tells him. He is stung by her words, and looks away, down into his empty glass. She indicates that he should help himself to the wine. "I'm sorry," she says, her tone softening a little.

He says, "At any rate, I was in the library and there was a telephone directory and I found you. This is where you used to live in my world, too, before we were married." He hesitates. "Do you mind if I ask— "

"What?"

"You're not married?"

"No. I live alone. And like it."

"You always were independent-minded."

"You talk as though you know me so well."

"I've been married to you for seven years."

"No. Not to me. Never to me. You don't know me at all."

He nods. "You're right. I don't really know you, Elizabeth, however much I think I do. But I want to. I feel drawn to you as strongly as I was to the other Elizabeth, that day in the mountains. It's always best right at the beginning, when two strangers reach toward one another, when the spark leaps the gap—" Tenderly he says, "May I spend the night here?"

"No."

Somehow the refusal comes as no surprise. He says, "You once gave me a different answer when I asked you that."

"Not I. Someone else."

"I'm sorry. It's so hard for me to keep you and her distinct in my mind, Elizabeth. But please don't turn me away.
I've come so far to be with you."

"You came uninvited. Besides, I'd feel so strange with
you—knowing you were thinking of her, comparing me
with her, measuring our differences, our points of similar-
ities——"

"What makes you think I would?"

"You would."

"I don't think that's sufficient reason for sending me
away."

"I'll give you another," she says. Her eyes sparkle mis-
chievously. "I never let myself get involved with married
men."

She is teasing him now. He says, laughing, confident
that she is beginning to yield, "That's the damndest far-
fetched excuse I've ever heard, Elizabeth!"

"Is it? I feel a great kinship with her. She has all my
sympathies. Why should I help you deceive her?"

"Deceive? What an old-fashioned word! Do you think
she'd object? She never expected me to be chaste on this trip.
She'd be flattered and delighted to know that I went looking
for you here. She'd be eager to hear about everything that
went on between us. How could she possibly be hurt by
knowing that I had been with you, when you and she
are——"

"Nevertheless, I'd like you to leave. Please."

"You haven't given me one convincing reason."

"I don't need to."

"I love you. I want to spend the night with you."

"You love someone else who resembles me," she replies.
"I keep telling you that. In any case, I don't love you. I don't
find you attractive, I'm afraid."

"Oh. She does, but you—don't. I see. How do you find me, then? Ugly? Overbearing? Repellent?"

"I find you disturbing," she says. "A little frightening. Much too intense, much too controlled, perhaps dangerous. You aren't my type. I'm probably not yours. Remember, I'm not the Elizabeth you met by that mountain lake. Perhaps I'd be happier if I were, but I'm not. I wish you had never come here. Now: please go. Please."

11.

Onward. This place is all gleaming towers and airy bridges, a glistening fantasy of a city. High overhead float glassy bubbles, silent airborne passenger vehicles, containing two or three people apiece who sprawl in postures of elegant relaxation. Bronzed young boys and girls lie naked beside soaring fountains spewing turquoise-and-scarlet foam. Giant orchids burst in tropical voluptuousness from the walls of colossal hotels. Small mechanical birds wheel and dart in the soft air like golden bullets, emitting sweet pinging sounds. From the tips of the tallest buildings comes a darker music, a ground-bass of swelling hundred-cycle notes oscillating around an insistent central rumble. This is a world two centuries ahead of his, at the least. He could never infiltrate here. He could never even be a tourist. The only role available to him is that of visiting savage, Jemmy Button among the Londoners, and what, after all, was Jemmy Button's fate? Not a happy one. Patagonia! Patagonia! Thees ticket eet ees no longer good here, sor. Colored rays dance in the sky, red, green, blue, exploding, showering the city with transcendental images. Cameron smiles. He will not let himself be overwhelmed, though this place is more confusing than the world of the halftrack automobiles. Jauntily he plants himself at the center of a small park between two lanes of flowing, noiseless traffic. It is a formal garden lush with toothy orange-fronded ferns and thorny skyrockets of looping cactus. Lovers stroll past him arm in arm, offering one another swigs from glossy sweat-beaded green flasks that look like tubes of polished jade. Delicately they dangle blue grapes before each other's lips, playfully they smile, arch their necks, take the bait with eager pounces; then they laugh, embrace, tumble into the dense moist grass, which stirs and sways and emits gentle thrumming melodies. This place pleases him. He wanders through the garden, thinking of Elizabeth, thinking of springtime, and, coming ultimately to a sinuous brook in which the city's tallest towers are reflected as inverted needles, he kneels to drink. The water is cool, sweet, tart, much like young wine. A moment after it touches his lips a mechanism rises from the spongy earth, five slender brassy columns, three with eye-sensors sprouting on all sides, one marked with a pattern of dark gridwork, one bearing an arrangement of winking colored lights. Out of the gridwork come ominous words in an unfathomable language. This is some kind of police machine, demanding his credentials: that much is clear. "I'm sorry," he says. "I can't understand what you're saying." Other machines are extruding themselves from trees, from the bed of the stream, from the hearts of the sturdiest ferns. "It's all right," he says. "I don't mean any harm. Just give me a chance to learn the language and I promise to become a useful citizen." One of the machines sprays him with a fine azure mist. Another drives a tiny needle into his forearm and extracts a droplet of blood. A crowd is gathering. They point, snicker, wink. The music of the building-tops has become higher in pitch, more sinister in texture; it shakes the balmy air and threatens him in a personal way. "Let me stay," Cameron begs, but the music is shoving him, pushing him with a flat irresistible hand, inexorably squeezing him out of this world. He is too primitive for them. He is too coarse; he carries too many obsolete microbes. Very well. If that's what they want, he'll leave, not out of fear, not because they've succeeded in intimidating him, but out of courtesy alone. In a flamboyant way he bids them farewell, bowing with a flourish worthy of Raleigh, blowing a kiss to the five-columned machine, smiling, even doing a little dance. Farewell. Farewell. The music rises to a wild crescendo. He hears celestial trumpets and distant thunder. Farewell. Onward.

12.

Here some kind of oriental marketplace has sprung up, foul-smelling, cluttered, medieval. Swarthy old men, white-bearded, in thick gray robes, sit patiently behind open burlap sacks of spices and grains. Lepers and cripples roam everywhere, begging importunately. Slender long-legged men wearing only tight loincloths and jingling dangling earrings of bright copper stalk through the crowd on solitary orbits, buying nothing, saying nothing; their skins are dark red; their faces are gaunt; their solemn features are finely modeled. They carry themselves like Inca princes. Perhaps they *are* Inca princes. In the haggle and babble of the market Cameron hears no recognizable tongue spoken. He sees the flash of gold as transactions are completed. The women balance immense burdens on their heads and show brilliant teeth when they smile. They favor patchwork skirts that cover their ankles, but they leave their breasts bare. Several of them glance provocatively at Cameron but he dares not return their quick dazzling probes until he knows what is permissible here. On the far side of the squalid plaza he catches sight of a woman who might well be Elizabeth; her back is to him, but he would know those strong shoulders anywhere, that erect stance, that cascade of unbound golden hair. He starts toward her, sliding with difficulty between the close-packed marketgoers. When he is still halfway across the marketplace from her he notices a man at her side, tall, a man of his own height and build. He wears a loose black robe and a dark scarf covers the lower half of his face. His eyes are grim and sullen and a terrible cicatrice, wide and glaringly cross-hatched with stitchmarks, runs along his left cheek up to his hairline. The man whispers something to the woman who might be Elizabeth; she nods and turns, so that Cameron now is able to see her face, and yes, the woman does seem to be Elizabeth, but she bears a matching scar, angry and hideous, up the right side of her face. Cameron gasps. The scar-faced man suddenly points and shouts. Cameron senses motion to one side, and swings around just in time to see a short thickbodied man come rushing toward him wildly waving a scimitar. For an instant Cameron sees the scene as though in a photograph: he has time to make a leisurely examination of his attacker's oily beard, his hooked hairy-nostriled nose, his yellowed teeth, the cheap glassy-looking inlaid stones on the haft of the scimitar. Then the frightful blade descends, while the assassin screams abuse at Cameron in what might be Arabic. It is a sorry welcome. Cameron cannot prolong this investigation. An instant before the scimitar cuts him in two he takes himself elsewhere, with regret.

13.

Onward. To a place where there is no solidity, where the planet itself has vanished, so that he swims through space, falling peacefully, going from nowhere to nowhere. He is surrounded by a brilliant green light that emanates from every point at once, like a message from the fabric of the universe. In great tranquility he drops through this cheerful glow for days on end, or what seems like days on end, drifting, banking, checking his course with small motions of his elbows or knees. It makes no difference where he goes; everything here is like everything else here. The green glow supports and sustains and nourishes him, but it makes him restless. He plays with it. Out of its lambent substance he succeeds in shaping images, faces, abstract patterns; he conjures up Elizabeth for himself, he evokes his own sharp features, he fills the heavens with a legion of marching Chinese in tapered straw hats, he obliterates them with forceful diagonal lines, he causes a river of silver to stream across the firmament and discharge its glittering burden down a mountainside a thousand miles high. He spins. He floats. He glides. He releases all his fantasies. This is total freedom, here in this unworldly place. But it is not enough. He grows weary of emptiness. He grows weary of serenity. He has drained this place of all it has to offer, too soon, too soon. He is not sure whether the failure is in himself or in the place, but he feels he must leave. Therefore: onward.

14.

Terrified peasants run shrieking as he materializes in their midst. This is some sort of farming village along the eastern shore of the bay: neat green fields, a cluster of low wicker huts radiating from a central plaza, naked children toddling and crying, a busy sub-population of goats and geese and chickens. It is midday; Cameron sees the bright gleam of water in the irrigation ditches. These people work hard. They have scattered at his approach, but now they creep back warily, crouching, ready to take off again if he performs any more miracles. This is another of those bucolic worlds in which San Francisco has not happened, but he is unable to identify these settlers, nor can he isolate the chain of events that brought them here. They are not Indians, nor Chinese, nor Peruvians; they have a European look about them, somehow Slavic, but what would Slavs be doing in California? Russian farmers, maybe, colonizing by way of Siberia? There is some plausibility in that—their dark complexions, their heavy facial structure, their squat powerful bodies—but they seem oddly primitive, half-naked, in furry leggings or less, as though they are no subjects of the Tsar but rather Scythians or Cimmerians transplanted from the prehistoric marshes of the Vistula.

"Don't be frightened," he tells them, holding his upraised outspread arms toward them. They do seem less fearful of him now, timidly approaching, staring with big dark eyes. "I won't harm you. I'd just like to visit with you." They murmur. A woman boldly shoves a child forward, a girl of about five, bare, with black greasy ringlets, and Cameron scoops her up, caresses her, tickles her, lightly sets her down. Instantly the whole tribe is around him, no longer afraid; they touch his arm, they kneel, they stroke his shins. A boy brings him a wooden bowl of porridge. An old woman gives him a mug of sweet wine, a kind of mead. A slender girl drapes a stole of auburn fur over his shoulders. They dance; they chant; their fear has turned into love; he is their honored guest. He is more than that: he is a god. They take him to an unoccupied hut, the largest in the village. Piously they bring him offerings of incense and acorns. When it grows dark they build an immense bonfire in the plaza, so that he wonders in vague concern if they will feast on him when they are done honoring him, but they feast on slaughtered cattle instead, and yield to him the choicest pieces, and afterward they stand by his door, singing discordant, energetic hymns. That night three girls of the tribe, no doubt the fairest virgins available, are sent to him, and in the morning he finds his threshold heaped with newly plucked blossoms. Later two tribal artisans, one lame and the other blind, set to work with stone adzes and chisels, hewing an immense and remarkably accurate likeness of him out of a redwood stump that has been mounted at the plaza's center.

So he has been deified. He has a quick Faustian vision of himself living among these diligent people, teaching them advanced methods of agriculture, leading them eventually into technology, into modern hygiene, into all the contemporary advantages without the contemporary abominations. Guiding them toward the light, molding them, creating them. This world, this village, would be a good place for him to stop his transit of the infinities, if stopping were desirable: god, prophet, king of a placid realm, teacher, inculcator of civilization, a purpose to his existence at last. But there *is* no place to stop. He knows that. Transforming happy primitive farmers into sophisticated twentieth-century agriculturalists is ultimately as useless a pastime as training fleas to jump through hoops. It is tempting to live as a god, but even divinity will pall, and it is dangerous to become attached to an unreal satisfaction, dangerous to become attached at all. The journey, not the arrival, matters. Always.

So Cameron does godhood for a little while. He finds it pleasant and fulfilling. He savors the rewards until he senses that the rewards are becoming too important to him. He makes his formal renunciation of his godhead. Then: onward.

15.

And this place he recognizes. His street, his house, his garden, his green car in the carport, Elizabeth's yellow one parked out front. Home again, so soon? He hadn't expected that; but every leap he has made, he knows, must in some way have been a product of deliberate choice, and evidently whatever hidden mechanism within him that has directed these voyages has chosen to bring him home again. All right, touch base. Digest your travels, examine them, allow your experiences to work their alchemy on you: you need to stand still a moment for that. Afterward you can always leave again. He slides his key into the door.

Elizabeth has one of the Mozart quartets on the phonograph. She sits curled up in the living-room window seat, leafing through a magazine. It is late afternoon, and the San Francisco skyline, clearly visible across the bay through the big window, is haloed by the brilliant retreating sunlight. There are freshly cut flowers in the little crystal bowl on the redwood-burl table; the fragrance of gardenias and jasmine dances past him. Unhurriedly she looks up, brings her eyes into line with his, dazzles him with the warmth of her smile, and says, "Well, hello!"

"Hello, Elizabeth."

She comes to him. "I didn't expect you back this quickly, Chris. I don't know if I expected you to come back at all, as a matter of fact."

"This quickly? How long have I been gone, for you?"

"Tuesday morning to Thursday afternoon. Two and a half days." She eyes his coarse new beard, his ragged, sunbleached shirt. "It's been longer for you, hasn't it?"

"Weeks and weeks. I'm not sure how long. I was in eight or nine different places, and I stayed in the last one quite some time. They were villagers, farmers, some primitive Slavonic tribe living down by the bay. I was their god, but I got bored with it."

"You always did get bored so easily," she says, and laughs, and takes his hands in hers and pulls him toward her. She brushes her lips lightly against him, a peck, a play-kiss, their usual first greeting, and then they kiss more passionately, bodies pressing close, tongue seeking tongue. He feels a pounding in his chest, the old inextinguishable throb. When they release each other he steps back, a little dizzied, and says, "I missed you, Elizabeth. I didn't know how much I'd miss you until I was somewhere else and aware that I might never find you again."

"Did you seriously worry about that?"

"Very much."

"I never doubted we'd be together again, one way or another. Infinity's such a big place, darling. You'd find your way back to me, or to someone very much like me. And someone very much like you would find his way to me, if you didn't. How many Chris Camerons do you think there are, on the move between worlds right now? A thousand? A trillion trillion?" She turns toward the sideboard and says, without breaking the flow of her words, "Would you like some wine?" and begins to pour from a half-empty jug of red. "Tell me where you've been," she says.

He comes up behind her and rests his hands on her shoulders, and draws them down the back of her silk blouse to her waist, holding her there, kissing the nape of her neck. He says, "To a world where there was an atomic war here, and to one where there still were Indian raiders out by Livermore, and one that was all fantastic robots and futuristic helicopters, and one where Johnson was President before Kennedy and Kennedy is alive and President now, and one where—oh, I'll give you all the details later. I need a chance to unwind first." He releases her and kisses the tip of her earlobe and takes one of the glasses from her, and they salute each other and drink, draining the wine quickly. "It's so good to be home," he says softly. "Good to have gone where I went, good to be back." She fills his glass again. The familiar domestic ritual: red wine is their special drink, cheap red wine out of gallon jugs. A sacrament, more dear to him than the burnt offerings of his recent subjects. Halfway through the second glass he says, "Come. Let's go inside."

The bed has fresh linens on it, cool, inviting. There are three thick books on the night table: she's set up for some heavy reading in his absence. Cut flowers in here, too, fragrance everywhere. Their clothes drop away. She touches his beard and chuckles at the roughness, and he kisses the smooth cool place along the inside of her thigh and draws his cheek lightly across it, sandpapering her lovingly, and then she pulls him to her and their bodies slide together and he enters her. Everything thereafter happens quickly, much too quickly; he has been long absent from her, if not she from him, and now her presence excites him, there is a strangeness about her body, her movements, and it hastens him to his ecstasy. He feels a mild pang of regret, but no more: he'll make it up to her soon enough, they both know that. They drift into a sleepy embrace, neither of them speaking, and eventually uncoil into tender new passion, and this time all is as it should be. Afterward they doze. A spectacular sunset blazes over the city when he opens his eyes. They rise, they take a shower together, much giggling, much playfulness. "Let's go across the bay for a fancy dinner tonight," he suggests. "Trianon, Blue Fox, Ernie's, anywhere. You name it. I feel like celebrating."

"So do I, Chris."

"It's good to be home again."

"It's good to have you here," she tells him. She looks for her purse. "How soon do you think you'll be heading out again? Not that I mean to rush you, but——"

"You know I'm not going to be staying?"

"Of course I know."

"Yes. You would." She had never questioned his going. They both tried to be responsive to each other's needs; they had always regarded one another as equal partners, free to do as they wished. "I can't say how long I'll stay. Probably not long. Coming home this soon was really an accident, you know. I just planned to go on and on and on, world after world, and I never programmed my next jump, at least not consciously. I simply leaped. And the last leap deposited me on my own doorstep, somehow, so I let myself into the house. And there you were to welcome me home."

She presses his hand between hers. Almost sadly she says, "You aren't home, Chris."

"What?"

He hears the sound of the front door opening. Footsteps in the hallway.

"You aren't home," she says.

Confusion seizes him. He thinks of all that has passed between them this evening.

"Elizabeth?" calls a deep voice from the living room.

"In here, darling. I have company!"

"Oh? Who?" A man enters the bedroom, halts, grins. He is clean-shaven and dressed in the clothes Cameron had worn on Tuesday; otherwise they could be twins. "Hey, hello!" he says warmly, extending his hand.

Elizabeth says, "He comes from a place that must be very much like this one. He's been here since five o'clock, and we were just going out for dinner. Have you been having an interesting time?"

"Very," the other Cameron says. "I'll tell you all about it later. Go on, don't let me keep you."

"You could join us for dinner," Cameron suggests helplessly.

"That's all right. I've just eaten. Breast of passenger pigeon—they aren't extinct everywhere. I wish I could have brought some home for the freezer. So you two go and enjoy. I'll see you later. Both of you, I hope. Will you be staying with us? We've got notes to compare, you and I."

16.

He rises just before dawn, in a marvelous foggy stillness. The Camerons have been wonderfully hospitable, but he must be moving along. He scrawls a thank-you note and slips it under their bedroom door. *Let's get together again someday. Somewhere. Somehow.* They wanted him as a house guest for a week or two, but no, he feels like a bit of an intruder here, and anyway the universe is waiting for him. He has to go. The journey, not the arrival, matters, for what else is there but trips? Departing is unexpectedly painful, but he knows the mood will pass. He closes his eyes. He breaks his moorings. He gives himself up to his sublime restlessness. Onward. Onward. *Goodbye, Elizabeth. Goodbye, Chris. I'll see you both again.* Onward.

▼▲▼▲▼

IN
THE
HOUSE
OF
DOUBLE
MINDS

Now they bring in the new ones, this spring's crop of ten-year-olds—six boys, six girls—and leave them with me in the dormitory room that will be their home for the next dozen years. The room is bare, austere, with black slate floors and rough brick walls, furnished for the time being with cots and clothes-cabinets and little more. The air is chill, and the children, who are naked, huddle in discomfort.

"I am Sister Mimise," I tell them. "I will be your guide and counselor in the first twelve months of your new life in the House of Double Minds."

I have lived in this place for eight years, since I was fourteen, and this is the fifth year that I have had charge of the new children. If I had not been disqualified by my left-handedness, this is the year I would have been graduated into full oraclehood, but I try not to dwell on that. Caring for the children is a rewarding task in itself. They arrive scrawny and frightened, and slowly they unfold: they blossom; they ripen; they grow toward their destinies. Each year there is some special one for me, some favorite, in whom I take particular joy. In my first group, four years ago, it was long-legged laughing Jen, she who is now my lover. A year later it was soft beautiful Jalil, and then Timas, who I thought would become one of the greatest of all oracles; but after two years of training Timas cracked and was culled. And last year bright-eyed Runild, impish Runild, my pet, my darling boy, more gifted even than Timas and, I fear, even less stable. I look at the new ones, wondering who will be special among them for me this year.

The children are pale, slender, uneasy; their thin nude bodies look more than naked because of their shaven skulls. As a result of what has been done to their brains they move clumsily today. Their left arms often dangle as though they have entirely forgotten them, and they tend to walk in a shuffling sidewise motion, dragging their left legs a little. These problems soon will disappear. The last of the operations in this group was performed only two days ago, on the short wide-shouldered girl whose breasts have already begun to grow. I can see the narrow red line marking the place where the surgeon's beam sliced through her scalp to sever the hemispheres of her brain.

"You have been selected," I say in a resonant formal tone, "for the highest and most sacred office in our society. From this moment until you reach adulthood your lives and energies will be consecrated to the purpose of attaining the skills and wisdom an oracle must have. I congratulate you on having come so far."

And I envy you.

I do not say that part aloud.

I feel envy and pity both. I have seen the children come and go, come and go. Out of each year's dozen, one or two usually die along the way of natural causes or accidents. At least three go insane under the terrible pressure of the disciplines and have to be culled. So only about half the group is likely to complete the twelve years of training, and most of those will prove to have little value as oracles. The useless ones will be allowed to remain, of course, but their lives will be meaningless. The House of Double Minds has been in existence for more than a century; there are at present just one hundred forty-two oracles in residence—seventy-seven women and sixty-five men—of whom all but about forty are mere drones. A thin harvest out of some twelve hundred novices since the beginning.

These children have never met before. I call upon them to introduce themselves. They give their names in low self-conscious voices, eyes downcast.

A boy named Divvan asks, "Will we wear clothes soon?"

Their nakedness disturbs them. They hold their thighs together and stand at odd storklike angles, keeping apart from one another, trying to conceal their undeveloped loins. They do this because they are strangers. They will forget their shame before long. As the months pass they will become closer than brothers and sisters.

"Robes will be issued this afternoon," I tell him. "But clothing ought not to be important here, and you need have no reason to wish to hide your bodies." Last year when this same point arose—it always does—the mischievous boy Runild suggested that I remove my own robe as a gesture of solidarity. Of course I did, but it was a mistake: the sight of a mature woman's body was more troubling to them than even their own bareness.

Now it is the time for the first exercises, so that they may learn the ways in which the brain operation has altered the responses of their bodies. At random I choose a girl named Hirole and ask her to step forward, while the rest form a circle around her. She is tall and fragile-looking and it must be torment to her to be aware of the eyes of all the others upon her.

Smiling, I say gently, "Raise your hand, Hirole."

She raises one hand.

"Bend your knee."

As she flexes her knee, there is an interruption. A wiry naked boy scrambles into the room, fast as a spider, wild as a monkey, and bursts into the middle of the circle, shouldering Hirole aside. Runild again! He is a strange and moody and extraordinarily intelligent child, who, now that he is in his second year at the House, has lately been behaving in a reckless, unpredictable way. He runs around the circle, seizing several of the new children briefly, putting his face close to theirs, staring with crazy intensity into their eyes. They are terrified of him. For a moment I am too astonished to move. Then I go to him and seize him.

He struggles ferociously. He spits at me, hisses, claws my arms, makes thick wordless grunting sounds. Gradually I get control of him. In a low voice I say, "What's wrong with you, Runild? You know you aren't supposed to be in here!"

"Let me go."

"Do you want me to report this to Brother Sleel?"

"I just want to see the new ones."

"You're frightening them. You'll be able to meet them in a few days, but you're not allowed to upset them now." I pull him toward the door. He continues to resist and nearly breaks free. Eleven-year-old boys are amazingly strong, sometimes. He kicks my thigh savagely: I will have purple bruises tonight. He tries to bite my arm. Somehow I get him out of the room, and in the corridor he suddenly goes slack and begins to tremble, as though he has had a fit that now is over. I am trembling too. Hoarsely I say, "What's happening to you, Runild? Do you want to be culled the way Timas and Jurda were? You can't keep doing things like this! You——"

He looks up at me, wild-eyed, and starts to say something, and stifles it, and turns and bolts. In a moment he is gone, a brown naked streak vanishing down the hallway. I feel a great sadness: Runild was a favorite of mine, and now he is going insane, and they will have to cull him. I should report the incident immediately, but I am unable to bring myself to do it, and, telling myself that my responsibility lies with the new ones, I return to the dorm room.

"Well!" I say briskly, as if nothing unusual has happened. "He's certainly playful today, isn't he! That was Runild. He's a year ahead of you. You'll meet him and the rest of his group a little later. Now, Hirole——"

The children, preoccupied with their own altered state, quickly grow calm; they seem much less distressed by Runild's intrusion than I am. Shakily I begin again, asking Hirole to raise a hand, to flex a knee, to close an eye. I thank her and call a boy named Mulliam into the center of the circle. I ask him to raise one shoulder above the other, to touch his hand to his cheek, to make a fist. Then I pick a girl named Fyme and instruct her to hop on one foot, to put an arm behind her back, to kick one leg in the air.

I say, "Who can tell me one thing that was true of every response?"

Several of them answer at once, "It was always the right side! The right eye, the right hand, the right leg——"

"Correct." I turn to a small dark-visaged boy named Bloss and ask, "Why is that? Do you think it's just coincidence?"

"Well," he says, "everybody here is right-handed, because left-handers aren't allowed to become oracles, and so everybody tended to use the side that he——"

Bloss falters, seeing heads shaking all around the circle.

Galaine, the girl whose breasts have begun to sprout, says, "It's because of the operation! The right side of our brains doesn't understand words very well, and it's the Right that controls the left side of the body, so when you tell us in words to do something, only our Left understands and moves the muscles it controls. It gets the jump on the Right because the Right can't speak or be spoken to."

"Very good, Galaine. That's it exactly."

I let it sink in. Now that the connections between the two halves of their brains have been cut, the Rights of these children are isolated, unable to draw on the skills of the language center in the Left. They are only now realizing what it means to have half a brain rendered illiterate and inarticulate, to have their Left respond as though it is the entire brain, activating only the muscles it controls most directly.

Fyme says, "Does that mean we won't ever be able to use our left sides again?"

"Not at all. Your Right isn't paralyzed or helpless. It just isn't very good at using words. So your Left is quicker to react when I give a verbal instruction. But if the instruction isn't phrased in words, the Right will be able to take control and respond."

"How can you give an instruction that isn't in words?" Mulliam asks.

"In many ways," I say. "I could draw a picture, or make a gesture, or use some sort of symbol. I'll show you what I mean by going through the exercises again. Sometimes I'll give the instructions in words, and sometimes by acting them out. When I do that, imitate what you see. Is that clear?"

I wait a moment to allow the sluggish word-skills of their Rights to grasp the scheme.

Then I say, "Raise a hand."

They lift their right arms. When I tell them to bend a knee, they bend their right knees. But when I wordlessly close my left eye, they imitate me and close their left eyes. Their Rights are able to exert muscular control in a normal way when the instructions are delivered non-verbally; but when I use words, the Left alone perceives and acts.

I test the ability of their Lefts to override the normal

motor functions of their Rights by instructing them verbally to raise their left shoulders. Their Rights, baffled by my words, take no action, forcing their Lefts to reach beyond a Left's usual sphere of dominance. Slowly, with great difficulty, a few of the children manage to raise their left shoulders. Some can manage only a mere twitch. Fyme, Bloss, and Mulliam, with signs of struggle evident on their faces, are unable to budge their left shoulders at all. I tell the entire group to relax, and the children collapse in relief, sprawling on their cots. There is nothing to worry about, I say. In time they will all regain full motor functions in both halves of their bodies. Unless they are driven insane by the split-brain phenomena, that is, but no need to tell them that.

"One more demonstration for today," I announce. This one will show them in another way how thoroughly the separation of the hemispheres affects the mental processes. I ask Gybold, the smallest of the boys, to seat himself at the testing table at the far end of the room. There is a screen mounted on the table; I tell Gybold to fix his eyes on the center of the screen, and I flash a picture of a banana on the left side of the screen for a fraction of a second.

"What do you see, Gybold?"

"I don't see anything, Sister Mimise," he replies, and the other children gasp. But the "I" that is speaking is merely Gybold's Left, which gets its visual information through his right eye; that eye did indeed see nothing. Meanwhile Gybold's Right is answering my question in the only way it can: the boy's left hand gropes among several objects lying on the table hidden behind the screen, finds the banana that is there, and triumphantly holds it up. Through sight and touch Gybold's Right has prevailed over its wordlessness.

"Excellent," I say. I take the banana from him and,

drawing his left hand behind the screen where he is unable to see it, I put a drinking-glass into it. I ask him to name the object in his hand.

"An apple?" he ventures. I frown, and quickly he says, "An egg? A pencil?"

The children laugh. Mulliam says, "He's just guessing!"

"Yes, he is. But which part of Gybold's brain is making the guesses?"

"His Left," Galaine cries. "But it's the Right that knows it's holding a glass."

They all shush her for giving away the secret. Gybold pulls his hand out from under the screen and stares at the glass, silently forming its name with his lips.

I put Herik, Chith, Simi, and Clane through related experiments. Always the results are the same. If I flash a picture to the right eye or put an object in the right hand, the children respond normally, correctly naming it. But if I transmit information only to the left eye or the left hand, they are unable to use words to describe the objects their Rights see or feel.

It is enough for now. The children are silent and have withdrawn into individual spheres of privacy. I know that they are working things out within their minds, performing small self-devised experiments, testing themselves, trying to learn the full extent of the changes the operation has brought about. They glance from one hand to another, flex fingers, whisper little calculations. They should not be allowed to look inward so much, not at the beginning. I take them to the storeroom to receive their new clothing, the simple gray monastic robes that we wear to set us apart from the ordinary people of the city. Then I turn them free, sending them romping into the broad fields of soft green grass behind the dormitory, to relax and play. They may be oracles in the making; but they are also, after all, ten-year-old children.

It is my afternoon rest period. On my way through the dark cool corridors to my chamber I am stopped by Brother Sleel, one of the senior oracles. He is a white-haired man, tall and of powerful build, and his blue eyes work almost independently of one another, constantly scanning his surroundings in restless separate searches. Sleel has never been anything but warm and kind to me, and yet I have always been afraid of him, I suppose more out of awe for his office than out of fear for the man himself. Really I feel timid with all the oracles, knowing that their minds work differently from mine and that they see things in me that I may not see myself. Sleel says, "I saw you having difficulties with Runild in the hall this morning. What was happening?"

"He wandered into my orientation meeting. I asked him to leave."

"What was he doing?"

"He said he wanted to see the new children. But of course I couldn't let him bother them."

"And he started to fight with you?"

"He made some trouble. Nothing much."

"He was fighting with you, Mimise."

"He was rather unruly," I admit.

Sleel's left eye stares into mine. I feel a chill. It is the oracle-eye, the all-seeing one. Quietly he says, "I saw you fighting with him."

I look away from him. I study my bare feet. "He wouldn't leave. He was frightening the new ones. When I tried to lead him from the room he jumped at me, yes. But he didn't hurt me and it was all over in a moment. Runild is high-spirited, Brother."

"Runild is a troubled child," Sleel says heavily. "He is disturbed. He is becoming wild, like a beast."

"No, Brother Sleel." How can I face that terrible eye? "He has extraordinary gifts. You know—surely *you* must know—that it takes time for one like him to settle down, to come to terms with——"

"I've had complaints from his counselor, Voree. She says she hardly knows how to handle him."

"It's only a phase. Voree's had responsibility for him only a couple of weeks. As soon as she——"

"I know you want to protect him, Mimise. But don't let your love for the boy cloud your judgment. I think this is Timas happening all over again. It's an old, old pattern here, the brilliant novice who is unable to cope with his changes, who——"

"Are you going to cull him?" I blurt.

Sleel smiles. He takes both my hands in his. I am engulfed by his strength, by his wisdom, by his power. I sense the unfathomable flow of perception from his mystic Right to his calm, analytic Left. He says, "If Runild gets any worse, I'll have to. But I want to save him. I like the boy. I respect his potential. What do you suggest we do, Mimise?"

"What do *I*——"

"Tell me. Advise me."

The senior oracle is playing a little game with me, I suppose. Shrugging, I say, "Obviously Runild's trying to gain attention through all these crazy pranks. Let's try to reach him and find out what he really wants, and perhaps there'll be some way we can give it to him. I'll speak to Voree. I'll talk to his sister, Kitrin. And tomorrow I'll talk to

Runild. I think he trusts me. We were very close last year, Runild and I."

"I know," Sleel says gently. "Very well: see what you can do."

Still later that afternoon, as I cross the central court-yard, Runild erupts from the second-year house and rushes up to me. His face is flushed; his bare chest is shiny with sweat. He clings to me, pulls me down to his height, looks me in the eye. His eyes have already begun to stray a little; one day they may be like Sleel's.

I think he wants to apologize for his invasion of my group. But all he manages to say is: "I am sorry for you. You wanted so much to be one of us." And he runs off.

To be one of them. Yes. Who does not long to dwell in the House of Double Minds, living apart from the noise and chaos of the world, devoting oneself to oracular contemplation and the service of mankind? My mother's father's sister was of that high company, and in early girlhood I was taken to visit her. How awesome it was to stand in the presence of her all-knowing Right, to feel the flood of warmth and understanding that emanated from her wise eyes. It was my dream to join her here, a dream doubly thwarted, for she died when I was eight, and by then the fact of my left-handedness was irremediably established.

Left-handers are never selected to undergo the oracle-making operation. The two halves of our brains are too symmetrical, too ambidextrous: we have speech centers on both sides, most of us left-handers, and so we are not likely to develop those imbalances of cerebral powers that oracles must have. Right-handers, too, are born with symmetrically functioning brains, each hemisphere developing independently and duplicating the operations of the other. But by the time they are two years old, their Lefts and Rights are linked in a way that gives them a shared pool of skills, and therefore each half is free to develop its own special capabilities, since the gifts of one half are instantly available to the other.

At the age of ten this specializing process is complete. Language, sequential thought, all the analytic and rational functions, center in the Left. Special perception, artistic vision, musical skill, emotional insight, center in the Right. The brain's left side is the scientist, the architect, the general, the mathematician. The brain's right side is the minstrel, the sculptor, the visionary, the dreamer. Normally the two halves operate as one. The Right experiences a flash of poetic intuition, the Left clothes it in words. The Right sees a pattern of fundamental connections, the Left expresses it in a sequence of theorems. The Right conceives the shape of a symphony, the Left sets the notes down on paper. Where there is true harmony between the hemispheres of the brain, works of genius are created.

Too often, though, one side seizes command. Perhaps the Right becomes dominant, and we have a dancer, an athlete, an artist, who has trouble with words, who is inexpressive and inarticulate except through some nonverbal medium. More often, because we are a word-worshipping people, it is the Left that rules, choking the subordinate Right in a welter of verbal analysis and commentary, slowing and hindering the spontaneous intuitive perceptions of the mind. What society gains in orderliness and rationality it loses in vision and grace. We can do nothing about these imbalances—except to take advantage of their existence by accentuating and exploiting them.

And so the children come here, a dozen of our best each year, and our surgeons sever the isthmus of neural tissue that links Left and Right. Some kind of communication between the hemispheres continues to operate, since each half remains aware of what the other is immediately experiencing, if not of its accumulated memories and skills. But the Right is cut free from the tyranny of the word-intoxicated Left. The Left continues to operate its normal routines of reading and writing and conversation and computation, while the Right, now its own master, observes and registers and analyzes in a way that has no need of words. Because its verbal skills are so feeble, the newly independent Right must find some other means of expression if it is to make its perceptions known: and, through the dozen years of training in the House of Double Minds, some of the children succeed in achieving this. They are able—I do not know how, no one who is not an oracle can ever know how—to transmit the unique insights of fully mature and wholly independent Rights to their Lefts, which can transmit them to the rest of us. It is a difficult and imperfect process; but it gives us access to levels of knowledge that few have ever reached before our time. Those who master that skill are our functional oracles. They dwell in realms of beauty and wisdom that, in the past, only saints and prophets and the greatest artists and a few madmen have reached.

I would, if I could, have entered those realms. But I came forth left-handed from the womb and my brain, though it is a decent one, therefore lacked the required asymmetry of function. If I could not be an oracle I could at least serve them, I decided. And thus I came here as a girl, and asked to be of use, and in time was given the important task of easing the new children into their new lives. So I have come to know Jen and Timas and Jalil and Runild and the others, some of whom will live to be among the most famous of oracles, and so now I welcome Hirole and Mulliam and Gybold and Galaine and their companions. And I am content, I think. I am content.

We gather in the main hall for the evening meal. My new group has not come before the older novices until now, and so my twelve undergo close scrutiny, which they find embarrassing, as I lead them to their place. Each year-group sits together at its own circular table. My dozen dine with me; at the table to my left is my group of last year, now in Voree's charge. Runild sits there with his back to me, and his mere presence creates a tension in me as if he is giving off an electric radiation. To my right is the third-year group, reduced now to nine by the culling of Timas and two deaths; the fourth-year children are just in front of me and the fifth-year ones, my darling Jen among them, at my rear. The older children are in the center of the hall. Along the sides of the great room are the tables of the instructors, those who have daily care of the ordinary education of the twelve groups of novices, and the senior oracles occupy long tables at the hall's far end, beneath a panoply of gay red and green banners.

Sleel makes a brief speech of welcome for my twelve, and the meal is served.

I send Galaine to Voree's table with a note: "*See me on the porch after dinner.*"

My appetite is poor. I finish quickly, but I stay with my group until it is time to dismiss them. All the children troop off to the auditorium for a show. A warm drizzle is falling;

Voree and I stand in the shelter of the eaves. She is much older than I am, a stocky woman with kinky orange hair. Year after year I pass my fledglings on to her. She is strong, efficient, stolid, insensitive. Runild baffles her. "He's like a monkey," she says. "Running around naked, chattering to himself, singing crazy songs, playing pranks. He isn't doing his lessons. He isn't even doing his disciplines, half the time. I've warned him he'll be culled, but he doesn't seem to care."

"What do you think he wants?"

"To have everyone notice him."

"Yes, surely, but *why?*"

"Because he's a naturally mischievous boy," Voree says, scowling. "I've seen many of his sort before. They think rules are for other people. Two more weeks of this and I'll recommend a cull."

"He's too brilliant to waste like that, Voree."

"He's wasting himself. Without the disciplines how can he become an oracle? And he's upsetting all the others. My group's a shambles. Now he's bothering yours. He won't leave his sister alone either. Culling, Mimise, that's where he's heading. Culling."

There is nothing to be gained from talking to Voree. I join my group in the auditorium.

Bedtime for the younger ones comes early. I see my children to their room; then I am free until midnight. I return to the auditorium, where the older children and the off-duty staff are relaxing, playing games, dancing, drifting off in couples. Kitrin, Runild's sister, is still there. I draw her aside. She is a slender, delicate girl of fourteen, a fifth-year novice. I am fond of her because she was in my very first group, but I have always found her shy, elusive, opaque. She is more so than ever now: I question her about her brother's behavior and she answers me with shrugs, vague unfinished sentences, and artful evasions. Runild is wild? Well, of course, many boys are wild, she says, especially the bright ones. The disciplines seem to bore him. He's far ahead of his group—you know that, Mimise. And so on. I get nothing from her except the strong feeling that she is hiding something about her brother. My attempts to probe fail; Kitrin is still a child, but she is halfway to oraclehood, nearly, and that gives her an advantage over me in any duel of wits. Only when I suggest that Runild is in immediate peril of culling do I break through her defenses.

"No!" she gasps, eyes widening in fear, cheeks turning pale. "They mustn't! He has to stay! He's going to be greater than any of them!"

"He's causing too much trouble."

"It's just a thing he's going through. He'll settle down, I promise you that."

"Voree doesn't think so. She's going to request a cull."

"No. No. What will happen to him if he's culled? He was *meant* to be an oracle. His whole life will have been thrown away. We have to save him, Mimise."

"We can do that only if he can control himself."

"I'll talk to him in the morning," Kitrin says.

I wonder what she knows about Runild that she does not want to tell me.

At the evening's end I bring Jen to my chamber, as I do three or four nights a week. She is tall and supple and looks more than her fourteen years. Her counselor tells me she is moving well through her mid-novitiate and will be a splendid oracle. We lie together, lips to lips, breasts against breasts, and we stroke and caress and tickle one another, we smile with our eyes, we enter into all the rituals of love. Afterward, in the stillness that follows passion, she finds the bruise of this morning's struggle on my thigh and questions me with a frown. "Runild," I say. I tell her about his erratic behavior, about Sleel's uneasiness, about my conversation with Voree.

"They mustn't cull him," Jen says solemnly. "I know he's troublesome. But the path he's taking is so important for all of us."

"Path? What path is that?"

"You don't know?"

"I know nothing, Jen."

She catches her breath, rolls away, studies me a moment. At length she says, "Runild sees into minds. When he puts his head very close to people, there's transmission. Without using words. It's—it's a kind of broadcast. His Right can read the Rights of other oracles, the way you'd open a book and read it. If he could get close enough to Sleel, say, or any of them, he could read what's in their Rights."

"What?"

"More, Mimise. His own Right talks to his Left the same way. He can transmit messages completely, quickly, making better contact between the halves than any of the oracles can do. He hasn't had the disciplines, even, and he has full access to his Right's perceptions. So whatever his Right sees, including what it gets from the Rights of others, can be transmitted to his Left and expressed in words more clearly even than Sleel himself can do it!"

"I don't believe this," I say, barely comprehending.

"It's true! It's true, Mimise! He's only just learning how, and it gets him terribly excited, it makes him wild, don't you see, when all that contact comes flooding in? He can't quite handle it yet, which is why he acts so strange. But once he gets his power under control——"

"How do you know anything about this, Jen?"

"Why, Kitrin told me."

"Kitrin? I spoke to Kitrin and she never even hinted that——"

"Oh," Jen says, looking pained. "Oh. I guess I wasn't supposed to say. Not even to you, I guess. Oh, now I'll be in trouble with Kitrin, and——"

"You won't be. She doesn't need to know how I found out. But—Jen, Jen, can this be? Can anyone have such powers?"

"Runild does."

"So he claims. Or Kitrin claims on his behalf."

"No," Jen says firmly. "He *does*. They showed me, he and Kitrin. I felt him touch my mind. I felt him read me. He can read anyone. He can read *you*, Mimise."

I must speak with Runild. But carefully, carefully, everything in its proper moment. In the morning I must first meet with my group and take them through the second-day exercises. These are designed to demonstrate that their Rights, although mute and presently isolated, are by no means inferior, and have perceptions and capabilities which in some ways are superior to those of their Lefts.

"Never think of your Right as a cripple," I warn them. "See it, rather, as some kind of extremely intelligent animal—an animal that is sharp-witted, quick to respond, imaginative, with only one flaw, that it has no vocabulary and is never going to be able to acquire more than a few simple words at best. Nobody pities a tiger or an eagle because it doesn't know how to speak. And there are ways of training tigers and eagles so that we can communicate with them without using words."

I flash a picture of a house on the screen and ask the children to copy it, first using their left hands, then the right. Although they are all right-handed, they are unable to draw anything better than simple, crude two-dimensional representations with their right hands. Their left-handed drawings, while shakily drawn because of their left arms' relatively backward muscular development and motor control, show a full understanding of the techniques of perspective. The right hand has the physical skill, but it is the left, drawing on the vision of the brain's right hemisphere, that has the artistic ability.

I ask them to arrange colored plastic cubes to match an intricate pattern on the screen. Left-handed, they carry out the exercise swiftly and expertly. Right-handed, they become confused, frown and bite their lips, hold the cubes long moments without knowing where to put them down, eventually array the cubes in chaotic mazes. Clane and Bloss give up entirely in a minute or two; Mulliam perseveres grimly like one who is determined to climb a mountain too steep for his strength, but he accomplishes little; Luabet's left hand keeps darting across to do the task that is beyond the right's powers, as if she is at war with herself. She must keep the impatient left hand behind her back in order to proceed at all. No one can complete the block design correctly with the right hand, and when I allow the children to work with both hands the hands fight for control, the formerly dominant right one unable to accept its new inferiority and angrily slapping at the cubes the left one tries to put in place.

We go on to the split-screen exercises in facial recognition and pattern analysis, to the musical exercises, and the rest of the usual second-day routine. The children are fascinated by the ease with which their Rights function in all but word-linked operations. Ordinarily I am delighted, too, to watch the newly liberated Rights come to life and assert their powers. But today I am impatient to be off to Runild and I give only perfunctory attention to my proper work.

At last the session ends. The children move off to the classroom where they will receive regular school-subject instruction. Runild's group, too, should be at school until noon. Possibly I can draw him aside after lunch. But, as though I have conjured him with a wish, I see him now, tumbling by himself in the meadow of crimson flowers by the auditorium. He sees me, too: halts in his gambol, winks, smiles, does a handspring, blows me a kiss. I go to him.

"Are you excused from classes this morning?" I ask, mock-stern.

"The flowers are so pretty," he replies.

"The flowers will be just as pretty after school."

"Oh, don't be so stuffy, Mimise! I know my lessons. I'm a clever boy."

"Perhaps too clever, Runild."

He grins. I do not frighten him. He seems to be patronizing me; he appears to be at once very much younger and very much wiser than his years. I take him gently by the wrist and draw him down, easily, until we are sprawled side by side in the grass. He plucks a flower for me. His look is flirtatious. I accept both the flower and the look and respond with a warm smile; I am flirtatious myself. No doubt of his charm; and I can never win him by acting as an authority-figure, only as a co-conspirator. There was always an underlying sexuality in our relationship, incestuous, as if I were an older sister.

We talk in banter, teasing each other. Then I say,

"Something mysterious has been happening to you lately, Runild. I know that. Share your mystery with me."

At first he denies all. He pretends innocence, but lets me know it is only pretense. His sly smile betrays him. He speaks in cryptic ellipses, hinting at arcane knowledge and defying me to pry details from him. I play his game, acting now intrigued, now eager, now skeptical, now wholly uninterested: we are stalking one another, and both of us know it. His oracle-eye pierces me. He toys with me with such subtlety that I must remind myself, with a glance at his slim hairless body, that I am dealing with a child. I ought never forget that he is only eleven. Finally I press directly once more, asking him outright what strange new gift he is cultivating.

"Wouldn't you like to know!" he cries, and pulls an outrageous face, and dashes away.

But he comes back. We talk on a more serious level. He admits that he has discovered, these past few months, that he is different from the other children and from the senior oracles, that he has a talent, a power. It disturbs and exalts him both. He is still exploring the scope of it. He will not describe the power in any specific way. Of course I know from Jen its nature, but I prefer not to reveal that. "Will you ever tell me?" I ask.

"Not today," he says.

Gradually I win his trust. We meet casually, in corridors or courtyards, and exchange easy pleasantries, the sort I might trade with any of my former charges. He is testing me, seeing whether I am a friend or simply Sleel's spy. I let him know of my concern for him. I let him know that his eccentric behavior has placed him in jeopardy of culling.

"I suppose so," he says gloomily. "But what can I do? I'm not like the others. I can't sit still for long. Things are jumping inside my head all the time. Why should I bother with arithmetic when I can——"

He halts, suddenly guarded again.

"When you can what, Runild?"

"*You* know."

"I don't."

"You will. Soon enough."

There are days when he seems calm. But his pranks have not ended. He finds poor Sister Sestoine, one of the oldest and dimmest of the oracles, and puts his forehead against hers and does something to her that sends her into an hour's tears. Sestoine will not say what took place during that moment of contact, and after a while she seems to forget the episode. Sleel's face is dark. He looks warningly at me as if to say, *Time's running short; the boy must go.*

On a day of driving rain I am in my chamber in midafternoon when Runild unexpectedly enters, soaked, hair plastered to his scalp. Puddles drip from him. He strips and I rub him with my towel and stand him before the fire. He says nothing all this while; he is tense, taut, as if a mighty pressure is building within him and the time has not yet come for its release. Abruptly he turns to me. His eyes are strange: they wander, they quiver, they glow. "Come close!" he whispers hoarsely, like a man calling a woman to his bed.

He grasps my shoulders, he pulls me down to his height, he pushes his blazing forehead roughly against mine. And the world changes. I see tongues of purple flame. I see crevasses opening in the earth. I see the oceans engulfing the shore. I am flooded with contact; I am swept with wild energies.

I know what it is to be an oracle.

My Right and my Left are asunder. It is not like having one brain cleft in two; it is like having two brains, independent, equal. I feel them ticking like two clocks, with separate beats; and the Left goes tick-tock-tick-tock, machine-dreary, while the Right leaps and dances and soars and sings in lunatic rhythms. But they are not lunatic rhythms, for their frantic pulses have a regularity of irregularity, a pattern of patternlessness. I grow used to the strangeness; I become comfortable within both brains, the Left which I think of as "me," and the Right which is "me" too, but an altered and unfamiliar self without a name. My earliest memories lie open to me in my Right. I see into a realm of shadows. I am an infant again; I have access to the first hours of my life, to all my first years, those years in which words meant nothing to me. The pre-verbal data all rests within my Right, shapes and textures and odors and sounds, and I do not need to give names to anything, I do not need to denote or analyze, I need only feel, experience, relive. All that is there is clear and sharp. I see how it has always been with me, how that set of recorded experiences had directed my behavior even as the experiences of later years have done so. I can reach that hidden realm now, and understand it, and use it.

I feel the flow of data from Right to Left—the wordless responses, the intuitive reactions, the quick spontaneous awareness of structures. The world holds new meanings for me. I think, but not in words, and I tell myself things, but not in words, and my Left, groping and fumbling (for it has not had the disciplines) seeks words, sometimes finding them, to express what I am giving it. So this is what oracles do. This is what they feel. This is the knowledge they have. I am transfigured. It is my fantasy come true: they have snipped that rubbery band of connective tissue; they have set free my Right; they have made me one of them. And I will never again be what once I was. I will think in tones and colors now. I will explore kingdoms unknown to the wordbound ones. I will live in a land of music. I will not merely speak and write; I will feel and know.

Only it is fading now.

The power is leaving me. I had it only a moment; and was it my own power or only a glimpse of Runild's? I cling, I grapple, and yet it goes, it goes, it goes, and I am left with shreds and bits, and then not even those, only an aftertaste, an echo of an echo, a diminishing shaft of feeble light. My eyes open. I am on my knees; sweat covers my body; my heart is pounding. Runild stands above me. "You see now?" he says. "You see? This is what it's like for me all the time. I can connect minds. *I can make connections, Mimise.*"

"Do it again," I beg.

He shakes his head. "Too much will hurt you," he says. And goes from me.

I have told Sleel what I have learned. Now they have the boy with them in the inner oracle-house, nine of them, the highest oracles, questioning him, testing him. I do not see how they can fail to welcome his gift, to give him special honor, to help him through his turbulent boyhood so that he can take his place supreme among oracles. But Jen thinks otherwise. She thinks he distresses them by scrabbling at their minds in his still unfocused attempts at making contact, and that they will fear him once they have had an explicit demonstration of what he can do; she thinks, too, that he is a threat to their authority, for his way of joining the perceptions of his Right to the analytic powers of his Left by a direct mental flow is far superior to their own laborious method of symbolic translation. Jen thinks they will surely cull him and may even put him to death. How can I believe such things? She is not yet an oracle herself; she is still a girl; she may be wrong. The conference continues, hour after hour, and no one emerges from the oracle-house.

In the evening they come forth. The rain has stopped. I see the senior oracles march across the courtyard. Runild is among them, very small at Sleel's side. There are no expressions on any faces. Runild's eyes meet mine: his look is blank, unreadable. Have I somehow betrayed him in trying to save him? What will happen to him? The procession reaches the far side of the quadrangle. A car is waiting. Runild and two of the senior oracles get into it.

After dinner Sleel calls me aside, thanks me for my help, tells me that Runild is to undergo study by experts at an institute far away. His power of mind-contact is so remarkable, says Sleel, that it requires prolonged analysis.

Mildly I ask whether it would not have been better to keep him here, among the surroundings that have become home to him, and let the experts come to the House of Double Minds to examine him. Sleel shakes his head. There are many experts, the testing equipment is not portable, the tests will be lengthy.

I wonder if I will ever see Runild again.

In the morning I meet with my group at the usual time. They have lived here several weeks now, and their early fears are gone from them. Already I see the destinies unfolding: Galaine is fast-witted but shallow, Mulliam and Chith are plodders, Fyme and Hirole and Divvan may have the stuff of oracles, the rest are mediocrities. An average group. Hirole, perhaps, is becoming my favorite. There are no Jens among them, no Runilds.

"Today we start to examine the idea of nonverbal words," I begin. "For example, if we say, Let this green ball stand for the word 'same,' and this blue box stand for the word 'different,' then we can——"

My voice drones on. The children listen placidly. So the training proceeds in the House of Double Minds. Beneath the vault of my skull my dreaming Right throbs a bit, as though reliving its moment of freedom. Through the corridors outside the room the oracles move, deep in contemplation, shrouded in impenetrable wisdom, and we who serve them go obediently about our tasks.

THIS
IS
THE
ROAD

*L*eaf, lolling cozily with Shadow on a thick heap of furs in the airwagon's snug passenger castle, heard rain beginning to fall and made a sour face: very likely he would soon have to get up and take charge of driving the wagon, if the rain was the sort of rain he thought it was.

This was the ninth day since the Teeth had begun to lay waste to the eastern provinces. The airwagon, carrying four who were fleeing the invaders' fierce appetites, was floating along Spider Highway somewhere between Theptis and Northman's Rib, heading west, heading west as fast as could be managed. Jumpy little Sting was at the power-reins, beaming dream-commands to the team of six nightmares that pulled the wagon along; burly Crown was amidwagon, probably plotting vengeance against the Teeth, for that was what Crown did most of the time; that left Leaf and Shadow at their ease, but not for much longer. Listening to the furious drumming of the downpour against the wagon's taut-stretched canopy of big-veined stickskin, Leaf knew that this was no ordinary rain, but rather the dread purple rain that turns the air foul and brings the no-leg spiders out to hunt. Sting would never be able to handle the wagon in a purple rain. What a nuisance, Leaf thought, cuddling close against Shadow's sleek, furry blue form. Before long he heard the worried snorting of the nightmares and felt the wagon jolt and buck: yes, beyond any doubt, purple rain, no-leg spiders. His time of relaxing was just about over.

Not that he objected to doing his fair share of the work. But he had finished his last shift of driving only half an hour ago. He had earned his rest. If Sting was incapable of handling the wagon in this weather—and Shadow too, Shadow could never manage in a purple rain—then Crown ought to take the reins himself. But of course Crown would do no such thing. It was Crown's wagon, and he never drove it himself. "I have always had underbreeds to do the driving for me," Crown had said ten days ago, as they stood in the grand plaza of Holy Town with the fires of the Teeth blazing in the outskirts.

"Your underbreeds have all fled without waiting for their master," Leaf had reminded him.

"So? There are others to drive."

"Am I to be your underbreed?" Leaf asked calmly. "Remember, Crown, I'm of the Pure Stream stock."

"I can see that by your face, friend. But why get into philosophical disputes? This is my wagon. The invaders will be here before nightfall. If you would ride west with me, these are the terms. If they're too bitter for you to swallow, well, stay here and test your luck against the mercies of the Teeth."

"I accept your terms," Leaf said.

So he had come aboard—and Sting, and Shadow— under the condition that the three of them would do all the driving. Leaf felt degraded by that—hiring on, in effect, as an indentured underbreed—but what choice was there for him? He was alone and far from his people; he had lost all his wealth and property; he faced sure death as the swarming hordes of Teeth devoured the eastland. He accepted Crown's terms. An aristocrat knows the art of yielding better than most. Resist humiliation until you can resist no longer, certainly, but then accept, accept, accept. Refusal to bow to the inevitable is vulgar and melodramatic. Leaf was of the highest caste, Pure Stream, schooled from childhood to be pliable, a willow in the wind, bending freely to the will of the Soul. Pride is a dangerous sin; so is stubbornness; so too, more than the others, is foolishness. Therefore, he labored while Crown lolled. Still, there were limits even to Leaf's capacity for acceptance, and he suspected those limits would be reached shortly.

On the first night, with only two small rivers between them and the Teeth and the terrible fires of Holy Town staining the sky, the fugitives halted briefly to forage for jellymelons in an abandoned field, and as they squatted there, gorging on ripe succulent fruit, Leaf said to Crown, "Where will you go, once you're safe from the Teeth on the far side of the Middle River?"

"I have distant kinsmen who live in the Flatlands," Crown replied. "I'll go to them and tell them what has happened to the Dark Lake folk in the east, and I'll persuade them to take up arms and drive the Teeth back into the icy wilderness where they belong. An army of liberation, Leaf, and I'll lead it." Crown's dark face glistened with juice. He wiped at it. "What are your plans?"

"Not nearly so grand. I'll seek kinsmen too, but not to organize an army. I wish simply to go to the Inland Sea, to my own people, and live quietly among them once again. I've been away from home too many years. What better time to return?" Leaf glanced at Shadow. "And you?" he asked her. "What do you want out of this journey?"

"I want only to go wherever you go," she said.

Leaf smiled. "You, Sting?"

"To survive," Sting said. "Just to survive."

Mankind had changed the world, and the changed world had worked changes in mankind. Each day the wagon brought the travelers to some new and strange folk who claimed descent from the old ancestral stock, though they might be water-breathers or have skins like tanned leather or grow several pairs of arms. Human, all of them, human, human, human. Or so they insisted. If you call yourself human, Leaf thought, then I will call you human too. Still, there were gradations of humanity. Leaf, as a Pure Stream, thought of himself as more nearly human than any of the peoples along their route, more nearly human even than his three companions; indeed, he sometimes tended to look upon Crown, Sting, and Shadow as very much other than human, though he did not consider that a fault in them. Whatever dwelled in the world was without fault, so long as it did no harm to others. Leaf had been taught to respect every breed of mankind, even the underbreeds. His companions were certainly no underbreeds: they were solidly midcaste, all of them, and ranked not far below Leaf himself. Crown, the biggest and strongest and most violent of them, was of the Dark Lake line. Shadow's race was Dancing Stars, and she was the most elegant, the most supple of the group. She was the only female aboard the wagon. Sting, who sprang from the White Crystal stock, was the quickest of body and spirit, mercurial, volatile. An odd assortment, Leaf thought. But in extreme times one takes one's traveling companions as they come. He had no complaints. He found it possible to get along with all of them, even Crown. Even Crown.

The wagon came to a jouncing halt. There was the clamor of hooves stamping the sodden soil; then shrill high-pitched cries from Sting and angry booming bellowings from Crown; and finally a series of muffled hissing explosions. Leaf shook his head sadly. "To waste our ammunition on no-leg spiders——"

"Perhaps they're harming the horses," Shadow said. "Crown is rough, but he isn't stupid."

Tenderly Leaf stroked her smooth haunches. Shadow tried always to be kind. He had never loved a Dancing Star before, though the sight of them had long given him pleasure: they were slender beings, bird-boned and shallow-breasted, covered from their ankles to their crested skulls by fine dense fur the color of the twilight sky in winter. Shadow's voice was musical and her motions were graceful; she was the antithesis of Crown.

Crown now appeared, a hulking figure thrusting bluntly through the glistening beaded curtains that enclosed the passenger castle. He glared malevolently at Leaf. Even in his pleasant moments Crown seemed angry, an effect perhaps caused by his eyes, which were bright red where those of Leaf and most other kinds of humans were white. Crown's body was a block of meat, twice as broad as Leaf and half again as tall, though Leaf did not come from a small-statured race. Crown's skin was glossy, greenish-purple in color, much like burnished bronze; he was entirely without hair and seemed more like a massive statue of an oiled gladiator than a living being. His arms hung well below his knees; equipped with extra joints and terminating in hands the size of great baskets; they were superb instruments of slaughter. Leaf offered him the most agreeable smile he could find. Crown said, without smiling in return, "You better get back on the reins, Leaf. The road's turning into one big swamp. The horses are uneasy. It's a purple rain."

Leaf had grown accustomed, in these nine days, to obeying Crown's brusque orders. He started to obey now, letting go of Shadow and starting to rise. But then, abruptly, he arrived at the limits of his acceptance.

"My shift just ended," he said.

Crown stared. "I know that. But Sting can't handle the wagon in this mess. And I just killed a bunch of mean-looking spiders. There'll be more if we stay around here much longer."

"So?"

"What are you trying to do, Leaf?"

"I guess I don't feel like going up front again so soon."

"You think Shadow here can hold the reins in this storm?" Crown asked coldly.

Leaf stiffened. He saw the wrath gathering in Crown's face. The big man was holding his natural violence in check with an effort; there would be trouble soon if Leaf remained defiant. This rebelliousness went against all of Leaf's principles, yet he found himself persisting in it and even taking a wicked pleasure in it. He chose to risk the confrontation and discover how firm Crown intended to be. Boldly he said, "You might try holding the reins yourself, friend."

"*Leaf!*" Shadow whispered, appalled.

Crown's face became murderous. His dark, shining cheeks puffed and went taut; his eyes blazed like molten nuggets; his hands closed and opened, closed and opened, furiously grasping air. "What kind of crazy stuff are you trying to give me? We have a contract, Leaf. Unless you've suddenly decided that a Pure Stream doesn't need to abide by——"

"Spare me the class prejudice, Crown. I'm not pleading Pure Stream as an excuse to get out of working. I'm tired and I've earned my rest."

Shadow said softly, "Nobody's denying you your rest, Leaf. But Crown's right that I can't drive in a purple rain. I would if I could. And Sting can't do it either. That leaves only you."

"And Crown," Leaf said obstinately.

"There's only you," Shadow murmured. It was like her to take no sides, to serve ever as a mediator. "Go on, Leaf. Before there's real trouble. Making trouble like this isn't your usual way."

Leaf felt bound to pursue his present course, however perilous. He shook his head. "You, Crown. You drive."

In a throttled voice Crown said, "You're pushing me too far. We have a contract."

All Leaf's Pure Stream temperature was gone now. "Contract? I agreed to do my fair share of the driving, not to let myself be yanked up from my rest at a time when——"

Crown kicked at a low wickerwork stool, splitting it. His rage was boiling close to the surface. Swollen veins throbbed in his throat. He said, still controlling himself, "Get out there right now, Leaf, or by the Soul I'll send you into the All-Is-One!"

"Beautiful, Crown. Kill me, if you feel you have to. Who'll drive your damned wagon for you then?"

"I'll worry about that then."

Crown started forward, swallowing air, clenching fists.

Shadow sharply nudged Leaf's ribs. "This is going beyond the point of reason," she told him. He agreed. He had tested Crown and he had his answer, which was that Crown was unlikely to back down; now enough was enough, for Crown was capable of killing. The huge Dark Laker loomed over him, lifting his tremendous arms as though to bring them crashing against Leaf's head. Leaf held up his hands, more a gesture of submission than of self-defense.

"Wait," he said. "Stop it, Crown. I'll drive."

Crown's arms descended anyway. Crown managed to halt the killing blow midway, losing his balance and lurching heavily against the side of the wagon. Clumsily he straightened. Slowly he shook his head. In a low, menacing voice he said, "Don't ever try something like this again, Leaf."

"It's the rain," Shadow said. "The purple rain. Everybody does strange things in a purple rain."

"Even so," Crown said, dropping onto the pile of furs as Leaf got up. "The next time, Leaf, there'll be bad trouble. Now go ahead. Get up front."

Nodding to him, Leaf said, "Come up front with me, Shadow."

She did not answer. A look of fear flickered across her face.

Crown said, "The driver drives alone. You know that, Leaf. Are you still testing me? If you're testing me, say so and I'll know how to deal with you."

"I just want some company, as long as I have to do an extra shift."

"Shadow stays here."

There was a moment of silence. Shadow was trembling. "All right," Leaf said finally. "Shadow stays here."

"I'll walk a little way toward the front with you," Shadow said, glancing timidly at Crown. Crown scowled but said nothing. Leaf stepped out of the passenger castle; Shadow followed. Outside, in the narrow passageway leading to the midcabin, Leaf halted, shaken, shaking, and seized her. She pressed her slight body against him and they embraced, roughly, intensely. When he released her she said, "Why did you try to cross him like that? It was such a strange thing for you to do, Leaf."

"I just didn't feel like taking the reins again so soon."

"I know that."

"I wanted to be with you."

"You'll be with me a little later," she said. "It didn't

make sense for you to talk back to Crown. There wasn't any choice. You *had* to drive."

"Why?"

"You know. Sting couldn't do it. I couldn't do it."

"And Crown?"

She looked at him oddly. "Crown? How could Crown have taken the reins?"

From the passenger castle came Crown's angry growl: "You going to stand there all day, Leaf? Go on! Get in here, Shadow!"

"I'm coming," she called.

Leaf held her a moment. "Why not? Why couldn't he have driven? He may be proud, but not so proud that——"

"Ask me another time," Shadow said, pushing him away. "Go. Go. You have to drive. If we don't move along we'll have the spiders upon us."

On the third day westward they had arrived at a village of Shapechangers. Much of the countryside through which they had been passing was deserted, although the Teeth had not yet visited it, but these Shapechangers went about their usual routines as if nothing had happened in the neighboring provinces. These were angular, long-legged people, sallow of skin, nearly green in hue, who were classed generally somewhere below the midcastes, but above the underbreeds. Their gift was metamorphosis, a slow softening of the bones under voluntary control that could, in the course of a week, drastically alter the form of their bodies, but Leaf saw them doing none of that, except for a few children who seemed midway through strange transformations, one with ropy, seemingly boneless arms, one with grotesquely distended shoulders, one with stiltlike legs. The adults came close to the wagon, admiring its beauty with soft cooing sounds, and Crown went out to talk with them. "I'm on my way to raise an army," he said. "I'll be back in a month or two, leading my kinsmen out of the Flatlands. Will you fight in our ranks? Together we'll drive out the Teeth and make the eastern provinces safe again."

The Shapechangers laughed heartily. "How can anyone drive out the Teeth?" asked an old one with a greasy mop of blue-white hair. "It was the will of the Soul that they burst forth as conquerors, and no one can quarrel with the Soul. The Teeth will stay in these lands for a thousand thousand years."

"They can be defeated!" Crown cried.

"They will destroy all that lies in their path, and no one can stop them."

"If you feel that way, why don't you flee?" Leaf asked.

"Oh, we have time. But we'll be gone long before your return with your army." There were giggles. "We'll keep ourselves clear of the Teeth. We have our ways. We make our changes and we slip away."

Crown persisted. "We can use you in our war against them. You have valuable gifts. If you won't serve as soldiers, at least serve us as spies. We'll send you into the camps of the Teeth, disguised as——"

"We will not be here," the old Shapechanger said, "and no one will be able to find us," and that was the end of it.

As the airwagon departed from the Shapechanger village, Shadow at the reins, Leaf said to Crown, "Do you really think you can defeat the Teeth?"

"I have to."

"You heard the old Shapechanger. The coming of the Teeth was the will of the Soul. Can you hope to thwart that will?"

"A rainstorm is the will of the Soul also," Crown said

quietly. "All the same, I do what I can to keep myself dry. I've never known the Soul to be displeased by that."

"It's not the same. A rainstorm is a transaction between the sky and the land. We aren't involved in it; if we want to cover our heads, it doesn't alter what's really taking place. But the invasion of the Teeth is a transaction between tribe and tribe, a reordering of social patterns. In the great scheme of things, Crown, it may be a necessary process, preordained to achieve certain ends beyond our understanding. All events are part of some larger whole, and everything balances out, everything compensates for something else. Now we have peace, and now it's the time for invaders, do you see? If that's so, it's futile to resist."

"The Teeth broke into the eastlands," said Crown, "and they massacred thousands of Dark Lake people. My concern with necessary processes begins and ends with that fact. My tribe has nearly been wiped out. Yours is still safe, up by its ferny shores. I will seek help and gain revenge."

"The Shapechangers laughed at you. Others will also. No one will want to fight the Teeth."

"I have cousins in the Flatlands. If no one else will, they'll mobilize themselves. They'll want to repay the Teeth for their crime against the Dark Lakers."

"Your western cousins may tell you, Crown, that they prefer to remain where they are safe. Why should they go east to die in the name of vengeance? Will vengeance, no matter how bloody, bring any of your kinsmen back to life?"

"They will fight," Crown said.

"Prepare yourself for the possibility that they won't."

"If they refuse," said Crown, "then I'll go back east myself, and wage my war alone until I'm overwhelmed. But don't fear for me, Leaf. I'm sure I'll find plenty of willing recruits."

"How stubborn you are, Crown. You have good reason

to hate the Teeth, as do we all. But why let that hatred cost you your only life? Why not accept the disaster that has befallen us, and make a new life for yourself beyond the Middle River, and forget this dream of reversing the irreversible?"

"I have my task," said Crown.

Forward through the wagon Leaf moved, going slowly, head down, shoulders hunched, feet atickle with the urge to kick things. He felt sour of spirit, curdled with dull resentment. He had let himself become angry at Crown, which was bad enough; but worse, he had let that anger possess and poison him. Not even the beauty of the wagon could lift him: ordinarily its superb construction and elegant furnishings gave him joy, the swirl-patterned fur hangings, the banners of gossamer textiles, the intricate carved inlays, the graceful strings of dried seeds and tassels that dangled from the vaulted ceilings, but these wonders meant nothing to him now. That was no way to be, he knew.

The airwagon was longer than ten men of the Pure Stream lying head to toe, and so wide that it spanned nearly the whole roadway. The finest workmanship had gone into its making: Flower Giver artisans, no doubt of it, only Flower Givers could build so well. Leaf imagined dozens of the fragile little folk toiling earnestly for months, all smiles and silence, long, slender fingers and quick, gleaming eyes, shaping the great wagon as one might shape a poem. The main frame was of lengthy pale spars of light, resilient wingwood, elegantly laminated into broad curving strips with a colorless fragrant mucilage and bound with springy withes brought from the southern marshes. Over this elaborate armature tanned sheets of stickskin had been stretched and stitched into place with thick yellow fibers drawn from the stick-creatures' own gristly bodies. The floor was of dark shining nightflower-wood planks, buffed to a high finish and pegged together with great skill. No metal had been employed in the construction of the wagon, nor any artificial substances: nature had supplied everything. Huge and majestic though the wagon was, it was airy and light, light enough to float on a vertical column of warm air generated by magnetic rotors whirling in its belly; so long as the earth turned, so would the rotors, and when the rotors were spinning the wagon drifted cat-high above the ground, and could be tugged easily along by the team of nightmares.

It was more a mobile palace than a wagon, and wherever it went it stirred excitement: Crown's love, Crown's joy, Crown's estate, a wondrous toy. To pay for the making of it Crown must have sent many souls into the All-Is-One, for that was how Crown had earned his livelihood in the old days, as a hired warrior, a surrogate killer, fighting one-on-one duels for rich eastern princelings too weak or too lazy to defend their own honor. He had never been scratched, and his fees had been high; but all that was ended now that the Teeth were loose in the eastlands.

Leaf could not bear to endure being so irritable any longer. He paused to adjust himself, closing his eyes and listening for the clear tone that sounded always at the center of his being. After a few minutes he found it, tuned himself to it, let it purify him. Crown's unfairness ceased to matter. Leaf became once more his usual self, alert and outgoing, aware and responsive.

Smiling, whistling, he made his way swiftly through the wide, comfortable, brightly lit midcabin, decorated with Crown's weapons and other grim souvenirs of battle, and went on into the front corridor that led to the driver's cabin.

Sting sat slumped at the reins. White Crystal folk such as Sting generally seemed to throb and tick with energy; but Sting looked exhausted, emptied, half dead of fatigue. He was a small, sinewy being, narrow of shoulder and hip, with colorless skin of a waxy, horny texture, pocked everywhere with little hairy nodes and whorls. His muscles were long and flat; his face was cavernous, beaked nose and tiny chin, dark mischievous eyes hidden in bony recesses. Leaf touched his shoulder. "It's all right," he said. "Crown sent me to relieve you." Sting nodded feebly but did not move. The little man was quivering like a frog. Leaf had always thought of him as indestructible, but in the grip of this despondency Sting seemed more fragile even than Shadow.

"Come," Leaf murmured. "You have a few hours for resting. Shadow will look after you."

Sting shrugged. He was hunched forward, staring dully through the clear curving window, stained now with splashes of muddy tinted water.

"The dirty spiders," he said. His voice was hoarse and frayed. "The filthy rain. The mud. Look at the horses, Leaf. They're dying of fright, and so am I. We'll all perish on this road, Leaf, if not of spiders then of poisoned rain, if not of rain then of the Teeth, if not of the Teeth then of something else. There's no road for us but this one, do you realize that? This is the road, and we're bound to it like helpless underbreeds, and we'll die on it."

"We'll die when our turn comes, like everything else, Sting, and not a moment before."

"Our turn is coming. Too soon. Too soon. I feel death-ghosts close at hand."

"*Sting!*"

"I feel haunted on this wagon, Leaf."

Sting made a weird ratcheting sound low in his throat, a

sort of rusty sob. Leaf lifted him and swung him out of the driver's seat, setting him gently down in the corridor. It was as though he weighed nothing at all. Perhaps just then that was true. Sting had many strange gifts. "Go on," Leaf said. "Get some rest while you can."

"How kind you are, Leaf."

"And no more talk of ghosts."

"Yes," Sting said. Leaf saw him struggling against fear and despair and weariness. Sting appeared to brighten a moment, flickering on the edge of his old vitality; then the brief glow subsided, and, smiling a pale smile, offering a whisper of thanks, he went aft.

Leaf took his place in the driver's seat.

Through the window of the wagon—thin, tough sheets of stickskin, the best quality, carefully matched, perfectly transparent—he confronted a dismal scene. Rain dark as blood was falling at a steep angle, scourging the spongy soil, kicking up tiny fountains of earth. A bluish miasma rose from the ground, billows of dark, steamy fog, the acrid odor of which had begun to seep into the wagon. Leaf sighed and reached for the reins. Death-ghosts, he thought. Haunted. Poor Sting, driven to the end of his wits.

And yet, and yet, as he considered the things Sting had said, Leaf realized that he had been feeling somewhat the same way, these past few days: tense, driven, haunted. *Haunted.* As though unseen presences, mocking, hostile, were hovering near. Ghosts? The strain, more likely, of all that he had gone through since the first onslaught of the Teeth. He had lived through the collapse of a rich and intricate civilization. He moved now through a strange world, all ashes and seaweed. He was haunted, perhaps, by the weight of the unburied past, by the memory of all that he had lost.

A rite of exorcism seemed in order.

Lightly he said, aloud, "If there are any ghosts in here, I want you to listen to me. *Get out of this cabin.* That's an order. I have work to do."

He laughed. He picked up the reins and made ready to take control of the team of nightmares.

The sense of an invisible presence was overwhelming.

Something at once palpable and intangible pressed clammily against him. He felt surrounded and engulfed. It's the fog, he told himself. Dark blue fog, pushing at the window, sealing the wagon into a pocket of vapor. Or was it? Leaf sat quite still for a moment, listening. Silence. He relinquished the reins, swung about in his seat, carefully inspected the cabin. No one there. An absurdity to be fidgeting like this. Yet the discomfort remained. This was no joke now. Sting's anxieties had infected him, and the malady was feeding on itself, growing more intense from moment to moment, making him vulnerable to any stray terror that whispered to him. Only with a tranquil mind could he attain the state of trance a nightmare-driver must enter; and trance seemed unattainable so long as he felt the prickle of some invisible watcher's gaze on the back of his neck. This rain, he thought, this damnable rain. It drives everybody crazy. In a clear, firm voice Leaf said, "I'm altogether serious. Show yourself and get yourself out of this cabin."

Silence.

He took up the reins again. No use. Concentration was impossible. He knew many techniques for centering himself, for leading his consciousness to a point of unassailable serenity. But could he achieve that now, jangled and distracted as he was? He would try. He had to succeed. The wagon had tarried in this place much too long already. Leaf summoned all his inner resources; he purged himself, one by one, of every discord; he compelled himself to slide into trance.

It seemed to be working. Darkness beckoned to him. He stood at the threshold. He started to step across.

"Such a fool, such a foolish fool," said a sudden dry voice out of nowhere that nibbled at his ears like the needle-toothed mice of the White Desert.

The trance broke. Leaf shivered as if stabbed and sat up, eyes bright, face flushed with excitement.

"Who spoke?"

"Put down those reins, friend. Going forward on this road is a heavy waste of spirit."

"Then I wasn't crazy and neither was Sting. There *is* something in here!"

"A ghost, yes, a ghost, a ghost, a ghost!" The ghost showered him with laughter.

Leaf's tension eased. Better to be troubled by a real ghost than to be vexed by a fantasy of one's own disturbed mind. He feared madness far more than he did the invisible. Besides, he thought he knew what this creature must be.

"Where are you, ghost?"

"Not far from you. Here I am. Here. Here." From three different parts of the cabin, one after another. The invisible being began to sing. Its song was high-pitched, whining, a grinding tone that stretched Leaf's patience intolerably. Leaf still saw no one, though he narrowed his eyes and stared as hard as he could. He imagined he could detect a faint veil of pink light floating along the wall of the cabin, a smoky haze moving from place to place, a shimmering film like thin oil on water, but whenever he focused his eyes on it the misty presence appeared to evaporate.

Leaf said, "How long have you been aboard this wagon?"

"Long enough."

"Did you come aboard at Theptis?"

"Was that the name of the place?" asked the ghost disingenuously. "I forget. It's so hard to remember things."

"Theptis," said Leaf. "Four days ago."

"Perhaps it was Theptis," the ghost said. "Fool! Dreamer!"

"Why do you call me names?"

"You travel a dead road, fool, and yet nothing will turn you from it." The invisible one snickered. "Do you think I'm a ghost, Pure Stream?"

"I know what you are."

"How wise you've become!"

"Such a pitiful phantom. Such a miserable drifting wraith. Show yourself to me, ghost."

Laughter reverberated from the corners of the cabin. The voice said, speaking from a point close to Leaf's left ear, "The road you choose to travel has been killed ahead. We told you that when you came to us, and yet you went onward, and still you go onward. Why are you so rash?"

"Why won't you show yourself? A gentleman finds it discomforting to speak to the air."

Obligingly the ghost yielded, after a brief pause, some fraction of its invisibility. A vaporous crimson stain appeared in the air before Leaf, and he saw within it dim, insubstantial features, like projections on a screen of thick fog. He believed he could make out a wispy white beard, harsh glittering eyes, lean curving lips; a whole forbidding face, a fleshless torso. The stain deepened momentarily to scarlet and for a moment Leaf saw the entire figure of the stranger revealed, a long narrow-bodied man, dried and withered, grinning ferociously at him. The edges of the figure softened and became mist. Then Leaf saw only vapor again, and then nothing.

"I remember you from Theptis," Leaf said. "In the tent of Invisibles."

"What will you do when you come to the dead place on the highway?" the invisible one demanded. "Will you fly over it? Will you tunnel under it?"

"You were asking the same things at Theptis," Leaf replied. "I will make the same answer that the Dark Laker gave you then. We will go forward, dead place or no. This is the only road for us."

They had come to Theptis on the fifth day of their flight—a grand city, a splendid mercantile emporium, the gateway to the west, sprawling athwart a place where two great rivers met and many highways converged. In happy times any and all peoples might be found in Theptis, Pure Streams and White Crystals and Flower Givers and Sand Shapers and a dozen others jostling one another in the busy streets, buying and selling, selling and buying, but mainly Theptis was a city of Fingers—the merchant caste, plump and industrious, thousands upon thousands of them concentrated in this one city.

The day Crown's airwagon reached Theptis much of the city was ablaze, and they halted on a broad streamsplit plain just outside the metropolitan area. An improvised camp for refugees had sprouted there, and tents of black and gold and green cloth littered the meadow like new nightshoots. Leaf and Crown went out to inquire after the news. Had the Teeth sacked Theptis as well? No, an old and sagging Sand Shaper told them. The Teeth, so far as anyone had heard, were still well to the east, rampaging through the coastal cities. Why the fires, then? The old man shook his head. His energy was exhausted, or his patience, or his courtesy. If you want to know anything else, he said, ask *them*. They know everything. And he pointed toward a tent opposite his.

Leaf looked into the tent and found it empty; then he looked again and saw upright shadows moving about in it, tenuous figures that existed at the very bounds of visibility and could be perceived only by tricks of the light as they changed places in the tent. They asked him within, and Crown came also. By the smoky light of their tentfire they were more readily seen: seven or eight men of the Invisible stock, nomads, ever mysterious, gifted with ways of causing beams of light to travel around or through their bodies so that they might escape the scrutiny of ordinary eyes. Leaf, like everyone else not of their kind, was uncomfortable among Invisibles. No one trusted them; no one was capable of predicting their actions, for they were creatures of whim and caprice, or else followed some code the logic of which was incomprehensible to outsiders. They made Leaf and Crown welcome, adjusting their bodies until they were in clear sight, and offering the visitors a flagon of wine, a bowl of fruit. Crown gestured toward Theptis. Who had set the city afire? A red-bearded Invisible with a raucous rumbling voice answered that on the second night of the invasion the richest of the Fingers had panicked and had begun to flee the city with their most precious belongings, and as their wagons rolled through the gates the lesser breeds had begun to loot the Finger mansions, and brawling had started once the wine-cellars were pierced, and fires broke out, and there was no one to make the fire wardens do their work, for they were all underbreeds and the masters had fled. So the city burned and was still burning, and the survivors were huddled here on the plain, waiting for the rubble to cool so that they might salvage valuables from it, and hoping that the Teeth would not fall upon them before they could do their sifting. As for the Fingers, said the Invisible, they were all gone from Theptis now.

Which way had they gone? Mainly to the northwest, by way of Sunset Highway, at first; but then the approach to that road had become choked by stalled wagons butted one up against another, so that the only way to reach the Sunset now was by making a difficult detour through the sand country north of the city, and once that news became general the Fingers had turned their wagons southward. Crown wondered why no one seemed to be taking Spider Highway westward. At this a second Invisible, white-bearded, joined the conversation. Spider Highway, he said, is blocked just a few days' journey west of here: a dead road, a useless road. Everyone knows that, said the white-bearded Invisible.

"That is our route," said Crown.

"I wish you well," said the Invisible. "You will not get far."

"I have to get to the Flatlands."

"Take your chances with the sand country," the red-bearded one advised, "and go by way of the Sunset."

"It would waste two weeks or more," Crown replied. "Spider Highway is the only road we can consider." Leaf and Crown exchanged wary glances. Leaf asked the nature of the trouble on the highway, but the Invisibles said only that the road had been "killed," and would offer no amplification. "We will go forward," Crown said, "dead place or no."

"As you choose," said the older Invisible, pouring more wine. Already both Invisibles were fading; the flagon seemed suspended in mist. So, too, did the discussion become unreal, dreamlike, as answers no longer followed closely upon the sense of questions, and the words of the Invisibles came to Leaf and Crown as though swaddled in thick wool. There was a long interval of silence, at last, and when Leaf extended his empty glass the flagon was not offered to him, and he realized finally that he and Crown were alone in the tent. They left it and asked at other tents about the blockage on Spider Highway, but no one knew anything of it, neither some young Dancing Stars nor three flatfaced Water Breather women nor a family of Flower Givers. How reliable was the word of Invisibles? What did they mean by a "dead" road? Suppose they merely thought the road was ritually impure, for some reason understood only by Invisibles. What value, then, would their warning have to those who did not subscribe to their superstitions? Who knew at any time what the words of an Invisible meant? That night in the wagon the four of them puzzled over the concept of a road that has been "killed," but neither Shadow's intuitive perceptions nor Sting's broad knowledge of tribal dialects and customs could provide illumination. In the end Crown reaffirmed his decision to proceed on the road he had originally chosen, and it was Spider Highway that they took out of Theptis. As they proceeded westward they met no one traveling the opposite way, though one might expect the eastbound lanes to be thronged with a flux of travelers turning back from whatever obstruction might be closing the road ahead. Crown took cheer in that; but Leaf observed privately that their wagon appeared to be the only vehicle on the road in either direction, as if everyone else knew better than to make the attempt. In such stark solitude they journeyed four days west of Theptis before the purple rain hit them.

Now the Invisible said, "Go into your trance and drive your horses. I'll dream beside you until the awakening comes."

"I prefer privacy."

"You won't be disturbed."

"I ask you to leave."

"You treat your guests coldly."

"Are you my guest?" Leaf asked. "I don't remember extending an invitation."

"You drank wine in our tent. That creates in you an obligation to offer reciprocal hospitality." The Invisible sharpened his bodily intensity until he seemed as solid as Crown; but even as Leaf observed the effect he grew thin again, fading in patches. The far wall of the cabin showed through his chest, as if he were hollow. His arms had disappeared, but not his gnarled long-fingered hands. He was grinning, showing crooked close-set teeth. There was a strange scent in the cabin, sharp and musky, like vinegar mixed with honey. The Invisible said, "I'll ride with you a little longer," and vanished altogether.

Leaf searched the corners of the cabin, knowing that an Invisible could always be felt even if he eluded the eyes. His probing hands encountered nothing. Gone, gone, gone, whisking off to the place where snuffed flames go, eh? Even that odor of vinegar and honey was diminishing. "Where are you?" Leaf asked. "Still hiding somewhere close?" Silence. Leaf shrugged. The stink of the purple rain was the dominant scent again. Time to move on, stowaway or no. Rain was hitting the window in huge murky windblown blobs. Once more Leaf picked up the reins. He banished the Invisible from his mind.

These purple rains condensed out of drifting gaseous clots in the upper atmosphere—dank clouds of chemical residues that arose from the world's most stained, most injured places and circled the planet like malign tempests. Upon colliding with a mass of cool air such a poisonous cloud öften discharged its burden of reeking oils and acids in the form of a driving rainstorm; and the foulness that descended could be fatal to plants and shrubs, to small animals, sometimes even to man.

A purple rain was the cue for certain somber creatures to come forth from dark places: scuttering scavengers that picked eagerly through the dead and dying, and larger, more dangerous things that preyed on the dazed and choking living. The no-leg spiders were among the more unpleasant of these.

They were sinister spherical beasts the size of large dogs, voracious in the appetite and ruthless in the hunt. Their bodies were plump, covered with coarse, rank brown hair; they bore eight glittering eyes above sharp-fanged mouths. No-legged they were indeed, but not immobile, for a single huge fleshy foot, something like that of a snail, sprouted from the underbellies of these spiders and carried them along at a slow, inexorable pace. They were poor pursuers, easily avoided by healthy animals; but to the numbed victims of a purple rain, they were deadly, moving in to strike with hinged, poison-barbed claws that leaped out of niches along their backs. Were they truly spiders? Leaf had no idea. Like almost everything else, they were a recent species, mutated out of the-Soul-only-knew-what during the period of stormy biological upheavals that had attended the end of the old industrial civilization, and no one yet had studied them closely, or cared to.

Crown had killed four of them. Their bodies lay upside down at the edge of the road, upturned feet wilting and drooping like plucked toadstools. About a dozen more spiders had emerged from the low hills flanking the highway and were gliding slowly toward the stalled wagon; already several had reached their dead comrades and were making ready to feed on them, and some of the others were eyeing the horses.

The six nightmares, prisoners of their harnesses, prowled about uneasily in their constricted ambits, anxiously scraping at the muddy ground with their hooves. They were big, sturdy beasts, black as death, with long feathery ears and high-domed skulls that housed minds as keen as many humans', sharper than some. The rain annoyed the horses but could not seriously harm them, and the spiders could be kept at bay with kicks, but plainly the entire situation disturbed them.

Leaf meant to get them out of here as rapidly as he could.

A slimy coating covered everything the rain had touched, and the road was a miserable quagmire, slippery as ice. There was peril for all of them in that. If a horse stumbled and fell it might splinter a leg, causing such confusion that the whole team might be pulled down; and as the injured nightmares thrashed about in the mud the hungry spiders would surely move in on them, venomous claws rising, striking, delivering stings that stunned, leaving the horses paralyzed, helpless, vulnerable to eager teeth and strong jaws. As the wagon traveled onward through this swampy rain-soaked district Leaf would constantly have to steady and reassure the nightmares, pouring his energy into them to comfort them, a strenuous task, a task that had wrecked poor Sting.

Leaf slipped the reins over his forehead. He became aware of the consciousness of the six fretful horses.

Because he was still awake, contact was misty and uncertain. A waking mind was unable to communicate with the animals in any useful way. To guide the team he had to enter a trance-state, a dream-state; they would not respond to anything so gross as conscious intelligence. He looked about for manifestations of the Invisible. No, no sign of him. Good. Leaf brought his mind to dead center.

He closed his eyes. The technique of trance was easy enough for him, when there were no distractions.

He visualized a tunnel, narrow-mouthed and dark, slanting into the ground. He drifted toward its entrance.

Hovered there a moment.

Went down into it.

Floating, floating, borne downward by warm, gentle currents: he sinks in a slow spiral descent, autumn leaf on a springtime breeze. The tunnel's walls are circular, crystalline, lit from within, the light growing in brightness as he drops toward the heart of the world. Gleaming scarlet and blue flowers, brittle as glass, sprout from crevices at meticulously regular intervals.

He goes deep, touching nothing. Down.

Entering a place where the tunnel widens into a round smooth-walled chamber, sealed at the end. He stretches full-length on the floor. The floor is black stone, slick and slippery; he dreams it soft and yielding, womb-warm. Colors are muted here, sounds are blurred. He hears far-off music, percussive and muffled, *rat-a-tat*, *rat-a-tat*, *blllooom*, *blllooom*.

Now at least he is able to make full contact with the minds of the horses.

His spirit expands in their direction; he envelops them, he takes them into himself. He senses the separate identity of each, picks up the shifting play of their emotions, their prancing fantasies, their fears. Each mare has her own distinct response to the rain, to the spiders, to the sodden highway. One is restless, one is timid, one is furious, one is sullen, one is tense, one is torpid. He feeds energy to them. He pulls them together. Come, gather your strength, take us onward: this is the road, we must be on our way.

The nightmares stir.

They react well to his touch. He believes that they prefer him over Shadow and Sting as a driver: Sting is too manic, Shadow too permissive. Leaf keeps them together, directs them easily, gives them the guidance they need. They are intelligent, yes, they have personalities and goals and ideals, but also they are beasts of burden, and Leaf never forgets that, for the nightmares themselves do not.

Come, now. Onward.

The road is ghastly. They pick at it and their hooves make sucking sounds coming up from the mud. They complain to him. *We are cold, we are wet, we are bored.* He dreams wings for them to make their way easier. To soothe them he dreams sunlight for them, bountiful warmth, a dry highway, an easy trot. He dreams green hillsides, cascades of yellow blossoms, the flutter of hummingbirds' wings, the droning of bees. He gives the horses sweet summer, and they grow calm; they lift their heads; they fan their dream-wings and preen; they are ready now to resume the journey. They pull as one. The rotors hum happily. The wagon slides forward with a smooth coasting motion.

Leaf, deep in trance, is unable to see the road, but no matter; the horses see it for him and send him images, fluid, shifting dream-images, polarized and refracted and diffracted by the strangenesses of their vision and the distortions of dream-communication, six simultaneous and individual views. Here is the road, bordered by white birches whipped by an angry wind. Here is the road, an earthen swath slicing through a forest of mighty pines bowed down by white new snow. Here is the road, a ribbon of fertility, from which dazzling red poppies spring wherever a hoof strikes. Fleshy-finned blue fishes do headstands beside the road. Paunchy burghers of the Finger tribe spread brilliantly laundered tablecloths along the grassy margin and make lunch out of big-eyed reproachful oysters. Masked figures dart between the horses' legs. The road curves, curves again, doubles back on itself, crosses itself in a complacent loop. Leaf integrates this dizzying many-hued inrush of data, sorting the real from the unreal, blending and focusing the input and using it to guide himself in guiding the horses. Serenely he coordinates their movements with quick confident impulses of thought, so that each animal will pull with the same force. The wagon is precariously balanced on its column of air, and an unequal tug could well send it slewing into the treacherous thicket to the left of the road. He sends quicksilver messages down the thick conduit from his mind to theirs. Steady there, steady, watch that boggy patch coming up! Ah! Ah, that's my girl! Spiders on the left, careful! Good! Yes, yes, ah, yes! He pats their heaving flanks with a strand of his mind. He rewards their agility with dreams of the stable, of newly mown hay, of stallions waiting at journey's end.

From them—for they love him, he knows they love him—he gets warm dreams of the highway, all beauty and joy, all images converging into a single idealized view, majestic groves of wingwood trees and broad meadows through which clear brooks flow. They dream his own past life for him, too, feeding back to him nuggets of random autobiography mined in the seams of his being. What they transmit is filtered and transformed by their alien sensibilities, colored with hallucinatory glows and tugged and twisted into other-dimensional forms, but yet he is able to perceive the essential meaning of each tableau: his childhood among the parks and gardens of the Pure Stream enclave near the Inland Sea, his wanderyears among the innumerable, unfamiliar, not-quite-human breeds of the hinterlands, his brief, happy sojourn in the fog-swept western country, his eastward journey in early manhood, always following the will of the Soul, always bending to the breezes, accepting whatever destiny seizes him, eastward now, his band of friends closer than brothers in his adopted eastern province, his sprawling lakeshore home there, all polished wood and billowing tented pavilions, his collection of relics of mankind's former times—pieces of machinery, elegant coils of metal, rusted coins, grotesque statuettes, wedges of imperishable plastic—housed in its own wing with its own curator. Lost in these reveries he ceases to remember that the home by the lake has been reduced to ashes by the Teeth, that his friends of kinder days are dead, his estates overrun, his pretty things scattered in the kitchen-middens.

Imperceptibly, the dream turns sour.

Spiders and rain and mud creep back into it. He is reminded, through some darkening of tone of the imagery pervading his dreaming mind, that he has been stripped of everything and has become, now that he has taken flight, merely a driver hired out to a bestial Dark Lake mercenary who is himself a fugitive.

Leaf is working harder to control the team now. The horses seem less sure of their footing, and the pace slows; they are bothered about something, and a sour, querulous anxiety tinges their messages to him. He catches their mood. He sees himself harnessed to the wagon alongside the nightmares, and it is Crown at the reins, Crown wielding a terrible whip, driving the wagon frenziedly forward, seeking allies who will help him fulfill his fantasy of liberating the lands the Teeth have taken. There is no escape from Crown. He rises above the landscape like a monster of congealed smoke, growing more huge until he obscures the sky. Leaf wonders how he will disengage himself from Crown. Shadow runs beside him, stroking his cheeks, whispering to him, and he asks her to undo the harness, but she says she cannot, that it is their duty to serve Crown, and Leaf turns to Sting, who is harnessed on his other side, and he asks Sting for help, but Sting coughs and slips in the mud as Crown's whip flicks his backbone. There is no escape. The wagon heels and shakes. The right-hand horse skids, nearly falls, recovers. Leaf decides he must be getting tired. He has driven a great deal today, and the effort is telling. But the rain is still falling—he breaks through the veil of illusions, briefly, past the scenes of spring and summer and autumn, and sees the blue-black water dropping in wild handfuls from the sky—and there is no one else to drive, so he must continue.

He tries to submerge himself in deeper trance, where he will be less readily deflected from control.

But no, something is wrong, something plucks at his consciousness, drawing him toward the waking state. The horses summon him to wakefulness with frightful scenes. One beast shows him the wagon about to plunge through a wall of fire. Another pictures them at the brink of a vast impassable crater. Another gives him the image of giant boulders strewn across the road; another, a mountain of ice blocking the way; another, a pack of snarling wolves; another, a row of armored warriors standing shoulder to shoulder, lances at the ready. No doubt of it. Trouble. Trouble. Trouble. Perhaps they have come to the dead place in the road. No wonder that Invisible was skulking around. Leaf forces himself to awaken.

There was no wall of fire. No warriors, no wolves, none of those things. Only a palisade of newly felled timbers fac-

ing him some hundred paces ahead on the highway, timbers
twice as tall as Crown, sharpened to points at both ends and
thrust deep into the earth one up against the next and bound
securely with freshly cut vines. The barricade spanned the
highway completely from edge to edge; on its right it was
bordered by a tangle of impenetrable thorny scrub; on its left
it extended to the brink of a steep ravine.

They were stopped.

Such a blockade across a public highway was inconceivable. Leaf blinked, coughed, rubbed his aching forehead.
Those last few minutes of discordant dreams had left a murky,
gritty coating on his brain. This wall of wood seemed like
some sort of dream too, a very bad one. Leaf imagined he
could hear the Invisible's cool laughter somewhere close at
hand. At least the rain appeared to be slackening, and there
were no spiders about. Small consolations, but the best that
were available.

Baffled, Leaf freed himself of the reins and awaited the
next event. After a moment or two he sensed the joggling
rhythms that told of Crown's heavy forward progress through
the cabin. The big man peered into the driver's cabin.

"What's going on? Why aren't we moving?"

"Dead road."

"What are you talking about?"

"See for yourself," Leaf said wearily, gesturing toward
the window.

Crown leaned across Leaf to look. He studied the scene
an endless moment, reacting slowly. "What's that? A *wall?*"

"A wall, yes."

"A wall across a highway? I never heard of anything
like that."

"The Invisibles at Theptis may have been trying to
warn us about this."

"A wall. A wall." Crown shook with perplexed anger.

"It violates all the maintenance customs! Soul take it, Leaf, a public highway is——"

"——sacred and inviolable. Yes. What the Teeth have been doing in the east violates a good many maintenance customs too," Leaf said. "And territorial customs as well. These are unusual times everywhere." He wondered if he should tell about the Invisible who was on board. One problem at a time, he decided. "Maybe this is how these people propose to keep the Teeth out of their country, Crown."

"But to block a public road——"

"We were warned."

"Who could trust the word of an Invisible?"

"There's the wall," Leaf said. "Now we know why we didn't meet anyone else on the highway. They probably put this thing up as soon as they heard about the Teeth, and the whole province knows enough to avoid Spider Highway. Everyone but us."

"What folk dwell here?"

"No idea. Sting's the one who would know."

"Yes, Sting would know," said the high, clear, sharp-edged voice of Sting from the corridor. He poked his head into the cabin. Leaf saw Shadow just behind him. "This is the land of the Tree Companions," Sting said. "Do you know of them?"

Crown shook his head. "Not I," said Leaf.

"Forest-dwellers," Sting said. "Tree-worshippers. Small heads, slow brains. Dangerous in battle: they use poisoned darts. There are nine tribes of them in this region, I think, under a single chief. Once they paid tribute to my people, but I suppose in these times all that has ended."

"They worship trees?" Shadow said lightly. "And how many of their gods, then, did they cut down to make this barrier?"

Sting laughed. "If you must have gods, why not put them to some good use?"

Crown glared at the wall across the highway as he once might have glared at an opponent in the dueling ring. Seething, he paced a narrow path in the crowded cabin. "We can't waste any more time. The Teeth will be coming through this region in a few days, for sure. We've got to reach the river before something happens to the bridges ahead."

"The wall," Leaf said.

"There's plenty of brush lying around out there," said Sting. "We could build a bonfire and burn it down."

"Green wood," Leaf said. "It's impossible."

"We have hatchets," Shadow pointed out. "How long would it take for us to cut through timbers as thick as those?"

Sting said, "We'd need a week for the job. The Tree Companions would fill us full of darts before we'd been chopping an hour."

"Do you have any ideas?" Shadow said to Leaf.

"Well, we could turn back toward Theptis and try to find our way to Sunset Highway by way of the sand country. There are only two roads from here to the river, this and the Sunset. We lose five days, though, if we decide to go back, and we might get snarled up in whatever chaos is going on in Theptis, or we could very well get stranded in the desert trying to reach the highway. The only other choice I see is to abandon the wagon and look for some path around the wall on foot, but I doubt very much that Crown would——"

"Crown wouldn't," said Crown, who had been chewing his lip in tense silence. "But I see some different possibilities."

"Go on."

"One is to find these Tree Companions and compel them to clear this trash from the highway. Darts or no darts, one Dark Lake and one Pure Stream side by side ought to be able to terrify twenty tribes of pinhead forest folk."

"And if we can't?" Leaf asked.

"That brings us to the other possibility, which is that this wall isn't particularly intended to protect the neighborhood against the Teeth at all, but that these Tree Companions have taken advantage of the general confusion to set up some sort of toll-raising scheme. In that case, if we can't force them to open the road, we can find out what they want, what sort of toll they're asking, and pay it if we can and be on our way."

"Is that Crown who's talking?" Sting asked. "Talking about paying a toll to underbreeds of the forest? Incredible!"

Crown said, "I don't like the thought of paying toll to anybody. But it may be the simplest and quickest way to get out of here. Do you think I'm entirely a creature of pride, Sting?"

Leaf stood up. "If you're right that this is a toll station, there'd be some kind of gate in the wall. I'll go out there and have a look at it."

"No," said Crown, pushing him lightly back into his seat. "There's danger here, Leaf. This part of the work falls to me." He strode toward the midcabin and was busy there a few minutes. When he returned he was in his full armor: breastplates, helmet, face-mask, greaves, everything burnished to a high gloss. In those few places where his bare skin showed through, it seemed but a part of the armor. Crown looked like a machine. His mace hung at his hip, and the short shaft of his extensor sword rested easily along the inside of his right wrist, ready to spring to full length at a squeeze. Crown glanced toward Sting and said, "I'll need your nimble legs. Will you come?"

"As you say."

"Open the midcabin hatch for us, Leaf."

Leaf touched a control on the board below the front window. With a soft, whining sound a hinged door near the middle of the wagon swung upward and out, and a stepladder sprouted to provide access to the ground. Crown made a ponderous exit. Sting, scorning the ladder, stepped down: it was the special gift of the White Crystal people to be able to transport themselves short distances in extraordinary ways.

Sting and Crown began to walk warily toward the wall. Leaf, watching from the driver's seat, slipped his arm lightly about the waist of Shadow, who stood beside him, and caressed her smooth fur. The rain had ended; a gray cloud still hung low, and the gleam of Crown's armor was already softened by fine droplets of moisture. He and Sting were nearly to the palisade, now, Crown constantly scanning the underbrush as if expecting a horde of Tree Companions to spring forth. Sting, loping along next to him, looked like some agile little two-legged beast, the top of his head barely reaching to Crown's hip.

They reached the palisade. Thin, late-afternoon sunlight streamed over its top. Kneeling, Sting inspected the base of the wall, probing at the soil with his fingers, and said something to Crown, who nodded and pointed upward. Sting backed off, made a short running start, and lofted himself, rising almost as though he were taking wing. His leap carried him soaring to the wall's jagged crest in a swift blurred flight. He appeared to hover for a long moment while choosing a place to land. At last he alighted in a precarious, uncomfortable-looking position, sprawled along the top of the wall with his body arched to avoid the timbers' sharpened tips, his hands grasping two of the stakes and his feet wedged between two others. Sting remained in this desperate contortion for a remarkably long time, studying whatever lay beyond the barricade; then he let go his hold, sprang lightly outward, and floated to the ground, a distance some three times his own height. He landed upright, without stumbling. There was a brief conference between Crown and Sting. Then they came back to the wagon.

"It's a toll-raising scheme, all right," Crown muttered. "The middle timbers aren't embedded in the earth. They end just at ground level and form a hinged gate, fastened by two heavy bolts on the far side."

"I saw at least a hundred Tree Companions back of the wall," Sting said. "Armed with blow-darts. They'll be coming around to visit us in a moment."

"We should arm ourselves," Leaf said.

Crown shrugged. "We can't fight that many of them. Not twenty-five to one, we can't. The best hand-to-hand man in the world is helpless against little forest folk with poisoned blow-darts. If we aren't able to awe them into letting us go through, we'll have to buy them off somehow. But I don't know. That gate isn't nearly wide enough for the wagon."

He was right about that. There was the dry scraping squeal of wood against wood—the bolts were being unfastened—and then the gate swung slowly open. When it had been fully pushed back it provided an opening through which any good-sized cart of ordinary dimensions might pass, but not Crown's magnificent vehicle. Five or six stakes on each side of the gate would have to be pulled down in order for the wagon to go by.

Tree Companions came swarming toward the wagon,

scores of them—small, naked folk with lean limbs and smooth blue-green skin. They looked like animated clay statuettes, casually pinched into shape: their hairless heads were narrow and elongated, with flat sloping foreheads, and their long necks looked flimsy and fragile. They had shallow chests and bony, meatless frames. All of them, men and women both, wore reed dart-blowers strapped to their hips. As they danced and frolicked about the wagon they set up a ragged, irregular chanting, tuneless and atonal, like the improvised songs of children caught up in frantic play.

"We'll go out to them," Crown said. "Stay calm, make no sudden moves. Remember that these are underbreeds. So long as we think of ourselves as men and them as nothing more than monkeys, and make them realize we think that way, we'll be able to keep them under control."

"They're men," said Shadow quietly. "Same as we. Not monkeys."

"Think of them as like monkeys," Crown told her. "Otherwise we're lost. Come, now."

They left the wagon, Crown first, then Leaf, Sting, Shadow. The cavorting Tree Companions paused momentarily in their sport as the four travelers emerged; they looked up, grinned, chattered, pointed, did handsprings and headstands. They did not seem awed. Did Pure Stream mean nothing to them? Had they no fear of Dark Lake? Crown, glowering, said to Sting, "Can you speak their language?"

"A few words."

"Speak to them. Ask them to send their chief here to me."

Sting took up a position just in front of Crown, cupped his hands to his mouth, and shouted something high and piercing in a singsong language. He spoke with exaggerated, painful clarity, as one does in addressing a blind person or a foreigner. The Tree Companions snickered and exchanged little yipping cries. Then one of them came dancing forward, planted his face a handsbreath from Sting's, and mimicked Sting's words, catching the intonation with comic accuracy. Sting looked frightened, and backed away half a pace, butting accidentally into Crown's chest. The Tree Companion loosed a stream of words, and when he fell silent Sting repeated his original phrase in a more subdued tone.

"What's happening?" Crown asked. "Can you understand anything?"

"A little. Very little."

"Will they get the chief?"

"I'm not sure. I don't know if he and I are talking about the same things."

"You said these people pay tribute to White Crystal."

"Paid," Sting said. "I don't know if there's any allegiance any longer. I think they may be having some fun at our expense. I think what he said was insulting, but I'm not sure. I'm just not sure."

"Stinking monkeys!"

"Careful, Crown," Shadow murmured. "We can't speak their language, but they may understand ours."

Crown said, "Try again. Speak more slowly. Get the monkey to speak more slowly. The chief, Sting, we want to see the chief! Isn't there any way you can make contact?"

"I could go into trance," Sting said. "And Shadow could help me with the meanings. But I'd need time to get myself together. I feel too quick now, too tense." As if to illustrate his point he executed a tiny jumping moment, blur-snap-hop, that carried him laterally a few paces to the left. Blur-snap-hop and he was back in place again. The Tree Companion laughed shrilly, clapped his hands, and tried to imitate Sting's little shuttling jump. Others of the tribe came

over; there were ten or twelve of them now, clustered near
the entrance to the wagon. Sting hopped again: it was like a
twitch, a tic. He started to tremble. Shadow reached toward
him and folded her slender arms about his chest, as though
to anchor him. The Tree Companions grew more agitated;
there was a hard, intense quality about their playfulness
now. Trouble seemed imminent. Leaf, standing on the far
side of Crown, felt a sudden knotting of the muscles at the
base of his stomach. Something nagged at his attention, off
to his right out in the crowd of Tree Companions; he glanced
that way and saw an azure brightness, elongated and
upright, a man-sized strip of fog and haze, drifting and weaving among the forest folk. Was it the Invisible? Or only some
trick of the dying daylight, slipping through the residual
vapor of the rainstorm? He struggled for a sharp focus, but
the figure eluded his gaze, slipping ticklingly beyond sight as
Leaf followed it with his eyes. Abruptly he heard a howl
from Crown and turned just in time to see a Tree Companion duck beneath the huge man's elbow and go sprinting
into the wagon. "Stop!" Crown roared. "Come back!" And,
as if a signal had been given, seven or eight others of the lithe
little tribesmen scrambled aboard.

There was death in Crown's eyes. He beckoned savagely to Leaf and rushed through the entrance. Leaf followed. Sting, sobbing, huddled in the entranceway, making
no attempt to halt the Tree Companions who were streaming
into the wagon. Leaf saw them climbing over everything, ex-
amining, inspecting, commenting. Monkeys, yes. Down in
the front corridor Crown was struggling with four of them,
holding one in each vast hand, trying to shake free two
others who were climbing his armored legs. Leaf confronted
a miniature Tree Companion woman, a gnomish bright-eyed
creature whose bare lean body glistened with sour sweat, and

as he reached for her she drew not a dart-blower but a long narrow blade from the tube at her hip, and slashed Leaf fiercely along the inside of his left forearm. There was a quick, frightening gush of blood, and only some moments afterward did he feel the fiery lick of the pain. A poisoned knife? Well, then, into the All-Is-One with you, Leaf. But if there had been poison, he felt no effects of it; he wrenched the knife from her grasp, jammed it into the wall, scooped her up, and pitched her lightly through the open hatch of the wagon. No more Tree Companions were coming in, now. Leaf found two more, threw them out, dragged another out of the roofbeams, tossed him after the others, went looking for more. Shadow stood in the hatchway, blocking it with her frail arms outstretched. Where was Crown? Ah. There. In the trophy room. "Grab them and carry them to the hatch!" Leaf yelled. "We're rid of most of them!"

"The stinking monkeys," Crown cried. He gestured angrily. The Tree Companions had seized some treasure of Crown's, some ancient suit of mail, and in their childish buoyancy had ripped the fragile links apart with their tug-of-war. Crown, enraged, bore down on them, clamped one hand on each tapering skull—*"Don't!"* Leaf shouted, fearing darts in vengeance—and squeezed, cracking them like nuts. He tossed the corpses aside and, picking up his torn trophy, stood sadly pressing the sundered edges together in a clumsy attempt at repair.

"You've done it now," Leaf said. "They were just being inquisitive. Now we'll have war, and we'll be dead before nightfall."

"Never," Crown grunted.

He dropped the chain-mail, scooped up the dead Tree Companions, carried them dangling through the wagon, and threw them like offal into the clearing. Then he stood defiantly in the hatchway, inviting their darts. None came. Those Tree Companions still aboard the wagon, five or six of them, appeared empty-handed, silent, and slipped hastily around the hulking Dark Laker. Leaf went forward and joined Crown. Blood was still dripping from Leaf's wound; he dared not induce clotting nor permit the wound to close until he had been purged of whatever poison might have been on the blade. A thin, straight cut, deep and painful, ran down his arm from elbow to wrist. Shadow gave a soft little cry and seized his hand. Her breath was warm against the edges of the gash. "Are you badly injured?" she whispered.

"I don't think so. It's just a question of whether the knife was poisoned."

"They poison only their darts," said Sting. "But there'll be infection to cope with. Better let Shadow look after you."

"Yes," Leaf said. He glanced into the clearing. The Tree Companions, as though thrown into shock by the violence that had come from their brief invasion of the wagon, stood frozen along the road in silent groups of nine or ten, keeping their distance. The two dead ones lay crumpled where Crown had hurled them. The unmistakable figure of the Invisible, transparent but clearly outlined by a dark perimeter, could be seen to the right, near the border of the thicket: his eyes glittered fiercely, his lips were twisted in a strange smile. Crown was staring at him in slack-jawed astonishment. Everything seemed suspended, held floating motionless in the bowl of time. To Leaf the scene was an eerie tableau in which the only sense of ongoing process was supplied by the throbbing in his slashed arm. He hung moored at the center, waiting, waiting, incapable of action, trapped like the others in timelessness. In that long pause he realized that another figure had appeared during the melee, and stood now calmly ten paces or so to the left of the grinning Invisible: a Tree Companion, taller than the others of his kind, clad in beads and gimcracks but undeniably a being of presence and majesty.

"The chief has arrived," Sting said hoarsely.

The stasis broke. Leaf released his breath and let his rigid body slump. Shadow tugged at him, saying, "Let me clean that cut for you." The chief of the Tree Companions stabbed the air with three outstretched fingers, pointing at the wagon, and called out five crisp, sharp, jubilant syllables; slowly and grandly he began to stalk toward the wagon. At the same moment the Invisible flickered brightly, like a sun about to die, and disappeared entirely from view. Crown, turning to Leaf, said in a thick voice, "It's all going crazy here. I was just imagining I saw one of the Invisibles from Theptis skulking around by the underbrush."

"You weren't imagining anything," Leaf told him. "He's been riding secretly with us since Theptis. Waiting to see what would happen to us when we came to the Tree Companions' wall."

Crown looked jarred by that. "When did you find that out?" he demanded.

Shadow said, "Let him be, Crown. Go and parley with the chief. If I don't clean Leaf's wound soon——"

"Just a minute. I need to know the truth. Leaf, when did you find out about this Invisible?"

"When I went up front to relieve Sting. He was in the driver's cabin. Laughing at me, jeering. The way they do."

"And you didn't tell me? Why?"

"There was no chance. He bothered me for a while, and then he vanished, and I was busy driving after that, and then we came to the wall, and then the Tree Companions——"

"What does he want from us?" Crown asked harshly, face pushed close to Leaf's.

Leaf was starting to feel fever rising. He swayed and leaned on Shadow. Her taut, resilient little form bore him with surprising strength. He said tiredly, "I don't know. Does anyone ever know what one of them wants?" The Tree Companion chief, meanwhile, had come up beside them and in a lusty, self-assured way slapped his open palm several times against the side of the wagon, as though taking possession of it. Crown whirled. The chief coolly spoke, voice level, inflections controlled. Crown shook his head. "What's he saying?" he barked. "Sting? *Sting?*"

"Come," Shadow said to Leaf. "Now. Please."

She led him toward the passenger castle. He sprawled on the furs while she searched busily through her case of unguents and ointments; then she came to him with a long green vial in her hand and said, "There'll be pain for you now."

"Wait."

He centered himself and disconnected, as well as he was able, the network of sensory apparatus that conveyed messages of discomfort from his arm to his brain. At once he felt his skin growing cooler, and he realized for the first time since the battle how much pain he had been in: so much that he had not had the wisdom to do anything about it. Dispassionately he watched as Shadow, all efficiency, probed his wound, parting the lips of the cut without squeamishness and swabbing its red interior. A faint tickling, unpleasant but not painful, was all he sensed. She looked up, finally, and said, "There'll be no infection. You can allow the wound to close now." In order to do that Leaf had to re-establish the neural connections to a certain degree, and as he unblocked the flow of impulses he felt sudden startling pain, both from the cut itself and from Shadow's medicines; but quickly he induced clotting, and a moment afterward he was deep in the disciplines that would encourage the sundered flesh to heal. The wound began to close. Lightly Shadow blotted the fresh blood from his arm and prepared a poultice; by the time she had it in place, the gaping slash had reduced itself to a thin raw line. "You'll live," she said. "You were lucky they don't poison their knives." He kissed the tip of her nose and they returned to the hatch area.

Sting and the Tree Companion chief were conducting some sort of discussion in pantomime, Sting's motions sweeping and broad, the chief's the merest flicks of fingers, while Crown stood by, an impassive column of darkness, arms folded somberly. As Leaf and Shadow reappeared Crown said, "Sting isn't getting anywhere. It has to be a trance parley or we won't make contact. Help him, Shadow."

She nodded. To Leaf, Crown said, "How's the arm?"

"It'll be all right."

"How soon?"

"A day. Two, maybe. Sore for a week."

"We may be fighting again by sunrise."

"You told me yourself that we can't possibly survive a battle with these people."

"Even so," Crown said. "We may be fighting again by sunrise. If there's no other choice, we'll fight."

"And die?"

"And die," Crown said.

Leaf walked slowly away. Twilight had come. All vestiges of the rain had vanished, and the air was clear, crisp, growing chill, with a light wind out of the north that was gaining steadily in force. Beyond the thicket the tops of tall ropy-limbed trees were whipping about. The shards of the moon had moved into view, rough daggers of whiteness doing their slow dance about one another in the darkening sky. The poor old shattered moon, souvenir of an era long gone: it seemed a scratchy mirror for the tormented planet that owned it, for the fragmented race of races that was mankind. Leaf went to the nightmares, who stood patiently in harness, and passed among them, gently stroking their shaggy ears, caressing their blunt noses. Their eyes, liquid, intelligent, watchful, peered into his almost reproachfully. You promised us a stable, they seemed to be saying. Stallions, warmth, newly mown hay. Leaf shrugged. In this world, he told them wordlessly, it isn't always possible to keep one's promises. One does one's best, and one hopes that that is enough.

Near the wagon Sting has assumed a cross-legged position on the damp ground. Shadow squats beside him; the chief, mantled in dignity, stands stiffly before them, but Shadow coaxes him with gentle gestures to come down to them. Sting's eyes are closed and his head lolls forward. He is already in trance. His left hand grasps Shadow's muscular furry thigh; he extends his right, palm upward, and after a moment the chief puts his own palm to it. Contact: the circuit is closed.

Leaf has no idea what messages are passing among the three of them, but yet, oddly, he does not feel excluded from the transaction. Such a sense of love and warmth radiates from Sting and Shadow and even from the Tree Companion that he is drawn in, he is enfolded by their communion. And Crown, too, is engulfed and absorbed by the group aura; his rigid martial posture eases, his grim face looks strangely peaceful. Of course it is Sting and Shadow who are most closely linked; Shadow is closer now to Sting than she has ever been to Leaf, but Leaf is untroubled by this. Jealousy and competitiveness are inconceivable now. He is Sting, Sting is Leaf, they all are Shadow and Crown, there are no boundaries separating one from another, just as there will be no boundaries in the All-Is-One that awaits every living creature, Sting and Crown and Shadow and Leaf, the Tree Companions, the Invisibles, the nightmares, the no-leg spiders.

They are getting down to cases now. Leaf is aware of strands of opposition and conflict manifesting themselves in the intricate negotiation that is taking place. Although he is still without a clue to the content of the exchange, Leaf understands that the Tree Companion chief is stating a position of demand—calmly, bluntly, immovably—and Sting and Shadow are explaining to him that Crown is not at all likely to yield. More than that Leaf is unable to perceive, even when he is most deeply enmeshed in the larger consciousness of the trance-wrapped three. Nor does he know how much time is elapsing. The symphonic interchange—demand, response, development, climax—continues repetitively, indefinitely, reaching no resolution.

He feels, at last, a running-down, an attenuation of the experience. He begins to move outside the field of contact, or to have it move outside him. Spiderwebs of sensibility still connect him to the others even as Sting and Shadow and the chief rise and separate, but they are rapidly thinning and fraying, and in a moment they snap.

The contact ends.

The meeting was over. During the trance-time night had fallen, an extraordinarily black night against which the stars seemed unnaturally bright. The fragments of the moon had traveled far across the sky. So it had been a lengthy exchange; yet in the immediate vicinity of the wagon nothing seemed altered. Crown stood like a statue beside the wagon's entrance; the Tree Companions still occupied the cleared ground between the wagon and the gate. Once more a tableau, then: how easy it is to slide into motionlessness, Leaf thought, in these impoverished times. Stand and wait, stand and wait; but now motion returned. The Tree Companion pivoted and strode off without a word, signaling to his people, who gathered up their dead and followed him through the gate. From within they tugged the gate shut; there was the screeching sound of the bolts being forced home. Sting, looking dazed, whispered something to Shadow, who nodded and lightly touched his arm. They walked haltingly back to the wagon.

"Well?" Crown asked finally.

"They will allow us to pass," Sting said.

"How courteous of them." ´

"——but they claim the wagon and everything that is in it."

Crown gasped. "By what right?"

"Right of prophecy," said Shadow. "There is a seer among them, an old woman of mixed stock, part White Crystal, part Tree Companion, part Invisible. She has told them that everything that has happened lately in the world was caused by the Soul for the sake of enriching the Tree Companions."

"Everything? They see the onslaught of the Teeth as a sign of divine favor?"

"Everything," said Sting. "The entire upheaval. All for their benefit. All done so that migrations would begin and refugees would come to this place, carrying with them valuable possessions, which they would surrender to those whom the Soul meant should own them, meaning the Tree Companions."

Crown laughed roughly. "If they want to be brigands, why not practice brigandage outright, with the right name on it, and not blame their greed on the Soul?"

"They don't see themselves as brigands," Shadow said. "There can be no denying the chief's sincerity. He and his people genuinely believe that the Soul has decreed all this for their own special good, that the time has come——"

"*Sincerity!*"

"——for the Tree Companions to become people of substance and property. Therefore they've built this wall across the highway, and as refugees come west, the Tree Companions relieve them of their possessions with the blessing of the Soul."

"I'd like to meet their prophet," Crown muttered.

Leaf said, "It was my understanding that Invisibles were unable to breed with other stocks."

Sting told him, with a shrug, "We report only what we learned as we sat there dreaming with the chief. The witch-woman is part Invisible, he said. Perhaps he was wrong, but he was doing no lying. Of that I'm certain."

"And I," Shadow put in.

"What happens to those who refuse to pay tribute?" Crown asked.

"The Tree Companions regard them as thwarters of the Soul's design," said Sting, "and fall upon them and put them to death. And then seize their goods."

Crown moved restlessly in a shallow circle in front of the wagon, kicking up gouts of soil out of the hard-packed roadbed. After a moment he said, "They dangle on vines. They chatter like foolish monkeys. What do they want with the merchandise of civilized folk? Our furs, our statuettes, our carvings, our flutes, our robes?"

"Having such things will make them equal in their own sight to the higher stocks," Sting said. "Not the things themselves, but the possession of them, do you see, Crown?"

"They'll have nothing of mine!"

"What will we do, then?" Leaf asked. "Sit here and wait for their darts?"

Crown caught Sting heavily by the shoulder. "Did they give us any sort of time limit? How long do we have before they attack?"

"There was nothing like an ultimatum. The chief seems unwilling to enter into warfare with us."

"Because he's afraid of his betters!"

"Because he thinks violence cheapens the decree of the Soul," Sting replied evenly. "Therefore he intends to wait for us to surrender our belongings voluntarily."

"He'll wait a hundred years!"

"He'll wait a few days," Shadow said. "If we haven't yielded, the attack will come. But what will you do, Crown? Suppose they were willing to wait your hundred years. Are you? We can't camp here forever."

"Are you suggesting we give them what they ask?"

"I merely want to know what strategy you have in mind," she said. "You admit yourself we can't defeat them in battle. We haven't done a very good job of aweing them into submission. You recognize that any attempt to destroy their wall will bring them upon us with their darts. You refuse to turn back and look for some other westward route. You rule out the alternative of yielding to them. Very well, Crown: what do you have in mind?"

"We'll wait a few days," Crown said thickly.

"The Teeth are heading this way!" Sting cried. "Shall we sit here and let them catch us?"

Crown shook his head. "Long before the Teeth get here, Sting, this place will be full of other refugees, many of them, as unwilling to give up their goods to these folk as we are. I can feel them already on the road, coming this way, two days' march from us, perhaps less. We'll make alliance with them. Four of us may be helpless against a swarm of poisonous apes, but fifty or a hundred strong fighters would send them scrambling up their own trees."

"No one will come this way," said Leaf. "No one but fools. Everyone passing through Theptis knows what's been done to the highway here. What good is the aid of fools?"

"*We* came this way," Crown snapped. "Are we such fools?"

"Perhaps we are. We were warned not to take Spider Highway, and we took it anyway."

"Because we refused to trust the word of Invisibles."

"Well, the Invisibles happened to be telling the truth, this time," Leaf said. "And the news must be all over Theptis. No one in his right mind will come this way now."

"I feel marchers already on the way, hundreds of them," Crown said. "I can sense these things, sometimes. What about you, Sting? You feel things ahead of time, don't you? They're coming, aren't they? Have no fear, Leaf: we'll have allies here in a day or so, and then let these thieving Tree Companions beware." Crown gestured broadly. "Leaf, set the nightmares loose to graze. And then everybody inside the wagon. We'll seal it and take turns standing watch through the night. This is a time for vigilance and courage."

"This is a time for digging graves," Sting murmured sourly, as they clambered into the wagon.

Crown and Shadow stood the first round of watches while Leaf and Sting napped in the back. Leaf fell asleep at once and dreamed he was living in some immense brutal eastern city—the buildings and street plan were unfamiliar to him but the architecture was definitely eastern in style, gray and heavy, all parapets and cornices—that was coming under attack by the Teeth.

He observed everything from a many-windowed gallery atop an enormous square-sided brick tower that seemed like a survival from some remote prehistoric epoch. First, from the north, came the sound of the war song of the invaders, a nasty unendurable buzzing drone, piercing and intense, like the humming of high-speed polishing wheels at work on metal plates. That dread music brought the inhabitants of the city spilling into the streets—all stocks, Flower Givers and Sand Shapers and White Crystals and Dancing Stars and even Tree Companions, absurdly garbed in mercantile robes as though they were so many fat citified Fingers—but no one was able to escape, for there were so many people, colliding and jostling and stumbling and falling in helpless heaps, that they blocked every avenue and alleyway.

Into this chaos now entered the vanguard of the Teeth; shuffling forward in their peculiar bent-kneed crouch, trampling those who had fallen. They looked half-beast, half-demon: squat thick-thewed flat-headed long-muzzled creatures, naked, hairy, their skins the color of sand, their eyes glinting with insatiable hungers. Leaf's dreaming mind subtly magnified and distorted them so that they came hopping into the city like a band of giant toothy frogs, thump-thump, bare fleshy feet slapping pavement in sinister reverberations, short powerful arms swinging almost comically at each leaping stride. The kinship of mankind meant nothing to these carnivorous beings. They had been penned up too long in the cold, mountainous, barren country of the far northeast, living on such scraps and strings as the animals of the forest yielded, and they saw their fellow humans as mere meat stockpiled by the Soul against this day of vengeance. Efficiently, now, they began their roundup in the newly conquered city, seizing everyone in sight, cloistering the dazed prisoners in hastily rigged pens: these we eat tonight at our victory feast; these we save for tomorrow's dinner; these become dried meat to carry with us on the march; these we kill for sport; these we keep as slaves. Leaf watched the Teeth erecting their huge spits, kindling their fierce roasting-fires. Diligent search-teams fanned out through the suburbs. No one would escape. Leaf stirred and groaned, reached the threshold of wakefulness, fell back into dream. Would they find him in his tower? Smoke, gray and greasy, boiled up out of a hundred parts of town. Leaping flames. Rivulets of blood ran in the streets. He was choking. A terrible dream. But was it only a dream? This was how it had actually been in Holy Town hours after he and Crown and Sting and Shadow had managed to get away, this was no doubt as it had happened in city after city along the tormented coastal strip, very likely something of this sort was going on now in—where?—Bone Harbor? Ved-uru? Alsandar? He could smell the penetrating odor of roasting meat. He could hear the heavy lalloping sound of a Teeth patrol running up the stairs of his tower. They had him. Yes, here, now, now, a dozen Teeth bursting suddenly into his hiding place, grinning broadly—Pure Stream, they had captured a Pure Stream! What a coup! Beasts. Beasts. Prodding him; testing his flesh. Not plump enough for them, eh? This one's pretty lean. We'll cook him anyway. Pure Stream meat, it enlarges the soul, it makes you into something more than you were. Take him downstairs! To the spit, to the spit, to the—

"Leaf?"

"I warn you—you won't like—the flavor—"

"Leaf, wake up!"

"The fires—oh, the stink!"

"Leaf!"

It was Shadow. She shook him gently, plucked at his shoulder. He blinked and slowly sat up. His wounded arm was throbbing again; he felt feverish. Effects of the dream. A dream, only a dream. He shivered and tried to center himself, working at it, banishing the fever, banishing the shreds of dark fantasy that were still shrouding his mind.

"Are you all right?" she asked.

"I was dreaming about the Teeth," he told her. He shook his head, trying to clear it. "Am I to stand watch now?"

She nodded. "Up front. Driver's cabin."

"Has anything been happening?"

"Nothing. Not a thing." She reached up and drew her fingertips lightly along the sides of his jaws. Her eyes were warm and bright, her smile was loving. "The Teeth are far away, Leaf."

"From us, maybe. Not from others."

"They were sent by the will of the Soul."

"I know, I know." How often had he preached acceptance! This is the will, and we bow to it. This is the road, and we travel it uncomplainingly. But yet, but yet—he shuddered. The dream-mode persisted. He was altogether disoriented. Dream-Teeth nibbled at his flesh. The inner chambers of his spirit resonated to the screams of those on the spits, the sounds of rending and tearing, the unbearable reek of burning cities. In ten days, half a world torn apart. So much pain, so much death, so much that had been beautiful destroyed by relentless savages who would not halt until, the Soul only knew when, they had had their full measure of revenge. The will of the Soul sends them upon us. Accept. Accept. He could not find his center. Shadow held him, straining to encompass his body with her arms. After a moment he began to feel less troubled, but he remained scattered, diffused, present only in part, some portion of his mind nailed as if by spikes into that monstrous ash-strewn wasteland that the Teeth had created out of the fair and fertile eastern provinces.

She released him. "Go," she whispered. "It's quiet up front. You'll be able to find yourself again."

He took her place in the driver's cabin, going silently past Sting, who had replaced Crown on watch amidwagon. Half the night was gone. All was still in the roadside clearing; the great wooden gate was shut tight and nobody was about. By cold starlight Leaf saw the nightmares browsing patiently at the edge of the thicket. Gentle horses, almost human. If I must be visited by nightmares, he thought, let it be by their kind.

Shadow had been right. In the stillness he grew calm, and perspective returned. Lamentation would not restore the shattered eastland, expressions of horror and shock would not turn the Teeth into pious tillers of the soil. The Soul had decreed chaos: so be it. This is the road we must travel, and who dares ask why? Once the world had been whole and now it is fragmented, and that is the way things are because that is the way things were meant to be. He became less tense. Anguish dropped from him. He was Leaf again.

Toward dawn the visible world lost its sharp starlit edge; a soft fog settled over the wagon, and rain fell for a time, a light, pure rain, barely audible, altogether different in character from yesterday's vicious storm. In the strange light just preceding sunrise the world took on a delicate pearly mistiness; and out of that mist an apparition materialized. Leaf saw a figure come drifting through the closed gate—*through* it—a ghostly, incorporeal figure. He thought it might be the Invisible who had been lurking close by the wagon since Theptis, but no, this was a woman, old and frail, an attenuated woman, smaller even than Shadow, more slender. Leaf knew who she must be: the mixed-blood woman. The prophetess, the seer, she who had stirred up these Tree Companions to block the highway. Her skin had the White Crystal waxiness of texture and the White Crystal nodes of dark, coarse hair; the form of her body was essentially that of a Tree Companion, thin and long-armed; and from her Invisible forebears, it seemed, she had inherited that perplexing intangibility, that look of existing always on the borderland between hallucination and reality, between mist and flesh. Mixed-bloods were uncommon; Leaf had rarely seen one, and never had encountered one who combined in herself so many different stocks. It was said that people of mixed blood had strange gifts. Surely this one did. How had she bypassed the wall? Not even Invisibles could travel through solid wood. Perhaps this was just a dream, then, or possibly she had some way of projecting an image of herself into his mind from a point within the Tree Companion village. He did not understand.

He watched her a long while. She appeared real enough. She halted twenty paces from the nose of the wagon and scanned the entire horizon slowly, her eyes coming to rest at last on the window of the driver's cabin. She was aware, certainly, that he was looking at her, and she looked back, eye to eye, staring unflinchingly. They remained locked that way for some minutes. Her expression was glum and opaque, a withered scowl, but suddenly she brightened and smiled intensely at him and it was such a *knowing* smile that Leaf was thrown into terror by the old witch, and glanced away, shamed and defeated.

When he lifted his head she was out of view; he pressed

himself against the window, craned his neck, and found her down near the middle of the wagon. She was inspecting its exterior workmanship at close range, picking and prying at the hull. Then she wandered away, out to the place where Sting and Shadow and the chief had had their conference, and sat down crosslegged where they had been sitting. She became extraordinarily still, as if she were asleep, or in trance. Just when Leaf began to think she would never move again, she took a pipe of carved bone from a pouch at her waist, filled it with a gray-blue powder, and lit it. He searched her face for tokens of revelation, but nothing showed on it; she grew ever more impassive and unreadable. When the pipe went out, she filled it again, and smoked a second time, and still Leaf watched her, his face pushed awkwardly against the window, his body growing stiff. The first rays of sunlight now arrived, pink shading rapidly into gold. As the brightness deepened the witch-woman imperceptibly became less solid; she was fading away, moment by moment, and shortly he saw nothing of her but her pipe and her kerchief, and then the clearing was empty. The long shadows of the six nightmares splashed against the wooden palisade. Leaf's head lolled. I've been dozing, he thought. It's morning, and all's well. He went to awaken Crown.

They breakfasted lightly. Leaf and Shadow led the horses to water at a small clear brook five minutes' walk toward Theptis. Sting foraged a while in the thicket for nuts and berries, and, having filled two pails, went aft to doze in the furs. Crown brooded in his trophy room and said nothing to anyone. A few Tree Companions could be seen watching the wagon from perches in the crowns of towering red-leaved trees on the hillside just behind the wall. Nothing happened until mid-morning. Then, at a time when all four travelers were within the wagon, a dozen newcomers appeared, forerunners of the refugee tribe that Crown's intuitions had correctly predicted. They came slowly up the road, on foot, dusty and tired-looking, staggering beneath huge untidy bundles of belongings and supplies. They were square-headed muscular people, as tall as Leaf or taller, with the look of warriors about them; they carried short swords at their waists, and both men and women were conspicuously scarred. Their skins were gray tinged with pale green, and they had more fingers and toes than was usual among mankind.

Leaf had never seen their sort before. "Do you know them?" he asked Sting.

"Snow Hunters," Sting said. "Close kin to the Sand Shapers, I think. Midcaste and said to be unfriendly to strangers. They live southwest of Theptis, in the hill country."

"One would think they'd be safe there," said Shadow.

Sting shrugged. "No one's safe from the Teeth, eh? Not even on the highest hills. Not even in the thickest jungles."

The Snow Hunters dropped their packs and looked around. The wagon drew them first; they seemed stunned by the opulence of it. They examined it in wonder, touching it as the witch-woman had, scrutinizing it from every side. When they saw faces looking out at them, they nudged one another and pointed and whispered, but they did not smile, nor did they wave greetings. After a time they went on to the wall and studied it with the same childlike curiosity. It appeared to baffle them. They measured it with their outstretched hands, pressed their bodies against it, pushed at it with their shoulders, tapped the timbers, plucked at the sturdy bindings of vine. By this time perhaps a dozen more of them had come up the road; they too clustered about the wagon, doing as the first had done, and then continued toward the wall. More and more Snow Hunters were arriving, in groups of three or four. One trio, standing apart from the others, gave the impression of being tribal leaders; they consulted, nodded, summoned and dismissed other members of the tribe with forceful gestures of their hands.

"Let's go out and parley," Crown said. He donned his best armor and selected an array of elegant dress weapons. To Sting he gave a slender dagger. Shadow would not bear arms, and Leaf preferred to arm himself in nothing but Pure Stream prestige. His status as a member of the ancestral stock, he found, served him as well as a sword in most encounters with strangers.

The Snow Hunters—about a hundred of them now had gathered, with still more down the way—looked apprehensive as Crown and his companions descended from the wagon. Crown's bulk and gladiatorial swagger seemed far more threatening to these strong-bodied warlike folk than they had been to the chattering Tree Companions, and Leaf's presence too appeared disturbing to them. Warily they moved to form a loose semicircle about their three leaders; they stood close by one another, murmuring tensely, and their hands hovered near the hilts of their swords.

Crown stepped forward. "Careful," Leaf said softly. "They're on edge. Don't push them."

But Crown, with a display of slick diplomacy unusual for him, quickly put the Snow Hunters at their ease with a warm gesture of greeting—hands pressed to shoulders, palms outward, fingers spread wide—and a few hearty words of welcome. Introductions were exchanged. The spokesman for the tribe, an iron-faced man with frosty eyes and hard cheekbones, was called Sky; the names of his co-captains were Blade and Shield. Sky spoke in a flat, quiet voice, everything on the same note. He seemed empty, burned out, a man who had entered some realm of exhaustion far beyond mere fatigue. They had been on the road for three days and three nights almost without a halt, said Sky. Last week a major force of Teeth had started westward through the midcoastal lowlands bound for Theptis, and one band of these, just a few hundred warriors, had lost its way, going south into the hill country. Their aimless wanderings brought these straying Teeth without warning into the secluded village of the Snow Hunters, and there had been a terrible battle in which more than half of Sky's people had perished. The survivors, having slipped away into the trackless forest, had made their way by back roads to Spider Highway, and, numbed by shock and grief, had been marching like machines toward the Middle River, hoping to find some new hillside in the sparsely populated territories of the far northwest. They could never return to their old home, Shield declared, for it had been desecrated by the feasting of the Teeth.

"But what is this wall?" Sky asked.

Crown explained, telling the Snow Hunters about the Tree Companions and their prophetess, and of her promise that the booty of all refugees was to be surrendered to them. "They lie in wait for us with their darts," Crown said. "Four of us were helpless against them. But they would never dare challenge a force the size of yours. We'll have their wall smashed down by nightfall!"

"The Tree Companions are said to be fierce foes," Sky remarked quietly.

"Nothing but monkeys," said Crown. "They'll scramble to their treetops if we just draw our swords."

"And shower us with their poisoned arrows," Shield muttered. "Friend, we have little stomach for further warfare. Too many of us have fallen this week."

"What will you do?" Crown cried. "Give them your

swords, and your tunics and your wives' rings and the san dals off your feet?"

Sky closed his eyes and stood motionless, remaining silent for a long moment. At length, without opening his eyes, he said in a voice that came from the center of an immense void, "We will talk with the Tree Companions and learn what they actually demand of us, and then we wil make our decisions and form our plans."

"The wall—if you fight beside us, we can destroy this wall, and open the road to all who flee the Teeth!"

With cold patience Sky said, "We will speak with you again afterward," and turned away. "Now we will rest, and wait for the Tree Companions to come forth."

The Snow Hunters withdrew, sprawling out along the margin of the thicket just under the wall. There they huddled in rows, staring at the ground, waiting. Crown scowled, spat, shook his head. Turning to Leaf he said, "They have the true look of fighters. There's something that marks a fighter apart from other men, Leaf, and I can tell when it's there, and these Snow Hunters have it. They have the strength; they have the power; they have the spirit of battle in them. And yet, see them now! Squatting there like fat frightened Fingers!"

"They've been beaten badly," Leaf said. "They've been driven from their homeland. They know what it is to look back across a hilltop and see the fires in which your kinsmen are being cooked. That takes the fighting spirit out of a person, Crown."

"No. Losing makes the flame burn brighter. It makes you feverish with the desire for revenge."

"Does it? What do you know about losing? You were never so much as touched by any of your opponents."

Crown glared at him. "I'm not speaking of dueling. Do

you think my life has gone untouched by the Teeth? What am I doing here on this dirt road with all that I still own packed into a single wagon? But I'm no walking dead man like these Snow Hunters. I'm not running away, I'm going to find an army. And then I'll go back east and take my vengeance. While they—afraid of monkeys——"

"They've been marching day and night," Shadow said. "They must have been on the road when the purple rain was falling. They've spent all their strength while we've been riding in your wagon, Crown. Once they've had a little rest, perhaps they——"

"Afraid of *monkeys!*"

Crown shook with wrath. He strode up and down before the wagon, pounding his fists into his thighs. Leaf feared that he would go across to the Snow Hunters and attempt by bluster to force them into an alliance. Leaf understood the mood of these people: shattered and drained though they were, they might lash out in sudden savage irritation if Crown goaded them too severely. Possibly some hours of rest, as Shadow had suggested, and they might feel more like helping Crown drive his way through the Tree Companions' wall. But not now. Not now.

The gate in the wall opened. Some twenty of the forest folk emerged, among them the tribal chief and—Leaf caught his breath in awe—the ancient seeress, who looked across the way and bestowed on Leaf another of her penetrating comfortless smiles.

"What kind of creature is that?" Crown asked.

"The mixed-blood witch," said Leaf. "I saw her at dawn, while I was standing watch."

"Look!" Shadow cried. "She flickers and fades like an Invisible! But her pelt is like yours, Sting, and her shape is that of——"

"She frightens me," Sting said hoarsely. He was shaking. "She foretells death for us. We have little time left to us, friends. She is the goddess of death, that one." He plucked at Crown's elbow, unprotected by the armor. "Come! Let's start back along Spider Highway! Better to take our chances in the desert than to stay here and die!"

"Quiet," Crown snapped. "There's no going back. The Teeth are already in Theptis. They'll be moving out along this road in a day or two. There's only one direction for us.'

"But the wall," Sting said.

"The wall will be in ruins by nightfall," Crown told him.

The chief of the Tree Companions was conferring with Sky and Blade and Shield. Evidently the Snow Hunters knew something of the language of the Tree Companions, for Leaf could hear vocal interchanges, supplemented by pantomime and sign-language. The chief pointed to himself often, to the wall, to the prophetess; he indicated the packs the Snow Hunters had been carrying; he jerked his thumb angrily toward Crown's wagon. The conversation lasted nearly half an hour and seemed to reach an amicable outcome. The Tree Companions departed, this time leaving the gate open. Sky, Shield, and Blade moved among their people, issuing instructions. The Snow Hunters drew food from their packs—dried roots, seeds, smoked meat—and lunched in silence. Afterward, boys who carried huge water bags made of sewn hides slung between them on poles went off to the creek to replenish their supply, and the rest of the Snow Hunters rose, stretched, wandered in narrow circles about the clearing, as if getting ready to resume the march. Crown was seized by furious impatience. "What are they going to do?" he demanded. "What deal have they made?"

"I imagine they've submitted to the terms," Leaf said.

"No! No! I need their help!" Crown, in anguish, hammered at himself with his fists. "I have to talk to them," he muttered.

"Wait. Don't push them, Crown."

"What's the use? What's the use?" Now the Snow Hunters were hoisting their packs to their shoulders. No doubt of it; they were going to leave. Crown hurried across the clearing. Sky, busily directing the order of march, grudgingly gave him attention. "Where are you going?" Crown asked.

"Westward," said Sky.

"What about us?"

"March with us, if you wish."

"My wagon!"

"You can't get it through the gate, can you?"

Crown reared up as though he would strike the Snow Hunter in rage. "If you would aid us, the wall would fall! Look, how can I abandon my wagon? I need to reach my kinsmen in the Flatlands. I'll assemble an army; I'll return to the east and push the Teeth back into the mountains where they belong. I've lost too much time already. I *must* get through. Don't you want to see the Teeth destroyed?"

"It's nothing to us," Sky said evenly. "Our lands are lost to us forever. Vengeance is meaningless. Your pardon. My people need my guidance."

More than half the Snow Hunters had passed through the gate already. Leaf joined the procession. On the far side of the wall he discovered that the dense thicket along the highway's northern rim had been cleared for a considerable distance, and a few small wooden buildings, hostelries or depots, stood at the edge of the road. Another twenty or thirty paces farther along, a secondary path led northward into the forest; this was evidently the route to the Tree Companions' village. Traffic on that path was heavy just now. Hundreds of forest folk were streaming from the village to the highway, where a strange, repellent scene was being enacted. Each Snow Hunter in turn halted, unburdened himself of his pack, and laid it open. Three or four Tree Companions then picked through it, each seizing one item of value—a knife, a comb, a piece of jewelry, a fine cloak—and running triumphantly off with it. Once he had submitted to this harrying of his possessions, the Snow Hunter gathered up his pack, shouldered it, and marched on, head bowed, body slumping. Tribute. Leaf felt chilled. These proud warriors, homeless now, yielding up their remaining treasures to —he tried to choke off the word, and could not—to a tribe of monkeys. And moving onward, soiled, unmanned. Of all that he had seen since the Teeth had split the world apart, this was the most sad.

Leaf started back toward the wagon. He saw Sky, Shield, and Blade at the rear of the column of Snow Hunters. Their faces were ashen; they could not meet his eyes. Sky managed a half-hearted salute as he passed by.

"I wish you good fortune on your journey," Leaf said.

"I wish you better fortune than we have had," said Sky hollowly, and went on.

Leaf found Crown standing rigid in the middle of the highway, hands on hips. "Cowards!" he called in a bitter voice. "Weaklings!"

"And now it's our turn," Leaf said.

"What do you mean?"

"The time's come for us to face hard truths. We have to give up the wagon, Crown."

"Never."

"We agree that we can't turn back. And we can't go forward so long as the wall's there. If we stay here, the Tree

Companions will eventually kill us, if the Teeth don't overtake us first. Listen to me, Crown. We don't have to give the Tree Companions everything we have. The wagon itself, some of our spare clothing, some trinkets, the furnishings of the wagon—they'll be satisfied with that. We can load the rest of our goods on the horses and go safely through the gate as foot-pilgrims."

"I ignore this, Leaf."

"I know you do. I also know what the wagon means to you. I wish you could keep it. I wish I could stay with the wagon myself. Don't you think I'd rather ride west in comfort than slog through the rain and the cold? But we can't keep it. *We can't keep it*, Crown, that's the heart of the situation. We can go back east in the wagon and get lost in the desert, we can sit here and wait for the Tree Companions to lose patience and kill us, or we can give up the wagon and get out of this place with our skins still whole. What sort of choices are those? We have no choice. I've been telling you that for two days. Be reasonable, Crown!"

Crown glanced coldly at Sting and Shadow. "Find the chief and go into trance with him again. Tell him that I'll give him swords, armor, his pick of the finest things in the wagon. So long as he'll dismantle part of the wall and let the wagon itself pass through."

"We made that offer yesterday," Sting said glumly.

"And?"

"He insists on the wagon. The old witch has promised it to him for a palace."

"No," Crown said. "*NO!*" His wild roaring cry echoed from the hills. After a moment, more calmly, he said, "I have another idea. Leaf, Sting, come with me. The gate's open. We'll go to the village and seize the witch-woman. We'll grab her quickly, before anyone realizes what we're doing. They won't dare molest us while she's in our hands. Then, Sting, you tell the chief that unless they open the wall for us, we'll kill her." Crown chuckled. "Once she realizes we're serious, she'll tell them to hop to it. Anybody that old wants to live forever. And they'll obey her. You can bet on that. They'll obey her! Come, now." Crown started toward the gate at a vigorous pace. He took a dozen strides, halted, looked back. Neither Leaf nor Sting had moved.

"Well? Why aren't you coming?"

"I won't do it," said Leaf tiredly. "It's crazy, Crown. She's a witch, she's part Invisible—she already knows your scheme. She probably knew of it before you knew of it yourself. How can we hope to catch her?"

"Let me worry about that."

"Even if we did, Crown— No. No. I won't have any part of it. It's an impossible idea. Even if we did seize her. We'd be standing there holding a sword to her throat, and the chief would give a signal, and they'd put a hundred darts in us before we could move a muscle. It's insane, Crown."

"I ask you to come with me."

"You've had your answer."

"Then I'll go without you."

"As you choose," Leaf said quietly. "But you won't be seeing me again."

"Eh?"

"I'm going to collect what I own and let the Tree Companions take their pick of it, and then I'll hurry forward and catch up with the Snow Hunters. In a week or so I'll be at the Middle River. Shadow, will you come with me, or are you determined to stay here and die with Crown?"

The Dancing Star looked toward the muddy ground. "I don't know," she said. "Let me think a moment."

"Sting?"

"I'm going with you."

Leaf beckoned to Crown. "Please. Come to your senses, Crown. For the last time: Give up the wagon and let's get going, all four of us."

"You disgust me."

"Then this is where we part," Leaf said. "I wish you good fortune. Sting, let's assemble our belongings. Shadow? Will you be coming with us?"

"We have an obligation toward Crown," she said.

"To help him drive his wagon, yes. But not to die a foolish death for him. Crown has lost his wagon, Shadow, though he won't admit that yet. If the wagon's no longer his, our contract is voided. I hope you'll join us."

He entered the wagon and went to the midcabin cupboard where he stored the few possessions he had managed to bring with him out of the east. A pair of glistening boots made of the leathery skins of stick-creatures, two ancient copper coins, three ornamental ivory medallions, a shirt of dark-red silk, a thick, heavily worked belt—not much, not much at all, the salvage of a lifetime. He packed rapidly. He took with him a slab of dried meat and some bread; that would last him a day or two, and when it was gone he would learn from Sting or the Snow Hunters the arts of gathering food in the wilderness.

"Are you ready?"

"Ready as I'll ever be," Sting said. His pack was almost empty—a change of clothing, a hatchet, a knife, some smoked fish, nothing else.

"Let's go, then."

As Sting and Leaf moved toward the exit hatch, Shadow scrambled up into the wagon. She looked tight-strung and grave; her nostrils were flared, her eyes downcast. Without a word she went past Leaf and began loading her pack. Leaf waited for her. After a few minutes she reappeared and nodded to him.

"Poor Crown," she whispered. "Is there no way——"

"You heard him," Leaf said.

They emerged from the wagon. Crown had not moved. He stood as if rooted, midway between wagon and wall. Leaf gave him a quizzical look, as if to ask whether he had changed his mind, but Crown took no notice. Shrugging, Leaf walked around him, toward the edge of the thicket, where the nightmares were nibbling leaves. Affectionately he reached up to stroke the long neck of the nearest horse, and Crown suddenly came to life, shouting, "Those are my animals! Keep your hands off them!"

"I'm only saying goodbye to them."

"You think I'm going to let you have some? You think I'm that crazy, Leaf?"

Leaf looked sadly at him. "We plan to do our traveling on foot, Crown. I'm only saying goodbye. The nightmares were my friends. You can't understand that, can you?"

"Keep away from those animals! *Keep away!*"

Leaf sighed. "Whatever you say." Shadow, as usual, was right: poor Crown. Leaf adjusted his pack and moved off toward the gate, Shadow beside him, Sting a few paces to the rear. As he and Shadow reached the gate, Leaf looked back and saw Crown still motionless, saw Sting pausing, putting down his pack, dropping to his knees. "Anything wrong?" Leaf called.

"Tore a bootlace," Sting said. "You two go on ahead. It'll take me a minute to fix it."

"We can wait."

Leaf and Shadow stood within the frame of the gate

while Sting knotted his lace. After a few moments he rose and reached for his pack, saying, "That ought to hold me until tonight, and then I'll see if I can't——"

"*Watch out!*" Leaf yelled.

Crown erupted abruptly from his freeze, and, letting forth a lunatic cry, rushed with terrible swiftness toward Sting. There was no chance for Sting to make one of his little leaps: Crown seized him, held him high overhead like a child, and, grunting in frantic rage, hurled the little man toward the ravine. Arms and legs flailing, Sting traveled on a high arc over the edge; he seemed to dance in mid-air for an instant, and then he dropped from view. There was a long diminishing shriek, and silence. Silence.

Leaf stood stunned. "Hurry," Shadow said. "Crown's coming!"

Crown, swinging around, now rumbled like a machine of death toward Leaf and Shadow. His wild red eyes glittered ferociously. Leaf did not move; Shadow shook him urgently, and finally he pushed himself into action. Together they caught hold of the massive gate and, straining, swung it shut, slamming it just as Crown crashed into it. Leaf forced the reluctant bolts into place. Crown roared and pounded at the gate, but he was unable to force it.

Shadow shivered and wept. Leaf drew her to him and held her for a moment. At length he said, "We'd better be on our way. The Snow Hunters are far ahead of us already."

"Sting——"

"I know. I know. Come, now."

Half a dozen Tree Companions were waiting for them by the wooden houses. They grinned, chattered, pointed to the packs. "All right," Leaf said. "Go ahead. Take whatever you want. Take everything, if you like."

Busy fingers picked through his pack and Shadow's.

From Shadow the Tree Companions took a brocaded ribbon and a flat, smooth green stone. From Leaf they took one of the ivory medallions, both copper coins, and one of his stickskin boots. Tribute. Day by day, pieces of the past slipped from his grasp. He pulled the other boot from the pack and offered it to them, but they merely giggled and shook their heads. "One is of no use to me," he said. They would not take it. He tossed the boot into the grass beside the road.

The road curved gently toward the north and began a slow rise, following the flank of the forested hills in which the Tree Companions made their homes. Leaf and Shadow marched mechanically, saying little. The bootprints of the Snow Hunters were everywhere along the road, but the Snow Hunters themselves were far ahead, out of sight. It was early afternoon, and the day had become bright, unexpectedly warm. After an hour Shadow said, "I must rest."

Her teeth were clacking. She crouched by the roadside and wrapped her arms about her chest. Dancing Stars, covered with thick fur, usually wore no clothing except in the bleakest winters; but her pelt did her no good now.

"Are you ill?" he asked.

"It'll pass. I'm reacting. Sting——"

"Yes."

"And Crown. I feel so unhappy about Crown."

"A madman," Leaf said. "A murderer."

"Don't judge him so casually, Leaf. He's a man under sentence of death, and he knows it, and he's suffering from it, and when the fear and pain became unbearable to him he reached out for Sting. He didn't know what he was doing.

He needed to smash something, that was all, to relieve his own torment."

"We're all going to die sooner or later," Leaf said. "That doesn't generally drive us to kill our friends."

"I don't mean sooner or later. I mean that Crown will die tonight or tomorrow."

"Why should he?"

"What can he do now to save himself, Leaf?"

"He could yield to the Tree Companions and pass the gate on foot, as we've done."

"You know he'd never abandon the wagon."

"Well, then, he can harness the nightmares and turn around toward Theptis. At least he'd have a chance to make it through to the Sunset Highway that way."

"He can't do that either," Shadow said.

"Why not?"

"He can't drive the wagon."

"There's no one left to do it for him. His life's at stake. For once he could eat his pride and——"

"I didn't say *won't* drive the wagon, Leaf. I said *can't*. Crown's incapable. He isn't able to make dream-contact with the nightmares. Why do you think he always used hired drivers? Why was he so insistent on making you drive in the purple rain? He doesn't have the mind-power. Did you ever see a Dark Laker driving nightmares? Ever?"

Leaf stared at her. "You knew this all along?"

"From the beginning, yes."

"Is that why you hesitated to leave him at the gate? When you were talking about our contract with him?"

She nodded. "If all three of us left him, we were condemning him to death. He has no way of escaping the Tree Companions now unless he forces himself to leave the wagon, and he won't do that. They'll fall on him and kill him, today, tomorrow, whenever."

Leaf closed his eyes, shook his head. "I feel a kind of shame. Now that I know we were leaving him helpless. He could have spoken."

"Too proud."

"Yes. Yes. It's just as well he didn't say anything. We all have responsibilities to one another, but there are limits. You and I and Sting were under no obligation to die simply because Crown couldn't bring himself to give up his pretty wagon. But still—still—" He locked his hands tightly together. "Why did you finally decide to leave, then?"

"For the reason you just gave. I didn't want Crown to die, but I didn't believe I owed him my life. Besides, you had said you were going to go, no matter what."

"Poor, crazy Crown."

"And when he killed Sting—a life for a life, Leaf. All vows are cancelled now. I feel no guilt."

"Nor I.'"

"I think the fever is leaving me."

"Let's rest a few minutes more," Leaf said.

It was more than an hour before Leaf judged Shadow strong enough to go on. The highway now described a steady upgrade, not steep but making constant demands on their stamina, and they moved slowly. As the day's warmth began to dwindle, they reached the crest of the grade, and rested again at a place from which they could see the road ahead winding in switchbacks into a green, pleasant valley. Far below were the Snow Hunters, resting also by the side of a fair-sized stream.

"Smoke," Shadow said. "Do you smell it?"

"Campfires down there, I suppose."

"I don't think they have any fires going. I don't see any."

"The Tree Companions, then."

"It must be a big fire."

"No matter," Leaf said. "Are you ready to continue?"

"I hear a sound——"

A voice from behind and uphill of them said, "And so it ends the usual way, in foolishness and death, and the All-Is-One grows greater."

Leaf whirled, springing to his feet. He heard laughter on the hillside and saw movements in the underbrush; after a moment he made out a dim, faintly outlined figure, and realized that an Invisible was coming toward them, the same one, no doubt, who had traveled with them from Theptis.

"What do you want?" Leaf called.

"Want? Want? I want nothing. I'm merely passing through." The Invisible pointed over his shoulder. "You can see the whole thing from the top of this hill. Your big friend put up a mighty struggle, he killed many of them, but the darts, the darts——" The Invisible laughed. "He was dying, but even so he wasn't going to let them have his wagon. Such a stubborn man. Such a foolish man. Well, a happy journey to you both."

"Don't leave yet!" Leaf cried. But even the outlines of the Invisible were fading. Only the laughter remained, and then that too was gone. Leaf threw desperate questions into the air and, receiving no replies, turned and rushed up the hillside, clawing at the thick shrubbery. In ten minutes he was at the summit, and stood gasping and panting, looking back across a precipitous valley to the stretch of road they had just traversed. He could see everything clearly from here: the Tree Companion village nestling in the forest, the highway, the shacks by the side of the road, the wall, the clearing beyond the wall. And the wagon. The roof was gone and the sides had tumbled outward. Bright spears of flame shot high, and a black, billowing cloud of smoke stained the air. Leaf stood watching Crown's pyre a long while before returning to Shadow.

They descended toward the place where the Snow Hunters had made their camp. Breaking a long silence, Shadow said, "There must once have been a time when the world was different, when all people were of the same kind, and everyone lived in peace. A golden age, long gone. How did things change, Leaf? How did we bring this upon ourselves?"

"Nothing has changed," Leaf said, "except the look of our bodies. Inside we're the same. There never was any golden age."

"There were no Teeth, once."

"There were always Teeth, under one name or another. True peace never lasted long. Greed and hatred always existed."

"Do you believe that, truly?"

"I do. I believe that mankind is mankind, all of us the same whatever our shape, and such changes as come upon us are trifles, and the best we can ever do is find such happiness for ourselves as we can, however dark the times."

"These are darker times than most, Leaf."

"Perhaps."

"These are evil times. The end of all things approaches."

Leaf smiled. "Let it come. These are the times we were meant to live in, and no asking why, and no use longing for easier times. Pain ends when acceptance begins. This is what we have now. We make the best of it. This is the road we travel. Day by day we lose what was never ours, day by day we slip closer to the All-Is-One, and nothing matters, Shadow, nothing except learning to accept what comes. Yes?"

"Yes," she said. "How far is it to the Middle River?"

"Another few days."

"And from there to your kinsmen by the Inland Sea?"

"I don't know," he said. "However long it takes us is however long it will take. Are you very tired?"

"Not as tired as I thought I'd be."

"It isn't far to the Snow Hunters' camp. We'll sleep well tonight."

"Crown," she said. "Sting."

"What about them?"

"They also sleep."

"In the All-Is-One," Leaf said. "Beyond all trouble. Beyond all pain."

"And that beautiful wagon is a charred ruin!"

"If only Crown had had the grace to surrender it freely, once he knew he was dying. But then he wouldn't have been Crown, would he? Poor Crown. Poor crazy Crown." There was a stirring ahead, suddenly. "Look. The Snow Hunters see us. There's Sky. Blade." Leaf waved at them and shouted. Sky waved back, and Blade, and a few of the others. "May we camp with you tonight?" Leaf called. Sky answered something, but his words were blown away by the wind. He sounded friendly, Leaf thought. He sounded friendly. "Come," Leaf said, and he and Shadow hurried down the slope.